The Devil's Shallows

Debra Castaneda

SECOND
RODEO
— BOOKS —

ISBN: 9798430421014
Edited by: Lyndsey Smith, Horrorsmith Editing
Cover design by: James, GoOnWrite.com

For Alexandra

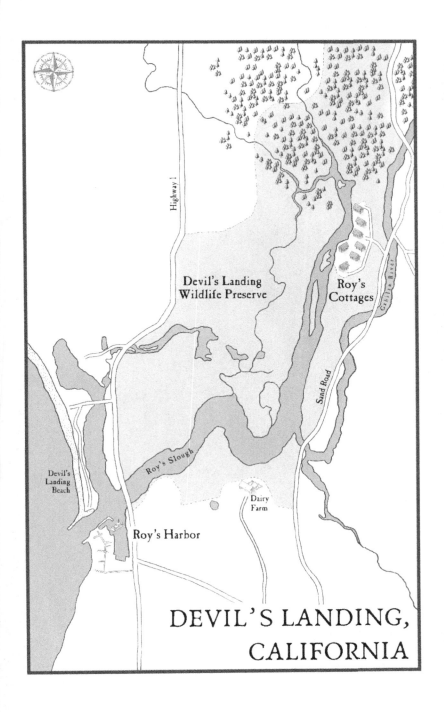

DEVIL'S LANDING, CALIFORNIA

Table of Contents

Chapter 1

Adam

My mother hated the slough. She's long dead, but I can still remember her shouting, "Adam, how many times do I have to tell you to stay away from the water!"

It wasn't deep where we lived, at the mouth near Devil's Landing, within sight of Roy's Harbor and the tangle of fishing boat masts, the cypress trees lining the marina. The water didn't even reach my shins, but it didn't matter. Not to Mom. Not to Dad either. Both believed the old stories which began circulating soon after a circus came to Devil's Landing in the early 1900s.

Just like the slough rarely looked the same twice—contingent on the interplay of sun, cloud, and fog—the stories were never quite the same either, depending on who was doing the telling.

Only one constant emerged in those many accounts.

After the chaos of the great 1906 earthquake, people began to see strange things at the back of the slough, far from the harbor, past where it narrowed and the trees, grass, and scrub eventually choked it dry.

In some tales, children went missing. In others, dairy farmers found their cows and goats dead and mangled. In one story, burning up my brain with feverish nightmares, a fisherman drifted by a teenage girl half in and half out of the water, her clothes ripped from her thin body.

Years later, when I finally returned to California's Central Coast after getting a degree in environmental science from

Brown—thanks to a full-ride scholarship—my mother dropped dead of a heart attack, and soon after, my grieving father became a BUI statistic. Boating under the influence.

It wasn't long before a stranger knocked on the door of the only house I'd ever known and dropped a bomb in the form of a letter—a thirty-day notice to vacate the property. The man with the steel wool eyebrows explained my parents had never gotten around to buying the house, even though he, the owner, had offered to sell it to them. All those years, I had assumed the tiny cottage would eventually pass on to me, their only child, but it was not to be. The man said he was sorry, and I believed him, but he'd already decided to sell the property to the marine lab next door so it could expand. So that was that.

I moved to a small, dank apartment in Monterey, which was all I could afford, and took over my dad's tour boat business. After spending a month refurbishing the pontoon boat, I got it inspected by the U.S. Coast Guard and began offering rides up Roy's Slough. There were other tour boats, but mine was the only one with a real naturalist to point out the sea otters, seals, and birds living in the wetland.

Nearly seventy-five percent of the customers shot their hands into the air at some point during the ride, and on every trip, at least one asked about the urban legend which had clung to the waterway with the sticky strength of slough mud in ebb tide.

Other places had the Chupacabra, The Loch Ness Monster, and the Beast of Bodmin Moor. But no such single-name clarity for the creature supposedly stalking the eight-mile stretch of ecological treasure that was Roy's Slough.

Over the years, the locals called the creature everything from "The Waterman," to "The Slough Devil," but tourists just asked, "Captain, how about that slough monster I read about online?"

Now, my father loved telling those stories, half of which he invented, but as a trained naturalist giving eco tours, I needed to walk the line between informing and entertaining, and since this legend was darker and uglier than its cryptid cousins, I didn't see much upside in amplifying the tale. It was best left in the past where it belonged.

The Slough Devil was no Nessie.

It was not beloved by local officials like the lake monster of the Scottish Highlands. The Slough Devil was too terrifying for that. Besides, no one had any idea what it looked like, so it was mostly depicted as a vague, shadowy creature, sometimes with four legs, sometimes with two, with red or yellow eyes.

I didn't believe in monsters.

The slough was a lonely, eerie place. On some days, it was easy to imagine dark shapes beneath the eel grass or mistake an old, gnarled oak for a monster lurking in the mist.

And then, on a spectacular fall afternoon, when the waters of the Monterey Bay sparkled in the sun and the temperature reached a perfect and glorious seventy-two degrees, I heard a shout from the back of the pontoon boat where the tourists with the professional-grade cameras liked to sit. At first, I thought the man had spotted a raft of otters. We hadn't come across one yet, and I knew the group from Germany was anxious to see otters resting and floating together.

I was piloting the boat that day, the sea breeze cool against my face. A graduate student from the University of California, Santa Cruz was giving the tour, when I heard her say, "What the effing heck is that?"

By that time, everyone on the boat—about twelve people—were standing up and leaning over the railing. We'd almost reached the turnaround point, where a thicket of oak trees obscured the view of the coastal prairie to the south. That's where the man was pointing.

The expression on his hard-angled face said it was something serious. Mountain lion, I thought. Maybe a feral pig. They were a big problem at the east end of the slough and mostly came out at night, but a day sighting was not unheard of.

The guy pointed his camera with its long lens, which must have cost thousands, and started shooting away. At what, I had no idea. But I could tell by the way he was standing, feet planted wide, leaning forward, one hand cupping the focus ring, it was something good. I anchored the boat and pushed my way through the crowd to see for myself. But whatever it was had gone, disappeared into the tangle of trees and brush.

Of everyone on the boat, only the guy with the camera and my college student had seen it, but they were too stunned to do anything more than sit there and repeat, "What the hell?" and "What the fuck!" between them.

"Show me," I demanded.

The German tourist silently handed me the camera, then began biting the nail of his thumb. A grunting noise escaped my throat while I scrolled through the video, my body tensing.

The camera had captured something not a man, but with two legs covered in patches of dark bristly fur, long arms, and a smallish head atop a tall and muscular body. It slithered out of the water onto the bank and shimmied up a tree.

The video lasted fourteen seconds.

The German tourist, Stefan Lorenz—a civil engineer—scurried back to his hotel along Monterey's Cannery Row and

4

uploaded the video, which within twenty-four hours racked up millions of views. Since then, experts studied it frame by frame and, each time, reluctantly acknowledged its authenticity with disclaimers designed to preserve their reputations.

A commentator on one of those cable shows, where guests talk over each other, not only called it a hoax, but he accused me of being the perpetrator. I can remember the exchange nearly word for word:

"Now look, we did a little digging into this Adam Gray character, and he's more than a little suspicious. He was an outspoken critic of the housing development going up next to Roy's Slough. He's about as pro-conservation as you can get. Some people call him an eco-warrior, and some people wouldn't put it past him to stage a hoax to scare off would-be buyers…"

The host interrupted the guest. "But Grady, we've learned that Adam Gray, despite his objections, entered the housing lottery and will be moving into the cottages. So for him to stage a hoax doesn't make complete sense, does it?"

No. No it did not. For all the "digging" the TV guys did, none of them bothered to contact me because I would have explained—grudgingly—I'd given up protesting after Phase One of Roy's Cottages had cleared its last hurdles, thanks to the cleverness of the Roy's Slough Trust. The trust promised to restore the wetlands in exchange for twenty-five percent of the land for the "innovative new housing development that will help ease the housing crisis." And when critics, like me, blasted the early plans pushing McMansions, the developer went back to the drawing board and downsized the residences to cottages to be sold as affordable properties in a democratic lottery.

At that point, even I could realize the inevitability of the project. And if cottages with slips into the slough were going up, then I wanted to live in one. It was simple as that. The project went into fast-track mode, and I began to feel the impact of the slough monster video.

The creature cast a dark shadow on every excursion up the eight-mile slough, even though it failed to materialize. My eyes did a nervous dance, scanning the muddy banks and the trees for the strange beast. It ruined the quiet of my solo kayak trips.

My tour business exploded. There was no way I could keep up with the demand for seats on my humble fifteen-seat pontoon, so it wasn't long before another outfit relocated from Pismo Beach to Roy's Harbor, launching with an advertising blitz boasting of its electric-powered catamaran and offering "Slough Monster Hunting Safari Rides."

For about two seconds, the arrival of a competitor had me nervous, but there were plenty of new tourists to go around, and bookings sold out months in advance. But all this business was not without its cost. Namely, my sanity.

The tourists clambered aboard with expectations of spotting the monster and left grumbling, picking their way down the aluminum ramp in their wrong shoes and stopping at the gift kiosks popping up at the harbor, which sold Slough Devil T-shirts, stickers, and plush toys.

Still, all my wondering and worry about what was on the video didn't stop me from jumping up and down when I learned I was one of the lucky winners of a Roy's Cottage. By that time, I couldn't stand living in my four hundred and fifty square foot rental which reeked of mold. The cottages were modern and beautiful, in a wide park-like setting surrounded by native plant landscaping. And of course, they were next to the marsh—magical, meandering, and filled with wildlife. Plenty of fresh ocean air. Who wouldn't want to live there?

To come up with the rest of the funds for the second half of the down payment, I started offering wilderness survival classes. Business had picked up enough, and I was able to buy good furniture for my new place. For that, the credit once again went to the elusive slough monster.

Enrollment in my bushcraft bootcamps skyrocketed. People who didn't know the difference between a lean-to and an A-frame shelter signed up, and at first, I was confused, until someone explained they'd read in an online forum I was offering slough monster fighting classes disguised as bushcraft basics.

In hindsight, that wouldn't have been such a bad idea.

Chapter 2

Christina

For someone who didn't like the beach, or anything waterfront, deciding to buy a cottage next to a slough sounded crazy. Putting down a deposit after a video surfaced showing a monster slithering out of it? Crazier still. But come on. Since when did Big Foot or the Mothman stop anyone from snapping up a good real estate deal when they saw one?

And it was California.

The only thing scarier than earthquakes, fire, and landslides were the housing prices. Also, my years spent working in the news business shaped my skepticism about viral videos of the supernatural and alien variety.

On the day the German tourist unleashed the Slough Devil video onto the world, we'd walked out of our morning editorial meeting, moaning about the lack of promotable stories with strong visuals. And then, like magic, the network assignment desk editor called and asked, in her snotty way, what we knew about the monster video and if we had anyone covering the story. It was news to us, but we weren't about to tell the network that, so we scrambled a reporter to Roy's Harbor to see what we could get, which was a few excited fishermen who swore they'd seen the creature before, except no one believed them.

And the naturalist Adam Gray. He was just as hot as the ladies at the station said.

In the interview, Adam looked thrilled, like we'd caught him waiting for a prostate exam, and picked his words with great care. He was borderline snippy, and if he hadn't been so good-looking, I'd have ordered the reporter to cut him from the story.

So to me, the video of the Slough Devil was just another crazy, out-there story, one I never took seriously and soon forgot. It also was the day I handed in my notice at the TV station where I worked as managing editor and six o'clock news anchor. Why? High stress, low pay, and terrible hours—the same reasons so many others ditched working in local news a few years into their careers.

I took a cushy job as head of communications for an agricultural startup. If I'd been willing to move to San Francisco or Silicon Valley, I could have found a better-paying job, but the only thing I hated more than the beach was traffic. The Central Coast was perfect for someone who loved a reasonable commute, walks in the redwoods, good Mexican food, and the occasional wine tasting. I didn't know much about agriculture, but that wasn't a problem. I could communicate a brand story and stay on message and pitch, and that's all the new bosses cared about.

My new salary was an enormous improvement over the pathetic pay I'd earned before—with lots more paid time off—and I thought about moving to a nicer place, but if I spent more money on a rental, then I wouldn't be saving for a down payment. When news of the housing lottery hit, I was all over it. Sure, the cottages weren't in the ideal location, and living next to the water was a waste on someone like me, but if I ever wanted to own my own place, that was my chance.

So, I entered the lottery for a Roy's Cottage. To my surprise, I won.

Later, when it came time to choose the lot at the developer's office, I studied the plans for all of five seconds and pointed at the cottage farthest from the slough, closest to the parking lot.

"Are you sure?" the agent asked, frowning. "It's the only one that doesn't face south, toward the water."

"That's why I like it," I said, then handed over an envelope with my second and final deposit.

The agent had gray smudgy circles under her eyes and sloping shoulders, weighed down by years of complaints. "Um, Christina. If at any point you change your mind, you won't be able to add a deck onto your property because of the way it's situated."

"I understand. Totally. If it makes you feel any better, would you like me to sign something?"

The agent brightened at this. "I think that would be best." She disappeared into the back to type up an addendum.

While I waited in the sterile office, with generic paintings of the Central Coast in washed out pastels, the door squeaked open, and a big man stumbled in, followed by a blast of musky perfume. A woman in tight jeans, a high ponytail, and cat eyeliner had both hands on his shoulders, pushing him forward. He gritted his teeth in a pained expression.

"Tell her," the woman snapped. She was around my age, closing in on mid-thirties.

The man's brown face turned a muddy red. "Anna," he groaned. "Please."

Both stared at me.

Before they dragged me into whatever they were up to, I held up a hand and said, "I don't work here." I sniffed. Anna's overpowering scent was making my nose run.

The man closed his eyes in relief, but his girlfriend, or wife, wasn't deterred.

"I want to speak to whoever is in charge," she said, eyes flashing, expecting me to argue.

I shrugged. "Go ahead. The agent will be back in a second." Then I snatched up my phone and tapped away, pretending I had urgent business.

A few minutes later, the agent reappeared, told the new visitors she'd be right with them, then beckoned me over to the counter.

The woman named Anna sidestepped me and launched at full volume. "We want our money back on the Royce Cottage…"

"Roy's Cottage, Anna," the man interrupted.

"Whatever, Michael." Anna put her hands on her hips. "I saw the video of that thing, and there is no way in hell I'm moving in there. No way, no how. Not me alone with the kids when he's away at work all day." She paused long enough to jerk her thumb in Michael's direction.

I had cousins like Anna and knew enough to stay out of it.

If Anna was expecting the agent to push back, she was quickly disappointed. The agent blinked, but managed a pleasant, professional smile.

"I'm sorry to hear that, but I understand. It won't be a problem. We have a waiting list of over five hundred people. If you can wait just a few minutes so I can finish helping this buyer, we can get the process started."

Without meeting my eyes, the agent pushed the two-page document across the counter. I read through it. It was straightforward enough, so I initialed both pages under the yellow sticky arrows, and she stapled them to my packet.

"Good luck," I said in a low voice.

The agent winked. "To you as well," she said with a smile, turning her full attention to the couple.

Before the door closed behind me, I heard Anna say, "Like I told my husband, I don't know what the fuck that was on the video, but there's no way I want it for a neighbor."

Turned out, Anna was the smartest woman in the world.

Chapter 3

Christina

Eighteen months after the German tourist caught the Slough Devil on video and shared it with the world, I moved into my Roy's Cottage on a bright Saturday morning in late March.

The creature hadn't resurfaced, much to everyone's relief, including the developers who had released a statement slamming the video as "nothing but a hoax intended to disrupt construction of the innovative, first-of-its kind project to help provide affordable, sustainable housing solutions while restoring the depleted Roy's Slough wetlands for the benefit of the entire community."

The developer had provided no evidence of a hoax, but it didn't need to. By ribbon-cutting time, the number of people who fell into Team Hoax seemed to outnumber Team Monster.

But as I learned on move-in day, some people were still nervous about living next door to an urban legend.

While rushing to my cottage, eager to open it for the first time, I ran into Ruth Burke, a former police chief. She was carrying a steel grey box that looked suspiciously heavy.

"Are you moving in?" I asked. Hopefully, because I liked her, and it never hurt to have someone with law enforcement connections living close by. Her retirement had come out of the blue. She was around fifty, and everyone expected her to stay on the job for another ten years. But, like me, Ruth burned out, and she'd admitted as much the last time I saw her.

She grinned. "Yeah. I couldn't believe my luck. Some people pulled out, and I was next on the wait list. So, are we neighbors, or are you just helping a friend?" Ruth had almond shaped eyes, luminous brown skin and a pixie cut.

"Nope. I'm here now too. What are you up to these days? Besides working out. Because you look great." And she did. She must have dropped twenty pounds, and she'd lost the pinched look around her mouth.

Ruth did a playful sideways lunge, bringing the metal box to her chest, holding it like a weight. "Thank you. I've got myself a trainer and darn, she pushes me. Hard. I went to work for a recruiting firm that specializes in law enforcement executives, so I get to keep my hand in. Without the stress. And since they're based in L.A., they're letting me work from home. Sweet! You still doing corporate communications?"

"I am and loving it. So far. Are you moving in with anyone?"

Ruth's perfectly arched eyebrows shot up. "If that's your way of asking me if I'm still single, that would be a yes, and at this rate, I'm going to die single. Apparently, I'm even too old for seventy-year-old men these days. I've even given up on dating apps. They're just too depressing. How about you? You still going out with that dentist?"

I shook my head. "No. He got way too serious too fast and then he got weird and clingy."

Basically, the same pattern every one of my relationships seemed to follow. My sister said the guys weren't the problem, I was. She said she'd read some articles about women like me: commitment-phobes. In my defense, I said, "Okay, but honestly, why should I continue to see someone if I know he's not...right? I mean, why waste the time?"

My sister said I had attachment and trust issues because I never got over my first serious boyfriend cheating on me. She even thought I should see a therapist because time was running out—I was pushing thirty-five.

Ruth gave a little shrug. "That's too bad. That dentist was hot."

I nodded, distracted by the box she was holding. "Is that a gun safe?"

"It is. I never go anywhere without my kids." Ruth clutched the box like I was threatening to snatch it from her.

"So you'll be ready in case the slough monster shows up," I joked.

Ruth set the metal case on the ground. "That video was such bullshit, but not everybody thinks so." She rolled her eyes. "Some people are so gullible. My trainer, Dawn, is moving in too, with her new husband. She hadn't heard about the video, and when she found out, she threw a fit and wanted to see if they could get out of their contract, but Paul talked her out of it. I just met him. He's a firefighter from Wyoming and he's got a gun locker that puts mine to shame. And, by the way, he said we—the homeowners—need to hold elections to vote board members onto our Home Owner's Association. He's going to run, and he asked me if I had any interest. I won't have time, but how about you? You'd be perfect."

"I'm not so sure about that." Being a board member meant meetings, and I already had to attend lots of them in my new job. Hopefully, other owners would step up. When I bought the place, I was surprised to learn it had an HOA, because each cottage was a separate building. The agent explained the small monthly association fee would cover landscaping, deck maintenance and other common areas, like the parking lot and the secure building for mail and deliveries.

Ruth scooped the gun locker off the ground. "I better put this thing away. After we get settled, let's get together for a drink sometime, okay?"

We updated our phone numbers and said goodbye.

The movers arrived with my furniture, and as soon as everything was in place, I could see it all looked wrong. My apartment in Pacific Grove had been old, with creaky wood floors, and lots of quirky charm. It was also expensive and impractical, with an outdated kitchen. By comparison, my new place gleamed like something out of an architectural magazine. With high ceilings throughout, it had a small foyer that opened to a "great room," a kitchen with high-end appliances, a half-bath and a mudroom leading to the back door. I'd use the downstairs bedroom as an office. Upstairs, there was a bedroom and bathroom.

Whoever designed the eleven hundred square foot cottage must have been a genius, because they'd packed a lot in without making it feel cramped. The outside was painted white with black trim. Some of the other cottages were bigger, with three bedrooms, or two bedrooms and an office, but none over fourteen hundred square feet.

My old dresser was too big for either of the bedrooms and my sofa was too small for the great room. It would be some time before I could afford new furniture, so I'd have to make do with what I had. The dresser would need to stay in the living area, and if I painted it and changed the handles, it could work as a TV console or bar.

I pulled my phone from the pocket of my jeans to search for decorating inspiration and saw with surprise I didn't have a signal, Then I vaguely remembered something about service being a problem until a new tower was installed. Except I couldn't recall when that was supposed to happen, and I couldn't look it up without a connection.

I also needed coffee, but with everything still in boxes, I couldn't make any. It occurred to me I didn't know where to find the closest cafe. I'd been so busy adjusting to my new job that I'd done nothing to familiarize myself with the area.

Roy's Cottages were oddly situated, off a rough rural road, about halfway between Santa Cruz and Monterey, some twenty miles from world class golfing at Pebble Beach, with the best Mexican food at El Charrito in Salinas a twenty-five-minute drive away. But it was also in the middle of nowhere, and if you stood on Sand Road and whirled around, you'd see nothing, but a long stretch of blacktop broken up with potholes in both directions and, on a clear day, the Gavilan Mountain range to the east.

Sand Road—scheduled for repaving in early summer—didn't have a single gas station, convenience store or fast-food drive through. I didn't even know where to find the closest grocery store. Another thing I needed to figure out if I wanted to make something for dinner instead of ordering pizza. Would they even deliver to such an out-of-the-way place?

My sister would have said this was typical of me to rush into things without thinking them through. Like deciding to spend an extra two years getting a master's degree in journalism only to get a job in a declining industry, where the hours were long and the pay was lousy. Like buying a house I could afford but that was out in the boonies.

My sister breezed through a two-year community college program and worked at a hospital in the radiology department doing diagnostic exams. She made almost as much as I did, worked fewer hours and never on holidays. My parents used to say she was the smart one. Before a drunk driver sped onto a freeway in Phoenix the wrong way and plowed into their car, killing them.

My temples were throbbing. What I needed was a jolt of caffeine. Preferably a nice hot cappuccino.

Roy's Harbor had to have a cafe, but I wasn't positive, because I'd only been there once for lunch at a restaurant famous for its clam chowder. I'd had a hard time finding it thanks to the worst fog I'd ever encountered. In fact, the fog was so thick I hadn't been able to see what else was there. For all I knew, there could be a Gucci store and a Cheesecake Factory, but all I wanted was a cafe with Wi-Fi and a grocery store.

Grabbing my keys and purse from the counter, I locked up and wandered around to see if there was someone I could ask about the lack of mobile service. The complex didn't have an office, but I'd heard the property manager from Monterey would be around on move-in day, and I found him near the mail building, surrounded by a small group of my new neighbors. The raised voices and shuffling feet hinted at a tense exchange, so I hung back and listened.

A tall guy with broad shoulders and a small waist said, "Are you saying what I think you're saying?"

An older man with sallow skin and rust-colored hair cleared his throat. "I'm sorry if this is coming as a surprise to some of you, but this was all in your disclosure packets, and my assistant emailed an update to all homeowners last week. We just found out that the phone company botched the order for the poles, so that means you won't have land lines until they can be installed. And as for cell service, that's going to take a while too. We're asking the carrier to stick to their original commitment and finish up the tower next week, but because of a staffing shortage, they're having to move workers around, and they're now saying it could be three to four weeks before they can get to it."

My heart sank as groans rippled through the group. Ruth appeared at my side, looking as dismayed as I felt. The property manager noticed us and raised a weary hand in greeting.

"Welcome. I'm Gary from the property management company. As you just heard, you won't have any mobile service until we can get the carrier to step up. This is a rural area, and the property is in a pocket between coverage areas and..."

An older woman standing on the other side of me interrupted. "I'm Liliana Garcia. I don't understand how this happened. Roy's Cottages have been in the works for what? Years? Didn't somebody think to get this done before we moved in? This is ridiculous. My husband has health issues. What if there's an emergency? How am I supposed to call for help?"

Gary's hair had that uneven reddish-brown shade that comes with home dye jobs. If he'd had the sense to go grey, he wouldn't look so jaundiced. He bit his lip and shoved his hands into the pockets of his baggy pants. "I understand your frustration, Mrs. Garcia. I really do. But I'll also be honest. From what I could gather, the responsibility for making sure this got done fell through the cracks, and since we only recently came onboard, we're still discovering some of these issues."

Mrs. Garcia wrinkled her nose as if someone had farted. She'd taken to glaring at the property manager with her arms folded in front of her chest. "So you say," she muttered.

Gary took a deep breath before he answered. "It's the truth, Mrs. Garcia. I have no reason to lie. I've been in this business for a long time, and you can ask anyone who's ever

21

worked with me. If my company blew it and got something wrong, I'd tell you and do my best to fix it. But this? This is out of my control, but we're going to straighten it out. Okay?"

I glanced over at Mrs. Garcia, who downgraded her glare to a wary appraisal. It was a chilly spring day with clouds moving in, but Gary's skin was shiny with perspiration. It was time to cut the man a break.

I said, "Thank you, Gary. Whatever you can do to expedite this, I'm sure everyone here will appreciate it. I know I will."

The group swiveled to give me the once over. The tall guy and the petite brunette in the black leggings, and a new arrival too. Another man. Whom I recognized immediately. The naturalist Adam Gray. He was shorter in person than I imagined. More like five-ten. But he was even better looking in real life with an arresting roman nose and longish black hair shot through with silver strands.

The brunette said, "Who put her in charge?" loud enough so everyone could hear. Her husband, who had to be the gun toting firefighter from Wyoming, clapped a hand over his mouth to hide his smile, like she was a toddler who'd just said something naughty and hilarious.

There was only one way to deal with someone like her. I stepped forward, stuck out my hand, and gave her my best smile. "Hi! I'm Christina. Very nice to meet you. I've heard you're an awesome personal trainer."

That was a stretch, but if there was one thing a small business owner couldn't resist it was more business. She looked me up and down, saw room for improvement, then her eyes widened. "Oh my god, I just recognized you. You used to be on the TV news, but we haven't seen you in a long time. I thought maybe you were on maternity leave or something."

Her eyes fell to my left hand (bare), then my stomach (reasonably flat), then dragged them back to my face. "And you let your hair go. I mean, you're not blond anymore. And I thought you'd be taller."

By that time, Paul no longer looked amused. His face had developed splotches of bright red. "Dawn," he said. "Um…" Clearly, he hadn't yet figured out how to reel in his new wife.

After years of being on television, I was used to personal remarks and found them only slightly annoying. The TV camera does weird things to people. It made me look taller and more angular. In real life, I'm five four. Dawn had one thing going for her besides a firm butt and a big mouth. She was observant. I had stopped bleaching my hair, and it was back to its natural shade of honey brown. Adam Gray was leaning against a wall, face expressionless. Watching.

The older woman with the sickly husband who was nowhere in sight, nudged me. "I'm Liliana. We just moved from Salinas. I never got to see you on TV. We watch the other station. No offense."

"None taken," I said.

Liliana was around seventy, with dangling earrings, eye popping neon green sneakers and silver spiked hair. "I got onto my computer to do a Zoom call with my kids. You know, to show them the place, but I couldn't get onto the internet. Is yours working?"

"I haven't tried yet," I said. My laptop was still sitting under a pile of junk next to an unopened box containing my desktop computer in the downstairs bedroom that I planned on using as an office. Then I made the connection. No phone service of any kind meant no internet connection. By the horrified expressions on my new neighbor's faces, they'd realized it too.

23

When I glanced over at Gary, the property manager was staring at us with his mouth open and a hand pressed against the side of his face. He cleared his throat again and waved his free hand over his head. "Everyone. If I can get your full attention. How many of you have read your disclosures?"

Dawn did one of those hip stretches, where you reach back, grab your ankle, and pull. "I skimmed them. Why do you ask?" The rest of the group nodded, including me. The disclosures were part of the buyer's paperwork, but I hadn't got around to reading the whole thing yet.

Gary closed his eyes and took a deep breath. Then he rolled his shoulders and said, "Then I have more bad news for you. There is no broadband in this area and the cable company has no plans to install it. There just aren't enough customers to justify the installation expense. The disclosures made that quite clear. If you want broadband, you'll have to pay for the cable run all the way out here. You can vote to cover the costs with a special assessment, but it will not be cheap. This is something the new HOA board can take up after board members are elected."

Stunned silence followed that bombshell. Dawn erupted first. "You've got to be fucking kidding me. There's no internet? How am I supposed to manage my business without the internet?"

Which was exactly what I was thinking. My new boss said I could work from home three days a week, but that cushy little arrangement wouldn't be possible if I couldn't get online. Which meant driving to Salinas for work every day.

Ruth groaned. "I can't believe this. I'm going to have to live at Starbucks or find an office to rent." Which wouldn't be cheap. Or nearby.

"I'm sorry," Dawn said, not sounding the least bit sorry. "But this is unacceptable. One hundred percent unacceptable. If we knew we wouldn't have a signal or internet, we would never have moved out here. Would we, Paul?" Paul gave an uneasy shrug.

"We certainly wouldn't have," Liliana piped up, her voice hard with bitterness. "Not with my husband's condition. No way, no how. I can't believe I'm about to say this, because we just moved in, but I think we may need to sell, and…"

A scream in the distance interrupted whatever she was about to say. Everyone froze. Except for Liliana, who flinched.

"That's Tommy," she cried, grabbing my arm.

Ruth, Paul, and Adam Gray raced toward the sound. Whatever was wrong with Liliana's husband hadn't affected his lungs. The piercing scream turned into a steady stream of shouts coming from the general direction of the marsh. Not wanting to abandon Liliana, I stayed by her side. With Dawn's help, we guided her toward the water.

When we hobbled up, Liliana murmuring, "Please god, please god," we found Paul crouched next to a balding man sitting in a chair on a dock that led to the slough. Paul had two fingers on the man's wrist, taking his pulse. Liliana sagged with relief at the sight of her husband, who was shaking his head and shivering.

Ruth was staring at the old guy with sharp, law enforcement eyes, while Adam Gray stood at the far end of the dock, gazing down at the water. Liliana recovered and rushed toward her husband on unsteady feet, arms outstretched.

"What happened?" she asked in a shrill voice.

The old man looked up at her with dark, confused eyes. "I saw it. It was in the water. Just like they said."

Liliana grabbed his hands in hers. "Like who said? What did you see?"

"The monster!" the man bellowed. "What the hell else would I be talking about? I told you we shouldn't move here. That's the trouble with you. You never listen."

Maybe whatever ailed the man made him cranky, too. Liliana, for all the feistiness she showed earlier, looked around nervously, then gave his hands an imploring shake. "Ai, Tommy. Settle down. Those new meds are messing with your head." She straightened up and turned to me. "The doctor gave him some new pills and when he's not sleeping, he's imagining things. He's the one who wanted to move here. We haven't been here half a day yet and I'm already having second thoughts about this place."

Talk about buyer's remorse. While I was sympathetic, we'd just met. Finding out we didn't have cell service or internet was enough of a blow without getting pulled into the personal problems of strangers. I slinked away down the dock, careful to keep to the middle. Water on both sides had the bizarre effect of triggering vertigo, and the last thing I needed was to fall into the water in front of Adam Gray.

The clouds overhead had turned the water a dark greenish gray. The slough was wider than I remembered when I toured my cottage for the first time. For once, there wasn't a kayaker in sight. Probably too foggy for that. Trees on the opposite bank rose out of the mist. A flock of brown pelicans preened on a sandbank, a rock's throw from where we stood, ignoring us. Up close, the birds were enormous. It was colder next to the water. My sweatshirt was no match against the damp, and I shivered.

"See anything out there?" I asked.

Without bothering to glance my way, the naturalist continued to stare out at the water, "Just what I see out here every day. I thought we'd have at least a couple of days before people started shouting 'monster,' but I guess I was wrong." Then he swung toward me and scraped a hand through his hair. "People," he said.

"People," I said in agreement. "I'm Christina, by the way. Christina Figueroa. Formerly of Pacific Grove."

"I know who you are. You used to be on billboards advertising your TV station. I'm Adam Gray. Formerly of Monterey, now resident of Cottage A-2." He paused long enough to point behind us, just to the left of where the others gathered around Mr. Garcia. "That's my place over there. Luckily, the Garcia's are in the second row back, so he won't be sitting around his living room staring out at the water, mistaking seals for monsters."

"Is that what you think happened?" I asked.

Adam nodded. "I do. The slough is full of seals and otters. One may have hopped onto the deck where Tommy was and scared him." He paused, studying me warily. "You're not one of those slough monster believers, are you?"

"If I was, I wouldn't admit it. That kind of thing can't be good for property values."

Adam's eyes narrowed. They were an unusual color. A cool gray. Like the clouds. Like his last name. "I would have thought you made way too much money to qualify for one of these places, working in TV."

I snorted. My sister had repeatedly warned me about not making that sound in front of attractive men. "Hah. Salaries suck in local TV. The starting pay is less than in fast food or a grocery store."

Adam's eyebrows jumped up. Unlike the hair on his head, they were dark, without a hint of silver. "Wow. I thought TV people made a lot of money."

Another snort escaped my throat. "Some do. In the big TV markets and at the national level. But the pay sucks in the smaller towns. But I have a new job and, luckily, my new salary came under the wire so I still qualified. I'm guessing being a tour operator isn't a get-rich job?"

"No, it's not. But it's what I love, and I'm building up my other business."

"And that would be?"

"Bushcraft," he replied.

For a second, I thought he was making a dirty joke. Because every time I've heard the word 'bush,' snickers usually followed., so I said nothing and waited for an explanation. A flush bloomed under his tan.

He cleared his throat and said, louder than necessary, "Wilderness survival. I do one and two-day boot camps, and when I can find someone I trust enough to handle my tour business on their own, I'll start offering the occasional one-week course."

"Nice," I lied. In fact, it sounded horrible. It probably involved sleeping outside in bad weather, learning how to rub two sticks together, without TV or wine. Adam shot me a look that told me he had a well-developed bullshit detector.

We were walking back to the others when he stopped and knelt where a part of the deck jutted about five feet over the water. I'd seen some marketing photos of a couple sitting in fancy deck chairs, sipping cocktails, and enjoying a cheese plate, not a harassing seagull in sight. Only the first row of cottage owners had decks jutting out onto the slough.

Adam's hair fell over his face, so I couldn't see his expression. He was running a hand along the side of the deck, which appeared to be made of a sturdy, fake wood material.

"What are you doing?" I asked.

Ignoring my question, he continued with his inspection, and when he finally stood up, his eyes fixed on me, and I felt a tingle race up my arms. Adam might never have worked a day of his life in a newsroom, but I knew that look. The one that directors get when technology delivers an unexpected problem they've never encountered. A mix of disbelief and indignation.

"I just found some pretty deep scratches," he said, then pointed.

I inched my way toward the edge of the deck and peered over the side where the fake wood met the lapping water. Sure enough. There were several deep grooves notched into the plank like something had clawed there to haul itself up.

"What made those?"

Adam shook his head. "I don't know."

"What do you mean you don't know? You're supposed to be the nature expert around here." The words came out more accusing than I intended, but his reaction to the scratches filled me with unease. "Could it have been an otter?" I asked. "Or maybe a worker installing the deck scratched it with a screwdriver or something."

"Sea otters have retractable claws on their front paws, but they aren't big enough to make those kinds of scratches, and that's not the pattern a screwdriver would make." He grimaced, then exhaled loudly. "I don't know what made those scratches but considering what just happened and the…" he paused, frowning as he searched for the right words, "…the atmosphere we find ourselves in, we might want to keep this to ourselves unless you want to freak out our new neighbors. If you get my meaning."

I did. Of course, I did. I didn't like it, but the alternative wasn't much better. Even the most casual announcement about mysterious scratches would alarm Mr. Garcia and Dawn, and all I wanted to do was grab a cup of coffee, and find a market to buy stuff for dinner, and get settled into my new place.

So, I said, "Yeah, sure," then watched as Adam slipped his phone from a pocket and quietly took pictures of the strange marks.

Chapter 4

Christina

Before leaving my new place, I set the odometer—five miles west on Sand Road, zig-zagging to avoid potholes, a heart-stopping left turn onto a busy two-lane highway, then another mile to Roy's Harbor. By the time I got there, those six miles felt like ten. It would feel even farther when I drove to Salinas for work, or to Monterey for shopping. I'd heard Sand City had decent options, but I hadn't had time to explore it yet. All that could wait. What I really needed was a cappuccino and something to eat.

I found both at The Otter Cafe at Roy's Harbor. It was far enough from the water I could sit outside and not freeze. The overhead heaters helped too. When the fog lifted, it was bright and clear enough to make me dig through my purse for my sunglasses.

A small gallery was attached to the back of the cafe. The owner—a furry-faced man the size of a door—painted delicate watercolors of otters and other wildlife. The gallery also had historical photos of Roy's Harbor. From the plaques, I learned the harbor started as a whaling station and fishing port, then was home to sardine processing plants and canneries. In 1906, the great San Francisco earthquake nearly destroyed the wharf, and the whole thing was rebuilt. Of course, before Captain Roy landed on the Central Coast, the area belonged to the Ohlone people, but there was just a mention of them and not a single illustration.

The harbor went through some rough patches after the whaling and sardine industries cratered. Eventually, bass, salmon, and crab fishing filled the void, and after the Monterey Bay became a wildlife sanctuary, Roy's Harbor took off as a port and tourist destination.

The server at the café said there was a market not far away, a short walk to the end of Marine Road, so I left my car in the lot and wandered around looking for it. Seagulls whirled overhead. The briny tang of the harbor filled my nose.

Halfway there, I came across a small crowd clustered outside a shop. "Blue Anchor Books" announced the sign overhead, along with a poster in the window advertising a book signing. "Meet the author of Bushcraft Basics" it read, underneath a picture of the book's cover.

Bells of recognition began ringing in my head. The photo on the cover made me do a double take.

It was Adam Gray, squinting into the distance with an axe over his shoulder, looking like he was trying to figure out which tree to chop. His scraggly, silver-threaded black hair looked like it needed a wash, but he also appeared to be the kind of guy you wanted at your campsite—rugged and capable.

The line outside the bookshop had grown so long it snaked around the corner, and when the door opened, about thirty people trooped inside. I followed them, curious.

Earlier, when we had gone our separate ways, Adam hadn't mentioned anything about a book signing. Most men I knew would have managed to drop that somehow. The crowd was an eclectic mix. College students in Cal State, Monterey Bay and University of California, Santa Cruz sweatshirts. A dozen or so men and women dressed like software engineers. A sprinkling of backpacker types wearing thick-soled hiking sandals. A few fishermen in brimmed caps. And a gaggle of women in leggings with the kind of sinewy bodies resulting from doing Pilates.

The bookshop owner clapped her hands in delight at the size of the crowd and batted her eyes in appreciation bordering on worship. Adam sat slouched behind a table, looking like he wished he was anywhere but there.

For god's sake, Adam, sit up, I wanted to shout at him.

Instead, I found a foldout chair in the last row and hid behind a broad-shouldered fisherman who smelled funky, like he'd just finished cleaning a fish. And maybe he had. The Pilates women whispered to each other loud enough I could hear.

"Oh my god, Amanda, you were right. He is so hot."

"I get why we're here, but can someone tell me what bushcraft is?"

"If it involves my bush, I'm all for it."

If Adam could feel the heat of their lust from where he was sitting, he showed no sign of it. Not even a peek in their direction.

The book shop owner had short bangs and a bowl haircut, and she clapped her hands again. "All right, everyone, I want to make sure we start on schedule so we leave enough time for questions. And I promised Adam we'd only take up an hour of his time, as he has a full schedule today."

She pushed her shoulders back and glanced at an index card in her left hand.

"Adam Gray is the owner of Gray Wildlife Tours, a business he inherited from his father. Adam grew up at Devil's Landing, and we're so glad he decided to return to the Central Coast after working as a ranger on the East Coast. Bushcraft Basics is Adam's debut book, and if you haven't read it, it's as beautifully written and entertaining as it is helpful and essential, so it's no surprise that it's made several best seller lists. So, without further ado, I present Adam Gray!"

The gushy speech made Adam squirm. After clearing his throat a few times, he said, "Thank you, Margie, for your kind words. I'm so glad to be here, and I want to thank all of you for taking time out of your Saturday."

His flat tone didn't quite match the gracious words of his opening remarks. I hoped he'd loosen up.

His gray eyes scanned the audience and eventually lighted on me. Oops. The broad-shouldered fisherman had shifted in his seat, leaving me exposed. His eyebrows lifted in surprise. I returned his stare with a sheepish wave and smile. The Pilates women swiveled and gave me the once over.

Adam started talking about his inspiration for the book, and within a few minutes, I found myself captivated like the rest of the audience.

"People asked me why I wrote this book," he began. "It's simple, really. In my first month working as a national park ranger, three day-hikers strayed from the trail and got lost. One fell into a creek and had no dry clothes to change into. Then a cold front moved in, and without jackets for warmth, two of them died of hypothermia. The woman who fell into the creek was just twenty-eight years old, and her partner, thirty. Both were healthy and physically fit. The only survivor was a friend, also thirty, who spent several nights in the hospital. Our search and rescue team managed to find him just in time.

"This tragedy was caused by a lack of planning, starting with not bringing the right jackets, the right layers. Then, they didn't tell anybody where they were going. They didn't have any way to light a fire that could have helped them survive the night. They were so convinced they were only hiking for a few hours, they didn't consider any other possibility." Adam sat back in his chair, shaking his head, grim.

The fisherman in front of me shot up his hand. "I thought bushcraft meant eating bugs and stuff to survive."

Adam managed an indulgent smile. "That's a bit extreme. Which is why I call this Bushcraft Basics. The kind of stuff you learn in the book is more along the lines of wrapping a lighter in duct tape to make it waterproof and packing things you might need, like giant trash bags to use for protection and shelter. And sure, the book shows you how to set up a camp and, the stuff no one likes to talk about, personal hygiene."

While the talk was more interesting than I imagined— who knew ash from a fire could be used as an antibacterial—it made me rethink my love of taking hikes in the redwoods. At least the way I took them, which involved hopping out of my car in joggers, a flannel shirt, and sneakers. Most of the time, I didn't even take a backpack with snacks, just a flask of water swinging from my hand. Now, my little treks through the woods seemed ignorant and foolhardy. Which, I supposed, was the point of his book. To share basic survival skills so rescue crews wouldn't have to risk their lives trying to save idiots like me. And I wasn't alone, based on the dumb questions people asked.

But the one thing they really wanted to know—the real reason they were there—became clear once Adam finished his talk and the Q&A started.

"Now, Adam," the fisherman said. "You've lived around here for most of your life. You ever see that Slough Devil?"

Adam hooked his hair behind an ear. "Hi Sig. I can't say I have."

"But you were giving the tour that day when the German fellow got that video, weren't you? You must have seen something then," the fisherman persisted. The leathery fat rolls on the back of his neck quivered with indignation.

Adam sucked in his lips and paused before answering. "I was busy piloting the boat, and by the time I was made aware of the video, whatever the camera caught was long gone. I didn't see anything myself that day, or any day, for that matter. But let me ask you this. You've been fishing around here for a long time. In all those years, have you ever seen anything that looks like the so-called Slough Devil?"

With his back to me, I couldn't see Sig's expression, but the way he puffed up hinted he was winding up with a good answer. "Can't say I have, but I'll tell you something interesting. I got to know your dad a bit down at the docks. Once, I asked him if he'd take me in that old boat of his to the end of the slough, and he flat out refused. He said he'd take me as far as the last dairy farm and no farther, and when I asked him why, he said he'd seen something at the end of the channel that scared the hell out of him. And when I asked him what it was, he said it was the Slough Devil."

Everyone had turned to stare at Sig, mouths slightly open. He had a deep, rumbly voice, the kind made for telling scary stories around a campfire. I shivered, even though the room was warm.

When I looked over at Adam, his arms were folded in front of his chest, and he was nodding. "Were you two drinking Jack Daniels by any chance?"

Sig hesitated, then barked out a laugh and pointed a beefy hand at Adam. "You got me. That's the truth. We used to knock 'em back at Doxie's before they tore it down to build the new laundromat."

"Sounds like my dad. Thank you for sharing that, Sig. All I can say is, my dad did love telling stories about the Slough Devil, mostly to keep me away from the water when I was a kid."

Sig gave a booming laugh. "You make it sound like your dad invented the Slough Devil, but that's something he can't take credit for. That story goes way back. Way, way back. And that's something you ought to know, Adam, as a local."

Adam gave a weary sigh. "Oh, I do. I just think it's an urban legend that refuses to die."

One of the Pilates women waved a hand over her head. "Okay, but what do you think it was? Based on your experience."

Like Adam Gray was an expert on monsters and not a naturalist.

Adam's eyes slid past the woman, and suddenly, he was staring right at me. I realized then I must have been smirking. Oops again. I quickly turned it into one of those encouraging half-smiles which says, you've got this buddy.

Not that he needed my help. Adam Gray was doing fine on his own.

He replied, "I must have watched that video a thousand times, and in all honesty, I just don't know."

The Pilates woman didn't give up easily. She jumped up and tugged at her leggings. "Do you think it was a hoax? Because if it wasn't real, then what was it? I've seen that video myself, and it was big. And it did not look like an animal. I guess what I'm really asking is, is the slough safe for people?" She paused and gestured to her friends sitting around her. "We're down here for the weekend, and we were thinking it would be fun to rent some kayaks to go up Roy's Slough to see the otters, but we're not sure that's such a good idea. What do you think?"

Since her back was to me, I couldn't see her face, but she sounded sincerely concerned. Again, I found myself locking eyes with Adam. I hoped I wasn't misreading his expression—

we'd just met, and I hardly knew him—but I could swear his eyes held a silent, desperate plea.

I rose and wriggled my shoulders straight. "I just moved into Roy's Cottages next to the slough, and I think you'll be just fine."

Adam sat back in his chair, blinking. Clearly, he hadn't expected me to barge in like that.

"Uh, I agree," he said. "I think if you want to take that kayak trip, you should. And you couldn't ask for better weather tomorrow. Just go in the morning. It gets windy in the afternoon, and it makes getting back to the harbor not so fun. And if you want any extra reassurance about the slough, I bought a place right next to it myself."

The Pilates women bent their heads together, whispered, then shot jealous glances in my direction.

The shop owner scurried over and profusely thanked Adam for attending the book signing. While people stood in line for him to sign their copies, I briefly debated hanging around. It seemed rude to leave, not offer my congratulations on his new book, but it also seemed presumptuous—the annoying new neighbor with expectations of instant friendship and, since he was a good-looking man, maybe even something more. That was my answer. I waved when he glanced up, then darted outside in search of the grocery store.

I thought about walking back to pick up the car, but I wanted to explore the rest of the harbor village in good weather, and I didn't plan to buy much. Just a few things for dinner. So, I walked. The chilly breeze blowing in from the ocean was a shock after the warmth of the bookstore, and I pulled up the collar of my jacket. Most of the buildings were Old West architecture—wood with high false fronts, some with second story balconies. I strolled past several gift and art shops, a post office, and a fish and chips restaurant. A sprawling marine lab followed, then a bed and breakfast with faded pink paint, a bar which looked like a saloon straight out of a Western movie, a place selling fishing gear along with beer and snacks, and then, finally, Roy's Harbor Market.

It was small, well-stocked, and ridiculously expensive. Not the kind of place where you went big shopping, unless you were rich or careless with your hard-earned money. The floors were so uneven—sagging and sloping in places—it reminded me of the funhouse I loved as a kid. I was browsing the aisles—collecting the ingredients for my Saturday calorie and carb splurge—spaghetti with clam sauce—when I nearly collided with Adam.

"Hey," he said, but not like he was surprised to see me.

I hadn't expected to run into him again. Otherwise, I wouldn't have pulled my hair into a messy, drunk girl bun. "Hi. Congratulations on your book. I planned on picking one up later. And wow. Your talk was great. Interesting. Well-done."

Adam gave a one-shouldered shrug. "Thanks, but I like giving tours better." He plunged his hands into the pockets of his hoodie.

It was then I realized he hadn't bothered to change for his appearance at the book shop. Then again, he seemed at home in what he was wearing, and if he'd shown up in anything else, he wouldn't have looked so...authentic. While he'd been giving his talk, my thoughts kept returning to when I first saw him earlier that day. Adam hadn't seemed surprised, and certainly not upset, when we learned we didn't have phone or internet service at Roy's Cottages.

Standing in the produce section, shoving a bunch of Italian parsley into a plastic bag, I said, "You read the disclosures, right? Before you bought your place?"

Adam nodded in that slow, thoughtful way of his. "Oh yeah. Every single word. This was the biggest purchase of my life, and I wanted to know what I was getting into." He paused, sucking air between his teeth. "Also, the packet seemed a little too thick to not have something in it."

He was right, of course. The disclosure packet had seemed a bit too substantial not to contain something more than just routine stuff, but I'd been so eager to grab my only shot at a mortgage on the Central Coast, I'd hadn't done my homework. Even if I had, it wouldn't have changed my mind. Those problems could be fixed later. How could they not be? Who lived without cell phones and the internet these days? Still, if I had read the disclosures, I wouldn't have been so surprised. I'd have known what I was getting into.

"It doesn't bother you?" I asked, curious.

Adam pushed onto the tips of his toes. "Not really. I'm one of those digital minimalist types. I have a computer for work, but I try to stay off it as much as I can, and I hate the phone." He shrugged. "I know. It sounds pretentious, or at least that's what my friends keep telling me. But I don't like being tethered to tech, you know?"

In fact, I didn't. Because I didn't have any friends like that. We were all enslaved to tech. But good for him. What he was talking about wasn't a new concept. I'd done a special report for my old TV station about the digital hijacking of our brains and our time.

"How about TV? We won't be able to watch that either." If he wasn't bothered, I was. How would I get through the evenings without my favorite pastime?

Adam shrugged. "If I want to watch a game, I go to a friend's house. He's got one of those big screen TVs, like eighty-five inches. Sometimes we watch sci-fi movies. But mostly, I read. Or listen to music. Or do other stuff."

"I like to read too, but this practically makes us Amish."

Adam laughed, but the smile faded a little too fast. "Well, I have to say, I am a little worried. It's not the best idea to be miles from anywhere without phones. For emergencies. And those are bound to happen. You know. People get sick. And stuff." Those last two words just sort of hung there between us like a dark cloud.

And stuff.

Like whatever scratched up the sides of the dock back at the cottages. Like whatever it was Tommy Garcia saw before he started shouting his head off. Like whatever Adam Gray seemed to be worrying about, even if he didn't want to admit it.

He followed me to the canned food section. I plucked a tin of chopped clams from a shelf and dropped it into the basket dangling from my arm.

"Isn't there anything we can do?" I asked over my shoulder. "Until the property management company can un-fuck this situation?"

A grandmother pulling along a small child glared at me.

Adam scooted around them, hands still shoved into the pockets of his jacket. "When you were on TV, did you ever accidentally F-bomb on the air?" he asked, like he really wanted to know.

I was a little taken aback by how close he was standing. If he kept that up, I'd grab another can of clams and a bottle of wine and invite him for dinner.

"Yes," I admitted. "Well, almost. The director saw it coming and cut my mic before it hit the air, or I definitely would have been fired."

41

Adam pulled out his phone and gave it a quick glance, then sighed. "Uh. I've got another book talk in Santa Cruz, and I better leave if I'm going to get there on time. They're doing this wine reception thing."

"Good luck," I said, doing my best to erase any thoughts of us splitting a bottle of red wine, surrounded by my unopened boxes, like a scene from a romance movie.

"Thanks. I hate these things, but I promised my agent I'd live up to my side of the marketing bargain. You should have seen her face when I told her I wasn't on social media, and I wasn't going to be just because of the book."

"It seems to be selling fine without it," I replied, fumbling around in my purse for my wallet.

At the end of the checkout lane, Adam reached into a pocket, pulled something out, and shook it. A blue cloth bag decorated with white jelly fish snapped open. He expertly bagged my groceries and handed the bag to me. "Maybe I can pick that up tomorrow?" he asked, glancing at it like he hated to part with it.

I was still trying to decide what level of smooth I'd just witnessed, and how best to answer, when Adam started walking backwards toward the exit.

"Well, good luck with all the unpacking. And I wasn't ignoring your question earlier, about whether there's anything we can do about our situation. I was going to talk to the property manager guy about maybe getting a sat phone. One we could keep in the mailroom, in case of emergencies. And I forgot to ask. What cottage are you in?"

"I'm in the one closest to the parking lot," I said, tapping my credit card on the payment screen.

"Good," he said.

I stared after him, wondering what that meant. Because when everybody else found out I lived furthest from the water, they offered their condolences. That was a strange response from a guy who made his living on the slough.

Chapter 5

Adam

Within a week after The Marsh Massacre Mystery—as it came to be known—a documentary filmmaker tracked us down in Sedona, Arizona.

Christina and I had plenty of offers to tell our story, but in the end, we decided to go with Tamara Rhodes. Not only had she produced several award-winning documentaries, but she'd also offered the largest appearance fee in exchange for signing an exclusive contract. Which was fine by us. Explaining what happened to a skeptical world with cameras rolling wasn't something we were eager to do more than once.

"At least we'll be one and done," Christina said, after looking over the contract Tamara had emailed.

Of course, we had a lawyer read it before we signed. The title of the documentary, The Slaughter at the Slough, made me swallow, hard, and sent my stomach churning. All those inescapable nouns—massacre, slaughter, bloodbath, annihilation, carnage, mass murder—attached themselves to every iteration of the story, which had attracted world-wide attention. Not that the words were wrong. The opposite, in fact. I felt slightly dizzy with the realization so many words existed to express what we'd somehow managed to survive. It all added to a sense of unreality I'd been unable to shake since...

Since...

I could hardly bring myself to say it. How would I manage to sit in front of a camera and give the interview I'd promised?

Christina said, as far as producers went, Tamara Rhodes was good. Very good. The best we could hope for, given the subject matter of the documentary. Any doubts I still had about her—and there were plenty—I shoved aside because the truth was, I needed the money to start over in a place far from Devil's Landing.

Whatever the future held was a worry I'd yet to have. It was out there, as inevitable as the incoming tide, but until it arrived, I was stuck in the past. Thinking about that damn slough. What came out of it. Over and over again in an endless, horrifying loop. Sometimes, it would begin with a sound. An unearthly chittering through the fog. The scratch of claws on wood. A wet plop against a kayak. Other times, it would start with an image. A dark, misshapen figure loping into the shadows of the opposite shore. The appearance of a mud-encrusted face in a window.

Get a fucking grip.

As many times as I'd thought it, muttered it, even prayed for it, controlling my thoughts and emotions was impossible, not even with therapy. There was no therapy for what I'd experienced. I could never hope to explain what happened without using that ridiculous word.

Monster.

And not the sort people often obsess over—serial killers, pedophiles, and Nazi war criminals.

Real monsters.

I'd chosen the outdoor life for its endless variety, the seasons on my face, and the natural guardrail against the temptations and overindulgence of technology. But how could I have known nature had hidden such creatures so close to tourists innocently enjoying the wonders of the Monterey Bay? And how could they have been hidden from me? The savvy

46

outdoorsman who thought he knew every inch of the slough. Prided himself on it. Humbly bragged about it.

"If something was out there, I would know about it," I'd said many a time.

But that was a lie. Even when those words came spilling out, I knew it. My attempts to explore the far end of the slough had ended in failure. The mud too boggy, the brush too thick, the wild expanse too wide, too deep. And I hadn't been the only one. Others had trekked in to explore. The determined surveyor, the scoffing survivalist, the naive and overly optimistic day hiker. But all had given up, emerging from that clump of coastal forest, embarrassed and bewildered they'd managed to get lost in those earthy-smelling woods. What was in there was anybody's guess. Until it decided we'd gotten a bit too close and sent out an unwelcoming party.

When Tamara Rhodes and her film crew arrived, panic set in. When I opened my mouth to answer her first question, sweat pooled at the base of my spine, and the words came out of my mouth in croaks, like a frog had lodged itself in my throat.

Christina's brown eyes widened, and she held up a hand. "Can we have a moment?" she said to the producer.

The crew had chosen to film in the backyard under the shade of a tree, Sedona's famous red rocks in the distance. Tamara didn't look happy but replied with a clipped, "Of course."

Christina hauled me inside to the kitchen and snatched an amber pill bottle from a cupboard, shaking out two tablets. "I think you forgot this," she said quietly, placing one in my outstretched palm.

I gazed down at the oval-shaped pill, scored in the middle. "I didn't think I needed it."

"That makes two of us." Christina swallowed a pill, dry.

That first day of filming was rough. For me. Christina's on-camera experience kicked in around the same time as the medication, and I could hear the crew exchanging whispers about how good she was.

The second day of filming went marginally better. We took our anti-anxiety meds an hour before the crew arrived, and by the time they left, I felt drained, and my throat was parched.

I poured myself a beer. Christina said I better get my shit together and start talking, really talking, if I wanted that nice fat check the producer promised.

"They'll pay me. They need me," I said, cracking open another beer. Another thing I needed to get a grip on. There was always another beer.

Christina looked up from her book. A space fantasy, like earth wasn't fantastical enough. "No, they don't. Not if you're going to sit there and grunt at them. They'll cut you loose, and they'll work around you if they have to."

She was too thin, her lower back still bearing scars from what happened on the beach. When we first met, she'd had curves. But now, she was a more angular version of herself. Still feisty though. Thank God.

My phone vibrated in a pocket. I kept it on me, or close by, just in case. When I glanced at the screen, a message from Tamara awaited and I groaned.

Christina glanced up from her book, frowning. "What's up?"

"It's Tamara. She said she's sent a video she wants me to watch. They interviewed the crazy podcast lady I told you about. The urban legend expert, or whatever she calls herself."

A faint smile played around Christina's lips. "Sounds like Tamara is trying to fire you up."

"Piss me off is more like it. Want to watch it with me?"

"No thank you."

I swiped my laptop off the lumpy couch and went into the wood-paneled kitchen to sit at the table. Tam's email glowed white in my inbox. Dark mode had a way of making even the most boring communication look slightly sinister. I clicked on the link, then entered the password the producer had provided and hit play.

A riot of color blasted my eyes. Patti Nelson had a mop of curly purple hair, a neon yellow-green top, and an electric blue scarf wrapped around her neck. I'd never seen her before. Only listened to her once for a few minutes, out of curiosity, and found her compelling, even if what she said was ridiculous for someone who had a Ph.D. in anthropology.

Or so I used to think.

The camera focused on Patti, who sat on a carved throne-like chair next to a cluttered desk. The wall behind her had several framed prints—woodblocks of Bigfoot and the Mothman. Tamara talked somewhere out of view, issuing last minute instructions to the crew darting around, adjusting the lighting and the clip-on mic attached to Patti's scarf.

Tamara plunged in with the first question. "I understand you've tracked down some new information about the Slough Devil. What can you tell us about that?"

Patti was older than I'd imagined. Seventy at least. With the telltale signs of good plastic surgery and a lifetime of healthy choices, she looked better than some women twenty years younger. She sniffed.

"Slough Devils, plural. There's no way just one was responsible for all that carnage."

"Yes, of course," Tamara said off-camera.

Patti settled back in her chair. "Well, let's start off with the first sign that anything was amiss at Roy's Slough. This dates to May 1906, when a ten-year-old boy went missing. Families from around Devil's Landing searched for him, but his body was never found. His parents said he was prone to wandering, and he disappeared during high tides. It was assumed he'd been swept away by what today we call a sneaker wave."

Christina's parents had never updated the kitchen, and the old pine cabinets smelled musty. I got up, cranked open a sticky window, and began to pace. So the story my parents told had been true.

I used to think they invented it to scare some sense into me, keep me away from the docks and the sand banks I loved to explore. Whenever my mother sensed my distraction, my eagerness to leave the safety of the house for the outdoors, she'd switch to her native Japanese, the language she reverted to whenever she was agitated. Back then, I knew enough to understand the gist of what she was saying. Many years ago, a Devil's Landing boy had gone out and never returned. He was ten. Small for his age, like me, with black hair, like mine.

When I asked how she knew what he looked like, she'd turn white with anger. "Are you calling your mother a liar?" I remember her saying.

My father thought these exchanges were funny. He'd throw an arm around her and say, "Oh, come on, admit it. Our kid's smart. Nothing gets past him."

Patti Nelson crossed her legs and continued. "The body of that missing boy was never found, but beginning in the summer of 1906, dairy farmers along the slough began to report something was killing their animals. Cows and goats mostly, that were allowed to graze close to the water. The farmers thought a mountain lion must have wandered down from the hills, so they decided to go hunting for it, and when they came back, they had quite a story to tell. They said they followed some tracks to the eastern end of the slough. It's heavily wooded there. They didn't make it very far in, when they came running out again, saying they'd seen something swinging in the trees and it came after them, but whatever it was, it was no mountain lion. That's when the rumors about the Slough Devil really got started."

Patti Nelson paused long enough to reach over for a notebook on the desk.

"Which brings us to what happened before the sighting I just mentioned, before the farm animals began turning up butchered, and before the boy disappeared."

She leaned toward the camera, tapping the notebook on her knees in a theatrical pause. "A circus came to town. And pay attention to the date because it's quite significant. The circus arrived on April 13, 1906. More like, blew ashore. It was storming, and the captain lost control of the ship. Crewmen were tossed overboard. Devil's Landing came by its name honestly. The whaling captain, and namesake of Roy's Harbor, said it best."

Patti closed her eyes and recalled the words.

"In 1856, Captain Roy wrote, 'It's a devil of a time to land here due to the treacherous weather conditions which seem to arrive without the usual proper notice.'" Her eyes popped open. "According to the newspaper accounts from the time, the circus came from an Eastern European country. Which one, I couldn't find, but it was called The Nightly Wonders Circus. The locals had never seen anything like it, so you can imagine the excitement. Roy's Harbor wasn't its final destination though. That was San Francisco. But first, the manager needed to hire some more workers and thought he could find them easier and cheaper on the Central Coast. Plus, he wanted a chance to work on some new acts, so he opened three rehearsals to the public, free of charge. The performances were held once nightly, beginning April 15th. I was able to find several articles written by a reporter from Monterey who attended the first performance, along with several dozen local families."

Patti reached across to her desk for a pair of bright red reading glasses.

"The reporter described it as, and I quote, 'equal parts entertaining and disturbing, aerialists spinning overhead without nets beneath them and freaks of such biological rarities as to defy belief. But it was the beasts that aroused the most interest. Fierce creatures that walked on two legs with the rocking gait of an ape, but able to run on all fours when prompted by the lash of a whip and, in some fleeting instances, when forced to demonstrate their prowess at climbing the poles supporting the tent. They would occasionally stop and gaze at the audience with a sudden and unexpected resemblance that was all too human.' End quote."

Patti whipped off her glasses, fluffed her scarf, and continued.

"The third and final rehearsal performance of the Nightly Wonders Circus at Roy's Harbor never happened. The earthquake that devastated San Francisco on April 18th also shook Roy's Harbor. It hit the area so hard that pilings and piers crumbled. Buildings and bridges collapsed. In other words, anything standing up got knocked down, like the circus tent and everything associated with it, including the cages holding the animals. Most of the animals were recovered, but not those 'beasts' the reporter talked about."

Off camera, Tamera gasped. "And then what happened?"

Patti shook her head. "The unimaginable. Whatever those animals were charged the carnival owner and their handler, killing them in a brutal and bloody assault. The circus folk claimed to be too terrified of the beasts to intervene, so they watched as the creatures escaped up the slough. Afterward, a reporter asked where they had come from, or what they were, but the circus workers swore they didn't know. Only one person had anything of interest to say—a three-legged woman who acted as the circus fortune teller."

Again, Patti paused to fumble for her glasses and read from the notebook.

"'They are not from anywhere,' the fortune teller scoffed. 'It was evil magic that made them, and black magic that made them weak. But when the earth shook, it rattled and broke the magic. Those bad men got what they deserved. I hope those poor creatures can finally find some peace.' As for the Nightly Wonders Circus, a man billed as 'the lion-faced marvel from Italy who can read and write in a half dozen languages!' led the troupe of performers south to Los Angeles instead of north to San Francisco, where the city was fighting an enormous fire that was more devastating than the earthquake. What happened to the circus after that, I haven't been able to discover."

A long silence followed. Finally, Tamera—still off camera—said, "And what do you make of all that?"

Patti ran a hand through her hair, which made it stick up in places. For a moment, I thought Tamara would stop filming to fix it before continuing, but she didn't. As Christina said, Tamara was too good of a producer to interrupt the flow.

53

"The story of the circus, and the animals that escaped, is the origin story of the Slough Devil urban legend, plain and simple. And, if there was any remaining doubt that a cryptid was on the loose in the marsh, then we only need to look at what happened to the poor young woman who was found dead—"

"What woman?" Tamara erupted.

The picture shook as the startled camera operator jumped.

Patti's red-lipsticked mouth formed a perfect O. "I forgot to tell you. I'm so sorry. I only found out yesterday."

"That's okay," Tamara said.

I could imagine her doing that annoying thing she did with her hands—pressing the palms together, fingers splayed, while her face flushed with agitation.

"It happens. You're doing great. We'll fix it in the edit. Okay. Tell us about this woman you found out about."

Patti nodded, then took a deep breath. "It's an awful story, really. Because this time, a body was found. The daughter of a fisherman from Russia. She'd only just turned eighteen. Her name was Sonya Orlov. It was just her and her father living at Devil's Landing. He'd been out whaling, and when he came back, there was no sign of Sonya. After a few days, she was found half in, half out of the water, midway up the slough. 'Brutalized,' is how the newspaper articles described it, a euphemism for sexual assault at the time."

Patti continued with her interview, but I could hardly follow, my mind stuck on those last two words—sexual assault. The ring of truth roared in my ears, made my knees go weak, and I sagged against the counter for support.

That day, that horrible day came flashing back. The sound of Christina's screams, bare legs frantically kicking.

Chapter 6

Adam

Not long after I met Christina, she turned me down. My friend Vic insisted she technically hadn't, but I had a hard time seeing it otherwise. I'm not sure why it bothered me so much, and when I admitted that to Vic, sitting around watching basketball at his Del Monte Beach condo, he laughed.

"Boo fucking hoo, dude. You're just not used to rejection. Now you know what it's like for the rest of us ordinary guys. Get over it. She's not even your type."

Which was true. Normally, I went for willowy, soft-spoken blondes who connected with nature. Christina was curvier, louder, and more interested in watching movies than getting outside. And she was blunt, with the mouth of a truck driver.

Vic used to watch her on TV. "She is so hot. You got to introduce me, bro."

"Only after I've had first crack," I'd muttered.

The joke was on me. I thought I'd detected a flicker of interest when she showed up for my book signing at Roy's Harbor, then again at the market, where I'd followed her like an idiotic teenager. And, as promised, when I knocked on her door to collect the shopping bag I'd loaned her, and she was all dressed up and distracted.

For one horrible moment, I thought she was headed to church because it was Sunday morning. When I asked her, her head snapped back.

"Fuck no," she said, and I couldn't help but laugh. In relief, mostly.

With her hair pulled up on her head, wearing a navy-blue dress and heels which made her taller, she looked camera-ready, and then I remembered she worked in corporate communications.

"Work?" I ventured.

Christina glanced over her shoulder at the stacks of boxes behind her in the living room and sighed. "Yeah. Ribbon-cutting for new farmworker housing. For once, they're not pieces of shit. People might actually want to live in these. Oh, you probably want your bag back. Let me get it."

"That's okay," I said. Then, because I wanted an excuse to see her again, "I can get it later. But hey, I was thinking. Maybe on your day off I can take you for a tour of the slough. I've got an extra kayak."

Christina's eyes widened, like I'd just suggested zip-lining over an alligator farm. Something I'd done.

When she didn't answer, my toes began to curl up. "Not into kayaking?"

"I hate the water," she said, pulling the door shut behind her.

I was so stunned all I could do was stare. She brushed past, smelling faintly of jasmine, heels clicking on the pavement.

She stopped and studied me, tucking a loose strand of hair behind an ear. "Did you figure out what made those marks on the dock?"

"No," I admitted. Somehow, with the back-to-back book signings of the previous day and a morning of unpacking, I'd managed to forget about them. "Just curious, why do you hate the water?" The disbelief I felt seeped into my voice.

Christina's eyes flicked upward. "Let me count the ways. If it's deep, you can drown. I didn't grow up near the ocean or lakes or anything, so I never learned how to swim. One of my cousins was killed rafting. He fell out and hit his head on a log. The idea of things lurking underneath me that I can't see freaks me out. So yeah, the idea of going kayaking in that slough"— she pointed over my shoulder in the direction of the waterway—"knowing that something came out of it and scared the shit out of Mr. Garcia, no thank you. And, in case you forgot, there's the video of that freakshow, whatever it was, that was shot by the tourist from your boat. So, no offense or anything, but kayaking is the last thing I want to do."

When I relayed all that to Vic, in painful detail, he'd put down his beer and laughed. "You're such a dumb ass. She said no to kayaking. Did you invite her someplace a normal woman might like to go? You know, like dinner? Wine tasting in Carmel?"

"No." My heart sank like a fluke anchor making straight for a muddy bottom.

Vic flicked a beer cap at me. "Idiot."

He had a point. I'd moped off like a kid who bungled his first prom invitation instead of coming up with something Christina might enjoy.

The next few days went by in a blur, and I didn't see Christina. Mostly because I was either stuck inside, getting my place together, or giving tours of the slough. I was booked solid for the next month, thanks to all those families with kids on spring break. Unless it rained, of course, or the fog drifted in. In either case, I'd have to cancel, citing the poor weather policy, and then experience the hassle of offering refunds or rescheduling. The tours had become as annoying as the book signings. Everyone asked about the slough monster.

I did manage a few solo trips—early morning kayak runs to keep an eye out for anything unusual. But it was no longer the peaceful escape I used to enjoy. The Lorenz video had thrown me into a constant state of watchfulness.

On high alert, I scanned the rippling waters of the salt marsh, its sandy shores, the long stretches of coastal grass, the clusters of twisted oaks. Once, when I paddled around a bend, the low tide had revealed an old piling. It rose out of the sulfurous water, covered in moss, the top rounded and worn smooth, bright green against the far bank encrusted white with pelican guano.

A sheaf of sea lettuce had draped itself on the piling, like a shroud. Its sudden and strange appearance startled me for a moment, and I scolded myself for turning into one of those people who see monsters everywhere.

It doesn't exist, I told myself. There were no slough monsters. There was no Slough Devil.

I didn't tell myself what the Lorenz video had captured because I didn't know. Couldn't guess. Nothing I saw on those morning paddles up Roy's Slough made me any wiser. Neither did my inspections of the new docks at Roy's Cottages. They were untouched except for those deep grooves in the slip below my place. A careless worker had probably done it. A screw sticking out of a pocket, maybe.

Whatever spare time I had I spent outfitting my garage with hooks and shelves and stacks of clear organizers. The luxury of having a garage meant I could ditch the storage unit I rented at Roy's Harbor. I was about to lose it anyway, with the expansion of the marine lab.

My expensive kayaks would be kept in the garage, I'd decided, along with my surfboards, wet suits, camping gear, and bushcraft kits. Now that I owned a nice place with new furniture, I wasn't about to junk it up with all that stuff, not even the loft I planned on using as an office. Unlike Christina, who had a two bedroom, my cottage was a "one bedroom plus," the developers called it. My old Land Cruiser would just have to stay outside. The elements couldn't do much more damage to the paint job anyway. When I bought it, rust had already discolored the wheel wells, and a galaxy of reddish-brown speckles stretched across the hood.

I had another reason for spending so much time in my garage. It was a few doors down from Christina's, and if I hung out long enough, maybe I'd see her, invite her to a wine tasting at a place I heard one of my customer's raving about.

"You have a lot of stuff," a voice behind me said. Female, but too thin and high to belong to Christina. Christina had a thick, back of the throat way of speaking which was undeniably sexy.

"I do," I said, turning around.

A teenage girl regarded me from a wheelchair.

"Where do you surf around here?" she asked, wheeling a bit closer.

"Depends on how much time I have. Sometimes, I go to the beach in Carmel. The waves are decent. But if I have a day off, I go to The Hook in Santa Cruz. I used to like Manressa, until more great white sharks started showing up."

The girl had blue eyes set in a heart-shaped face. With reddish-brown hair and shaggy style, she could have walked straight out of the seventies. If she'd been able to walk at all.

"What's with the wheelchair?" I asked.

She sighed, as if she'd heard the question a thousand times. "It's a long story. And it's really fucked up."

Feeling like an idiot for asking such an intrusive question, I said the first thing that popped into my head, "That sucks."

Her eyebrows shot up. "Yeah, it does. You want to know what sucks worse?" She slapped both hands against the

59

armrests. "Being stuck in this thing, out here, in the middle of nowhere."

I studied the wheelchair. It was the traditional kind you see everywhere but don't really see. Standard issue. Not that I was an expert. How was she supposed to get around in that? Roy's Cottages were new and ADA compliant, I'd seen that in the brochures, but without the right wheels, she'd never be able to leave the pathways or get close to the water.

"I think you need another kind of wheelchair," I blurted out.

The girl rolled her eyes. "You think?"

"I do."

"You can tell that to my dad, then, because he says they're too expensive, and they just spent a bunch of money on this place. And the baby. Plus, he says I'm not going to be here that long, just until my mom can find a new place in L.A. that's all one floor."

She swiped at her eyes with the back of her hand, and for an awful moment, I thought she was crying. Not that I blamed her. I'd cry too if I had all that to deal with at her age.

Not knowing what else to say, and because she'd already shared so much, I felt we were overdue for introductions. "My name is Adam. Adam Gray."

Her mouth formed an O. "Ohhh. You're that guy. I heard my stepmom talking about you. You're the guy with the boat who took the monster video. Awesome. I've watched it a hundred times. It was the only reason I wanted to come here. And I mean, the only reason."

I sighed. "Well, I hate to disappoint you, but I didn't take it. Some guy from Germany did. And since I told you my name, you have to tell me yours."

"Oh, yeah. Sure. Jordan. Lewis. I'm sixteen, almost seventeen, a junior."

Later, while I was unloading another haul from the storage unit, my thoughts kept returning to Jordan. Her chair couldn't make it across a patch of grass, never mind the rough, uneven ground comprising most of the property she now called home. She put on a tough act, but she seemed vulnerable in that thing. Vulnerable to what, I didn't want to think about, but there it was, simmering on my brain's back burner.

If there was a fire, say, or an earthquake, she wouldn't be able to flee. That's what I told myself. And that's what I told Vic later when I showed up at his place.

"You still got that electric mini dune buggy you never use?" I asked without preamble.

Vic stood in the doorway, scratching his bare, hairy stomach. He was a mechanical engineer, single, with lots of disposable income he wasted on toys. His garage was full of them. "Technically, it's a mini-ATV, but yeah, it's still in the garage. Why? You want to borrow it?"

"More like take it apart. For a good cause. If you'll let me have it."

Vic winced. "Oh, I gotta hear this one. Please."

So, I followed him inside and explained. With his donation, and his help, we could use the dune buggy as a base to build Jordan an electric all-terrain wheelchair.

"I don't know," Vic finally said, after a long silence. "I mean, a steering wheel is not going to work. We'll have to figure out how to add handles." Vic disappeared into his bedroom and came out a few minutes later wearing jeans and a sweatshirt. "And we're going to need another kind of seat. Something that will keep her more upright."

61

"Really? You'll let me have it?"

Vic had spent a few thousand bucks on the thing, and I was proposing to take it apart.

Vic frowned, arms akimbo. "It's not for you. It's for that poor kid. And I've been meaning to donate it to a charity, but I've never got around to it. So, this? This is even better, and the timing is perfect. I've got some PTO to burn off, and I'm in between projects at work." He rubbed his hands together. "I'll get started as soon as you find a used wheelchair with a good seat."

Luck was on my side. I searched online and found one for sale which looked like it would work. I ran downstairs to show Vic. He was circling the single-seat dune buggy in the garage, a hand cupping the side of his face.

When I shoved my phone at him, he peered at the screen and said, "Looks good. And I'm starving, so bring back pizza too."

When it was done, Jordan's new wheelchair was almost entirely Vic's creation. He spent three days, with little sleep, putting it together. I came by when I could, bringing sandwiches and offers of help, but Vic waved me off. Said he was really into the project and could manage on his own.

"At least go with me when I give it to her," I said while we wrangled it into the back of the Land Cruiser.

Vic made a face. "No. Weird. Awkward. Take a picture or something." He clapped me on the back and trudged up the steps back into his condo. The door slammed behind him.

When I rang the doorbell at Cottage B7, situated in the middle row at the far west end of the complex, a baby began to cry. Jordan's new sibling. I should have knocked quietly instead.

The door opened. A woman around my age stood there. Strawberry blonde hair. Tall, athletic build with a square face. She seemed too young to be Jordan's stepmother, but all evidence pointed to it—mostly the infant she held against her shoulder, and the exhausted look all new mothers seemed to wear.

"Can I help you?" she asked. Her tone was polite enough, but the words came out through gritted teeth.

I pointed at the tricked-out wheelchair at the bottom of the stairs. "I brought this for Jordan. She in?"

The woman's eyes widened as she took in the bright blue frame on rugged, off-road tires. "I don't understand. We didn't order that. There must be some mistake. Are you from an agency or something?"

I shook my head, kicking myself for not having talked to the Lewis family in advance. Maybe they wouldn't want the chair. Or worse, maybe they'd find it creepy a strange man wanted to give their daughter something so valuable. The thought hadn't occurred to me. I struggled to find the right words to carry me past that cringy moment.

"No, no," I said, feeling my cheeks burn. "My name is Adam Gray, and I'm your neighbor. I grew up around here, so I know how hard it is to get around once you get off the walkways. Jordan stopped by my garage a few days ago to say hello. She told me a little bit about what happened and…"

"Oh, you're Adam. You bought that for her?" she gasped.

My face felt like it was on fire. "Uh, no. A friend of mine made it. He does that kind of thing. Builds things." It was all coming out wrong. I hadn't given any thought about how I'd explain it.

The woman shook her head slowly, patting the baby's back, and eyed the wheelchair with open curiosity. "Wow.

That's like, really cool. It's amazing. I mean, that was nice of you and your friend. Beyond nice."

Jordan rolled into the living room, spotted me, and broke into a grin. "Oh, hi," she said. "What are you doing here?"

I stepped aside so she could see the all-terrain electric wonder Vic had built. Her blue eyes bulged.

As soon as she smiled and screamed, "What the fuck?" I knew it would all be okay.

Chapter 7

Christina

A week after I moved into Roy's Cottages, I went for a morning run down the lonely main road, then decided to walk around the complex. It felt like I'd hardly spent any time there, with my long hours at work in Salinas.

I'd spotted Adam a few times, but we always seemed to be hurrying off in opposite directions. By Wednesday, I'd given up hope he'd stop by to pick up the grocery bag he'd loaned me, and I spent the rest of the week kicking myself for not accepting his kayaking invitation. If I didn't tip the thing over, it might even have been fun. Okay, probably not because the idea of paddling around in a piece of plastic sounded like the opposite of fun, but Adam was smart and interesting and good looking, and single men my age were in short supply—at least the ones I'd want to go out with.

Each cottage had a porch, and by then, most had potted plants, spring wreaths, and colorful doormats. New patio furniture had sprung up on decks. Even some of the slips had tasteful outdoor furniture groupings. In five days, Roy's Cottages had transformed from a sterile new housing development to a lived-in looking place. A few kids zoomed around on bikes and scooters, their shouts competing with the shrieks of the gulls.

As I followed the path snaking along the front of the cottages closest to the slough, there was no sign of Adam Gray, but I did spot Tommy Garcia with a boy at the far end of a dock. By the way Tommy was waving his arms around, I could tell he was agitated. The child was sprawled, stomach down, as he gazed into the water. When Tommy spotted me, he waved me over, and I headed their way, a twinge of unease plucking my stomach like a bad guitar chord. The now familiar scent of salt and seaweed filled my nostrils.

"Hey, Mr. Garcia," I greeted him. "What are you two up to?"

The boy had thick black hair and a widow's peak, giving him an Eddie Munster look without the pointed ears. He pulled himself to a kneeling position. Dark eyes with long lashes only gifted to boys who could care less about them.

"I'm looking for bat rays," he said. "Adam Gray says the water is full of them. Some of them are so big they weigh two hundred pounds." The little boy ran Adam and Gray together like one word.

I stepped back from the edge with a swallow. Another reason to dislike the slough. "Is that something you should be doing? I mean, are they dangerous?"

The boy shrugged. "Maybe. They could stab you with their tail, but only if you try and grab them, and I just want to see them, not catch any. Adam Gray says the babies are called pups. My mom says we're going to take one of his tours so he can show me more stuff."

"That's cool," I said.

Tommy Garcia pulled at my sweatshirt, and when I turned toward him, his face was inches from mine. "He won't listen to me," he hissed, releasing a blast of bad coffee breath which made my eyes water. "I've been trying to tell him he has no business out here, all alone. I don't know what those parents of his are thinking."

I studied the boy. Not a teenager yet, but not a little kid either. And he'd shown enough sense not to stick his hands in the water where bat rays with stabby tails lurked.

"I think he's fine." I patted Mr. Garcia on the arm.

He pulled away as if I'd pinched him. "What the hell's wrong with you? That water is not safe." His voice had risen to a shout.

The boy eyed me nervously, and I faked a reassuring smile. "My name is Christina. What's yours? Which cottage do you live in?"

"I'm Noah Baggio." He pointed to the cottage next to Adam's. "I live just there. It's no big deal. My parents know I'm here. And this is our dock, so I'm not doing anything wrong."

Tommy Garcia's nostrils flared. "Stupid little shit head."

I was so shocked, I couldn't say anything for a moment. Noah opened his mouth to protest. Adult intervention was needed, and fast.

I gripped Mr. Garcia's elbow so firmly he yelped, "Ouch!"

Urging the old man forward with a couple of gentle pushes, I said, "Okay, Mr. Garcia, I think it's time we left Noah to do his thing and look for those bat rays. Why don't I walk you back to your place? I'd love to say hi to your wife."

Mr. Garcia's elbow was surprisingly bony and fragile under my fingers. I backed off the pressure and tugged him up the path away from the marsh.

"Quit manhandling me," he muttered, although he came along willingly enough.

We made our way to his cottage, and I noticed him shuffling and craning his neck forward. "You feeling okay, Mr. Garcia?"

"Don't henpeck me," he snapped. "I get enough of that from my wife."

Poor Liliana. No matter what ailed him, if he was like that all the time, she had a lot to put up with. Before we left the area, I paused for a final check on Noah. He was still there, hanging over the side of the deck. Boys.

Mrs. Garcia opened the door, and when she saw me, one hand still gripping her husband's elbow, she gave a little cry of dismay. "Oh, my goodness, is he okay? Did he fall?"

"For god's sake, Liliana, don't be so dramatic," he grumbled, pushing past her.

Liliana wore a baggy sweatshirt and pajama bottoms. Without her makeup, she looked faded and tired. "Did something happen?" she asked in a low voice.

"Not really," I said, then explained.

The simple story seemed to bother the woman more than it should. She rubbed her chest and took several deep breaths. "I hope Tommy didn't scare the little boy. I was just going to make some coffee. Come on in and join me."

She stepped aside, revealing the small entryway and living room. Not a box in sight. Everything in place. A colorfully painted wooden cross hung over the skinny entry table. A gold crucifix dangled from a chain around her neck. Old-school Catholic, probably, like my mom.

Something made me reach out and squeeze her hands. They were ice cold and slightly clammy. She could probably use some company, someone to talk to about whatever was going on with her husband. But I still had a lot on my to-do list, and before I knew it, Monday would roll around, followed by another long work week.

"Thank you, Liliana, but I've got to get back to unpacking."

"Are you going to the potluck?" she asked, eyeing me hopefully.

"What potluck?"

"The one this afternoon. I'm bringing quesadillas. Everyone likes those. Didn't you know about it? There's a sign at the mailboxes."

I sighed. The week had raced by without a single visit to the mailroom, and my email inbox was so full I had no idea what was in there. But that would have to change. I was a homeowner now, and part of a homeowner's association. Attending a potluck would mean less time making my place comfortable, but it was also a chance to meet and mingle with my new neighbors and, hopefully, see Adam. It would also mean driving to Roy's Harbor to hit the market to shop for whatever dish I decided to contribute. Great.

"I somehow missed the news," I admitted, then hurried off.

The potluck started at two o'clock, smack in the middle of the day.

Without bothering to shower, I grabbed my purse and keys, drove to the market, and bought the ingredients for enchilada meatballs because they were easy, even if my sister called them "fake Mexican."

I threw them together while I nibbled my tomato and smoked trout salad. It was the weekend, and I planned to drink my carbs later and watch a movie I'd downloaded onto my computer at work. Showered, I set out, carrying a crock pot to keep the fragrant meatballs warm, but realized I didn't know where everyone was meeting. I headed to the mailroom to check the flyer I hoped was still there and ran into a couple walking in the same direction. The woman had dark eyes with long lashes, and the man had shiny black hair and a distinctive widow's peak. The woman carried a plastic bowl of what looked like Asian chicken salad, while her partner toted several bottles of red wine. I liked them already.

"You must be Noah's parents," I guessed.

The man grinned. "Oh, oh. Sounds like you met our son. The kid gets around. He's already met more people than we have. I'm Rich Baggio, by the way."

The woman shot me a conspiratorial glance, then laughed. "I'm Cathy. It's the widow's peak, wasn't it? Am I right? Tell me I'm right."

The man groaned. "Oh please, Cathy. Not with the Eddie Munster jokes already. You know, it's possible some of our new neighbors might not have watched the show, and I'd have a chance at a fresh start in life."

Cathy leaned toward me. "Noah found out about that stupid hoax video, and now he won't shut up about it." Then, with a glance at her husband, she said, "Speaking of that son of ours, where is he? He was supposed to be back and get cleaned up before we went."

"He's probably still hunting for bat rays," Rich answered with a shrug. "I'll round him up after we drop this stuff off." Then turning to me, he added. "He's having the time of his life out here. We used to live off a busy street in a sketchy neighborhood, so we didn't allow him to just roam around. Which was especially tough for Cathy because she's home-schooling him."

I followed the Baggios to the western edge of our neighborhood and, to my surprise, found a small park, complete with a swing set, climbing structures, and picnic tables. Apparently, I'd failed to study the map which came along with the prospectus. When I first looked at the complex, I'd waved off the grand tour. The only thing I cared about, which was my cottage, was perfect in every way—new

70

construction, smart design, and even if I didn't love the coastal location, other people would, ensuring my investment would appreciate. What little I'd seen of the grounds had been enough for me.

A good-sized crowd had turned out for the potluck. It was sunny but chilly, with a slight breeze from the marsh off in the distance, so everyone was bundled up. No sign of Adam. He might not show up at all. It was, after all, a weekend, and he probably had tours to give. Or more book signings. The Garcias ambled in, both more pulled together than when I last saw them—Liliana wearing a silver parka and Tommy in a red plaid jacket. I gave them a friendly wave and began the circuit of introductions.

Two women who looked to be in their mid-twenties were organizing the main food table. I set down the crockpot, and they introduced themselves as Cassie and Abigail, newlyweds just back from their honeymoon and now first-time homeowners. When I was their age, I was working in my first job as an underpaid multimedia journalist and could barely cover my rent.

"So, what do you two do?" I asked, even though I hated that kind of question myself.

"Nurses," they said at the same time, then laughed.

"She's in pediatrics," said Cassie, pointing at her wife.

"ICU," said Abigail, pointing at Cassie.

Even with their combined incomes, they'd qualified to enter the housing lottery due to the staggering amount left to pay on their college loans. When they weren't working, they explained, they kayaked the slough and harbor and surfed. It seemed there was no getting away from aquatic sports this close to the water.

When I spotted Ruth, I excused myself and crossed the stretch of tanbark to say hello. But her personal trainer, Dawn Ashlock, and her hunky firefighter husband, Paul, beat me to it. Within seconds, I understood they had an ulterior motive for attending the potluck.

"So, Ruth," Dawn said, "you being a former police chief and all, you're definitely an influencer, and I was hoping we could count on you to support Paul's run for HOA president."

Which was funny, because my friends who lived in condos with homeowner's associations swore it was a nightmare getting people to volunteer for the board, never mind agreeing to lead one. A thankless, time suck of a job if there ever was one. If Paul wanted to run, I doubted he'd face any opposition.

Ruth opened her mouth to reply, but Dawn spotted me first.

"And there's the other influencer we'd been hoping to run into," she said, clutching my arm and pulling me into their circle.

Dawn only seemed to own two types of outfits—workout clothes for working out and workout clothes for everything else. She wore black leggings, a white stretchy top, a gray cape jacket with a hood, and sneakers, of course.

She nudged her husband and stared up at him with adoring eyes. "Tell them about your plan, Paul."

Paul cleared his throat and straightened his shoulders. He had sandy blond hair and a sculpted jawline, one of those big strong guys who make women ask, "Why are firefighters so hot?"

"Well, I've been looking into how we can pay for getting a cell tower installed, and broadband too, without all of us having to come up with a cash lump sum—"

Whatever he was about to say was interrupted by a ruckus behind us. Raised voices, people looking around, confused. At the center of it all were the Baggios. Rich and Cathy, wild-eyed.

"Has anyone seen our son?" Rich shouted.

"We've looked everywhere for him," Cathy cried. "He's missing."

The last I'd seen Noah, he'd been alone at the dock. But that wouldn't come as any news to his panicked parents. They knew he'd been there too, so presumably they'd looked. Ruth's jaw tightened, and she rolled her shoulders back, assuming the expression and posture I remembered from press conferences she'd held as police chief.

Ruth stepped forward and clapped her hands a few times. "Okay, we've got a lot of people here who can help look. But first, what is his name, when was the last time you saw him, and where was he?"

"His name is Noah," Rich exploded. "And who are you?"

Ruth clearly hadn't been expecting that reaction. Most locals recognized her on sight, even if they didn't know her name. "Ruth Burke," she said. "Former police chief and still involved with law enforcement.

That's all Cathy Baggio needed to hear. She grabbed Ruth by both arms. "You've got to help us, please. This isn't like him. He doesn't just wander off. He's never done that before. We saw him an hour ago. Down at our dock. Didn't we, Rich?"

Rich pressed a hand against the side of his head. "I don't know. He was back and forth between the house and the dock all morning."

Liliana whispered to her husband, Tommy, who scowled in response to whatever she was saying.

73

"I saw Noah about eleven-thirty down at the dock," I said. "He was looking for bat rays."

"Was he alone?" Ruth asked.

"He was when I last saw him. Before that, he was talking to that gentleman over there." I bit my lip, not sure how much to share, at least in front of the parents.

People had begun to gather around, eager to help. Everyone except for the Garcias, who kept their distance.

"I see," Ruth replied, in a way which hinted she didn't like my response. "Okay, let's take advantage of all these people who are willing to help. Everyone take out your cell phones and get ready to take my number. If anyone sees Noah, call me immediately." Turning to the Baggios, who's faces had gone from white to gray, she said, "I'm sure he's fine, and we'll find him soon, but I don't think we should waste any time. Rich, call 911 while I get the search organized."

"The phones don't work out here, Ruth," said Paul.

Ruth slapped her forehead. "I can't believe I forgot. Scratch that, everyone. Rich, I think you and your wife should stay here. Who else will volunteer to drive out and make that call?"

Dawn's hand shot into the air. "Me. I got it." Before waiting for approval, she ran toward the parking lot.

"We'll go check the docks," Abigail said.

When she'd finished calling out instructions, Ruth leaned toward me. "Have you seen Adam Gray around today?"

"No. Why?"

"He knows the slough, and he's got a boat. If we don't find Noah, fast, they'll want to send out the Coast Guard, but Adam can respond faster. Do you have his number?"

Biting my lip, I shook my head. I hardly knew Adam, but if there was anyone we needed at that moment, it was him.

Calm, capable. The man who'd worked as a ranger and written an entire book on wilderness survival tactics would certainly know how to help find a missing kid.

As if by some magical summoning, Adam's head appeared over the top of an embankment. His face was lit up, his eyes crinkling at the corners. And then a go-kart zipped over the top with a girl inside. The blue vehicle, and its occupant, raced toward us like we were the finish line.

"How awesome is this?" she shouted, circling around us.

Adam ran up while the girl, who appeared to be a teenager, took off down a path and disappeared behind a building.

He stopped when he saw our expressions. "Everything okay?"

Ruth sniffed. "No, but it's a blessing you turned up. A ten-year-old is missing. Noah Baggio. Last seen at the dock in front of his house. Looking for bat rays."

It was probably fifty-five degrees out, and Adam was dressed in nothing but a T-shirt and jeans. He went completely still. After a silence which seemed to last forever, he cleared his throat. "Looking for bat rays," he repeated in a flat voice.

"That's right." Ruth jerked her chin in the direction of the marsh. "What's the tide doing out there?"

Adam didn't hesitate. "It should be falling a bit by now. High tide was around eleven-thirty. So maybe about six feet. But Noah could handle that fine. When I asked if he knew how to swim, he said yes. He said he'd had swimming lessons since he was a baby, so even if he accidentally went in, he should be able to swim to the shore. There's rip currents out near Devil's Landing, but not this far up the slough."

"Unless that's not what happened," I blurted out, thinking of those nasty scratches on the dock we'd seen. The scratches Adam hadn't been able to explain.

Two pairs of eyes locked on mine.

"Pardon?" Ruth asked. Then, her eyes snapped wide. "Oh, come on, Christina. You're not saying what I think you're saying? That ridiculous monster video? Really?"

Adam shot me an exasperated look. Not now. Not that.

He had a point. What, exactly, would I tell the former police chief, who'd spent her career fighting monsters who were all too real?

Instead, I said, "Noah was looking for bat rays. He said their tails can stab people. Maybe he tried to catch one and..."

Adam paled. "No. No, he wouldn't do that."

Ruth scowled. "Well, as much as I'd like to think a ten-year-old boy would have more sense than that, it's just another reason to focus on the water. I'll head down to the docks. How long will it take to get your boat?

"For this, a kayak's better," Adam said, turning to leave. "I've got one in my garage."

The teenage girl was suddenly next to us. Her modified wheelchair, whatever it was, must have been electric because it was so quiet we hadn't heard her come up. She tugged Adam's T-shirt. "I just heard. That's awful. Can I help look?"

Adam and Ruth exchanged looks, and the former police chief gave a curt nod.

"Please," Ruth said. "Can you go off trail in that thing?"

"Absafuckinglutely!" The girl clapped a hand over her mouth. "Sorry. Adam made it for me from dune buggy parts. Okay, not just Adam, his friend too. And I'm Jordan Lewis."

By that time, Adam had gone. Jordan sped away, hands expertly guiding the steering levers. One day, I hoped to learn more about Jordan, her story, and her connection to Adam, but all that would have to wait.

I agreed to stay with the Baggios until the officers arrived. Before Ruth left to join the others, she pulled me aside and nodded in the direction of the Garcias.

She turned her back on them and in a low voice said, "Is that Thomas Garcia?" Her face looked even more stern than before.

"Yeah. Do you know him?"

"Yes. I guess there's no harm in telling you, but just keep it to yourself, please. And I'm a little surprised you don't remember the case since your station was all over it."

I raised my eyebrows. His name wasn't ringing any bells, but then again, so many cases crossed the news desk that, except for the big ones, they tended to blur together.

"Still nothing," I replied, glancing over at the Baggios, who were huddled together on a bench.

"He worked as a math teacher in Salinas. Took the kids on mathlete competitions and everything. Then, a few years back, one of his students said Mr. Garcia had become abusive, and then other kids came forward. One boy said he'd forced him into his car and drove around, yelling. Mr. Garcia claimed he was just trying to talk some sense into the boy because he was hanging out with gang bangers, and he was too smart for that. We investigated but couldn't find any proof he'd physically harmed anyone, and later, he admitted to losing his temper and yelling at some of the kids. But only because he cared."

Suddenly, I could remember, except I was having a hard time connecting the older, nearly frail man I'd met and the burly, intimidating figure I remembered from the photo we ran at the TV station. I glanced over at the Garcias, who were approaching, Liliana doing her best to restrain her husband while he tried to shake her off.

"Hello, Mr. Garcia," Ruth said, steering the couple away from the Baggios.

Tommy gave her a cold look. "I don't know who you are, and I don't care, but my wife says you're some kind of cop. I have something to say, and if you're smart, you'll listen to me."

"And what is that, Mr. Garcia?"

"That boy who went missing? The little shit wouldn't listen to me, and I warned him. Over and over again. And now, see what happened? That monster from the water, that cucuy, it took him. I saw it. I saw it with my own eyes just this morning. It crawled onto the dock and was sniffing around. I told that boy it wasn't safe, and if he wasn't careful, the cucuy was going to get him."

Ruth blinked. "The cucuy? I'm afraid I don't know what that is."

"The Mexican boogeyman," I explained, then turned to Tommy, who scowled at me. "Mr. Garcia, the cucuy doesn't live around here."

The cucuy hid under beds, behind bushes, ready to snatch children who didn't obey their parents. The monster my grandmother threatened with to keep me in line didn't hang out at the beach, as far as I knew.

Mr. Garcia stuck a quivering finger in my face. "That's where you're wrong, young lady. There's a cucuy here all right. And all of you are going to be sorry for not listening to me."

Liliana lifted her chin and glared at Ruth. "My husband had nothing to do with that little boy. He hasn't seen him since this morning." She spun him around, nearly knocking him off his feet. "Come on, Tommy. Let's go home."

I stared after them, shivering as electrified prickles ran up my arms. The cucuy didn't crawl around like an animal. But something with claws which scratched the side of decks might.

Chapter 8

Christina

It seemed everyone on the Central Coast showed up to search for Noah Baggio. People drove down from Santa Cruz and up from Big Sur. Police circulated photos of the adorable ten-year-old boy with the distinctive widow's peak and black hair. Friends and family of the Baggios joined the new residents of Roy's Cottages to scour the area where he was last seen when he vanished, looking for bat rays, wearing blue pants and a green hoodie.

Officers went through the contents of trash cans and two dumpsters kept in an enclosed area near the parking lot. Volunteers kayaked the slough, fishermen searched the harbor from one end to the other, and search and rescue teams dove into the water at Devil's Landing, where the marsh ended and the mouth of the harbor opened wide.

Adam inspected the docks for more mysterious scratches but found none.

Authorities questioned Thomas Garcia, the person last seen talking to Noah alone, but did not take him into custody. The word spread fast, though, and neighbors warned their children to stay away from Mr. Garcia.

A tabloid newspaper ran a story speculating the Slough Devil captured on the Lorenz film had taken Noah, and of course, social media blew it up too.

But the slough monster theory never gained traction at Roy's Cottages. It was just too ridiculous.

On the Wednesday following that awful Saturday when Noah disappeared in the middle of the day, someone made an anonymous call to the police. A white van had been spotted, parked on the side of Sand Road, less than a quarter mile from where he'd disappeared. And not just any van. Old, dirty, no windows on the sides. The kind where a door slides open and a hand emerges and grabs a woman, or a kid, and hauls them inside. Or shoves them in.

Police questioned the locals again, and this time, a half dozen people recalled the van. Overnight, the search for Noah Baggio shifted from an accidental drowning, with no body yet recovered, to an abduction. Someone had sneaked onto the property, skulked around, waited for just the right opportunity, then dragged Noah Baggio down the banks of the slough and eventually to the van. And sure enough, one of Noah's slip-on sneakers—bloodied—was found squashed into the stinky mud several hundred yards east of where he disappeared. His blood, tests confirmed.

The Baggios lost it. Understandably.

While walking to my car to go to work, I spotted Adam in his garage with Jordan Lewis, doing something to her tricked-out dune buggy wheelchair.

"Whatcha guys up to?" I asked.

Jordan rolled her eyes, but I could tell she was pleased. She was a cute girl, with big blue eyes and pointy chin. She reminded me of a fairy. And the way she looked at Adam. The big brother she never had. Dream crush. Superhero. It was hard to tell which one, or maybe it was a bit of all of them.

"He's freaking out that if something happens to me while I'm in this thing, I won't be able to call for help. So, he's attaching that."

That was an orange cannister with a black horn. Adam was in the process of lashing it to the part of the wheelchair frame closest to Jordan's right hip. She'd scooted as far as she could to the left so he could secure the zip ties.

"Is that an air horn?" I asked.

Adam looked up and smiled. "It is. It's marine grade. This thing can be heard from a mile away."

Jordan's hand drifted toward the horn.

Adam smacked it away. "Don't, Jordan. This is serious. You only use this in an emergency, and I mean it."

"Uh, it's just so...tempting." Jordan gripped the steering levers and gave them a good shake.

"Would you stop?" Adam snapped. "With you fidgeting, this is taking twice as long as it should."

Which, I suspected, was the point. Anything to prolong her time with Adam who, by the looks of it, was headed for a day of giving tours on the slough. His face was smeared with sunscreen he hadn't bothered to rub in, and he had his hair pulled back in a silver-streaked knot. The lotion had an intoxicating scent, like coconut and chocolate. It made me want to shove my nose in his face and take a big whiff.

"Is that thing really necessary?" I asked.

A marine grade air horn seemed a bit extreme. I surveyed the garage. Two kayaks—one red, the other yellow—sat in large hooks mounted to the wall. On the ceiling, a steel contraption held three surfboards and one paddle board. A wooden workspace took up the far wall, and on two sides, clear plastic storage bins lined the walls.

Before Adam could reply, Jordan shot me a sweet smile and said, "He's afraid the man in the white van is going to come after me, and he wants to give me a fighting chance."

"They make safety whistles for women, you know," I said, rattling my key chain to call attention to the bright purple disc.

Adam stared at it, blinking, then squeezed his eyes shut. Jordan laughed so hard I thought she'd choke. It was the first time anyone laughed that week. Something she seemed to realize because she clapped a hand over her mouth.

I patted her shoulder. "It's okay."

When she looked up at me, she had tears in her eyes, and I had to swallow a few times to get rid of the lump. Noah's disappearance had affected everyone, including Adam, who had dark circles under his eyes and looked like he hadn't slept much.

"I'm glad you're all having fun in there while my son is still missing," barked a voice from outside the garage.

It was Cathy Baggio, clothes rumpled like she'd slept in them, hair unwashed, greasy, chin broken out in a rash of tiny pimples. Jordan grabbed the levers and spun around. Adam got to his feet and came to stand next to me in a gesture of solidarity because there was no mistaking the waves of hostility coming from the distraught mother. Jordan shrank against the back of her wheelchair.

Face twisting, Cathy pointed at Adam. "It's your fault he's gone. If you wouldn't have told him about those stupid bat rays and got him all obsessed like that, he never would have been out there."

Adam opened his mouth to reply, but must have thought there wasn't any point, and he shut it again. He didn't drop his eyes or look away. "I'm sorry about what happened to Noah." His voice was low but steady.

"I'm sorry about what happened to Noah," Cathy mimicked.

When we first met on our way to the potluck, she'd been happy. Funny. Teased her husband. I wouldn't have thought her capable of such insulting behavior. But she wasn't the same anymore because her life wasn't the same.

"That's not fair," Jordan said. "I was there when Adam told him about the bat rays. We were down at the water, seeing if the wheels on my chair would get stuck, and Noah asked what we were doing. He freaked out when he saw something in the water, and Adam told him it was just a bat ray, and then Noah had a million questions. Adam was just being nice, that's all."

"It's okay, Jordan," Adam murmured.

Cathy took a few steps toward Jordan and shouted, "If he was so nice, he wouldn't be here, screwing around with his man toys. He'd be out there looking for my son." She swiveled on Adam, who'd shuffled off to the side, likely to draw Cathy's wrath away from Jordan. "And you're supposed to be some kind of survival expert? Give me a break. You try and survive what we're going through. I don't care what anybody says, Noah wouldn't have been down there if you hadn't started talking about bat rays."

Cathy Baggio stormed off, and not one of us could find something to say.

At work, I couldn't concentrate, thinking about Adam. He'd traipsed to his rust bucket of a truck, head down. Jordan had spoken the simple truth. Cathy Baggio had been horribly unfair to Adam, blaming him for something which was in no way his fault, but it was impossible to be angry with the woman. When she came to her senses, if she ever did, she'd regret those words. Maybe even apologize.

85

On some level, Adam must have understood that too, but her sharp words had cut him, slashed him deep. I had his number, so I called him, then messaged. But there was no reply. Probably out of signal range. There was also a chance he didn't feel like talking.

Before leaving Salinas, I stopped at El Charrito and bought half a dozen burritos—beef, two kinds of chicken, chorizo, and veggie. They were on the small side, so most guys could eat two. Then, I swung by Star Market and bought two bottles of red wine. I tried reaching Adam one more time while I had a signal, but still nothing. The spicy scent of the burritos made my stomach rumble on the drive home. When I pulled into the parking lot, I spotted Adam's Land Cruiser, nearly hidden by the fog rolling in so fast I could hardly see the path in front of me.

At home, I had a bit of a shock. A figure was pacing back and forth on the porch, blocking my doorway. The automatic light had come on, and the mist swirled around it like a scene out of that old movie, The Fog.

The figure turned out to be a man wearing an over-sized trench coat, an old man with a stooped posture.

"Mr. Garcia. What are you doing here?"

He turned with a gasp. "Oh, you scared me bad, Miss Figueroa."

That made two of us. Moments before, I'd nearly dropped my grocery bags.

"Is everything okay?" I asked, fumbling for my keys.

"Not exactly." His voice was loud.

I wondered if he was losing his hearing, on top of whatever else was going on with him. Whatever he wanted, I hoped it wouldn't take long. I was anxious to change out of my work clothes and head over to Adam's place. My desire to check on him, to comfort him, after the awful exchange with Cathy Baggio had intensified through the day.

He cleared his throat and continued. "I came to say I'm sorry. I haven't been feeling myself lately. Don't know what's wrong with me. I've been seeing things, except nobody will believe me. Especially Liliana. She says if I don't stop it, she'll take me back to the doctor to get my head examined."

Not the kind of conversation to have outdoors in the dark, so I invited him in, reluctantly, with an advance warning. "Why don't you come in, Mr. Garcia? I have some place I need to get to in a few minutes, but at least we'll be warm."

I reached for the doorknob, damp and slippery from the fog. Mr. Garcia followed me without a word while I flicked on the lights. I pointed to an easy chair, and he sat, hands on his knees, like he expected to spring up any moment. Looking around with open curiosity, he said, "You made it real nice in here. Very homey."

I'd been aiming for something a little more stylish, but "homey" wasn't so bad. And my place was colorful and cozy. I wanted to get to Adam's place, but I was also curious to hear the old man out, even though it felt like opening the door to a dark basement where unknown dangers lurked. There was nothing else to do but take the plunge.

"I remember the day Noah went missing. You said you'd seen the slough monster and tried to warn him. Is that what you're talking about?"

He clapped, so loudly I jumped. "That's exactly what I'm talking about, but no matter how many times I told my wife, or that stuck-up detective that came to see me, they won't believe it. I heard them. The two of them, talking about me."

"You mean Liliana and the detective?"

"Who else would I be talking about!" he thundered. "I can't trust that woman anymore. She's taken against me since those little bastards at the school started making up lies about me."

I steered him back to the original subject, as much as I wished to avoid it. "Can you describe this...thing you saw in the water?"

Tommy Garcia's brown skin paled. "No, not really. I didn't get a good look at it because the damn thing moved so fast. But it wasn't an animal, I can tell you that. Or a fish. It was hiding in the water, beneath all that seaweed. Just waiting, like. I told that kid to stay away from the edge because it would grab him and pull him over. It went away when you walked up. But I've seen it. There's more than one, you know. At night. I've been having real bad dreams, so I wake up a lot. And I've heard things. Like somebody walking around out there and a scratching on the glass. And then the other night, I saw it. That thing from the water was looking inside. It had yellow eyes, like a cat or a leopard or something."

"Could you have been dreaming, Mr. Garcia? Sometimes, nightmares are very vivid."

"Oh, I have plenty of nightmares, that's for damn sure. But that was no dream. It was there. Outside my window. Sniffing around. Casing the place. It's going to come back, you know. I can feel it in my bones. Maybe bring some of its friends with it. That monster took that kid, and if nobody stops it, it's going to come back because they're plenty more where that one came from." His eyes bored into mine, defiant. Mr. Garcia breathed heavily through gritted teeth, his jaw working.

There was no doubt in my mind he believed what he was saying. And he spoke with such conviction I nearly believed him too. Almost. But something could explain it. Something that made more sense, given what his wife had said when we first met. Tommy Garcia had health problems. Serious ones.

"Are you on any new medication, Mr. Garcia?" When he pursed his mouth, angrily, I held up a hand. "It's a fair question. Medications can mess with our heads. I had to take something once that made me want to jump out of my skin."

He sat back in the chair and folded his arms across his chest. "My new doctor has me doped up on so many pills, I don't know if I'm coming or going."

Relief. Tommy Garcia hallucinating monsters was easier to accept than a creature with yellow eyes running around. Just like the rest of the world, he'd seen the Lorenz video, and his addled mind had brought it to life, sent it swimming in the slough and skulking outside his kitchen window.

"What are the pills for, Mr. Garcia? If you don't mind me asking."

With a sigh, Tommy struggled to his feet and shuffled across the room to the door. With one hand on the knob, his face crumpled. "I must have seen a hundred doctors, but not one of them can figure out what's wrong. One of them says I have depression. Another says I've maybe got that disease, Parkinson's. So hell if I know."

The door banged shut behind him.

When he left, what little energy remaining after work drained from my body. My limbs felt heavy. Finding the right words to console Adam Gray suddenly seemed daunting, if not impossible. My own nightmares about Noah Baggio had wrecked my sleep, and his mother's grief and fury had stuck with me through the day, making it hard to focus on the endless emails, calls, and meetings.

After checking the locks and yanking down the blinds, I pulled a burrito out of the bag, shoved the rest into the refrigerator, opened a bottle of wine, and poured a glass. Eating alone and going to bed was all I could manage.

Chapter 9

Adam

After the incident with Noah Baggio's mother, I checked the tour schedule for the day. Luckily, there were only two. I'd be done by noon. If it had been more, with the mood I was in, I would have canceled. I could get through two.

But just barely as it turned out.

The tourists had heard about Noah's disappearance, and that's all they asked about. Not the otters, or the seals, or the bat rays. I didn't think I'd ever be able to look at another ray without thinking of that kid. The way his face had lit up with excitement when I mentioned there were lots of them in the slough that time of year. He'd asked questions, smart ones, and then he'd walked away, and that was the last time I saw him.

After lunch, I changed into my wet suit, drove north along Highway 1 to The Hook in Santa Cruz, and spent three hours surfing. The water temperature was fifty-five degrees. I did some stretching to get the blood flowing. The chilly water stung my feet and face when I first went in, and I paddled around between sets to keep warm. When a guy with rental gear, clearly not local, cut me off and nicked my board, I lost my temper and yelled at him. Surfers shouted and clapped their approval, but scolding the tourists wasn't my usual style. Later, I caught up with him in the little parking lot on the other side of East Cliff and apologized. I even bought him a quick beer at the brewery up the street, answered his questions about the area, then drove back to Roy's Cottages.

I wasn't exactly buzzed, but I was feeling a little bolder, so I knocked on Christina's door, hoping she was there. To collect the grocery bag I loaned her and never got back, I told myself, but I really wanted to talk through what happened with Cathy Baggio, exorcise those words I couldn't get out of my head. I needed someone to tell me Noah's disappearance wasn't my fault. No, not just anyone. Jordan had tried, in her righteous, teenage way.

Christina. I had to hear Christina say it, like only she could, in her firm, no-nonsense way. To take the accusation which had blown up into the size of a blimp and reduce it to a small, manageable ball. Something I could bounce away.

But she wasn't there.

I wandered to the dock outside my cottage, feeling lost. The wind from the ocean came up the marsh, cold against my face, and I shivered. My own personal slip, what had sold me on the place, what had helped me overcome my objections to living in an environmentally sensitive area. Of course, the cottage was the major sell, but the slip sealed the deal. Before, whenever I'd wanted to go out on the slough for personal recreation, I had to haul my kayak on top of the Land Cruiser, drive from Monterey to the harbor, pay ten bucks for parking, and put in there. Setting out whenever I felt like it, on a whim, proved too hard to resist.

Vic gave me a hard time, and so did other people. I'd protested, strongly, against Roy's Cottages back when the development was still in the planning stages. I'd attended every public meeting, made signs, written letters, gave interviews. And then, when the trust announced the big bribe—restoring the wetlands in exchange for a small part of the land—I had a change of heart, and then lost my heart to a thousand square feet and a slip leading to the marsh.

I'd enjoyed it for a week, from move-in day to the potluck when Noah Baggio disappeared. A kidnapper in a dirty van was the most obvious answer, as horrible as it was. If only my mind would stop replaying that Lorenz video. And that old man. What he'd said about seeing a monster and warning Noah. All of that wrecked the joy of having my very own dock because that's all I thought of now. All tangled up like a ball of seaweed, old fishing net, and trash.

I was feeling so down, if I had a signal, I would have called Vic to come over. He would have cheered me up. He always did. Picking up the mail, I ran into Jordan's stepmom and learned her name, Danielle. When she invited me over for dinner—taco night—I said yes, mostly because I didn't want to be alone with my dark thoughts and because I was curious about Jordan's family.

As I suspected, Mark Lewis was older than his second wife—by as much as fifteen years—and once served in the military. No surprise there. He looked ready to step back into uniform with a crew cut and green polo shirt tucked into khaki pants. He owned a plumbing supply shop in Seaside and worked long hours, which explained why I hadn't met him yet.

"That's really something, what you did for my daughter," he said, choking up.

I glanced over at him in surprise. "I was glad to do it, and really, my friend did all the hard work."

"We're suing the bastard who did this to her. And the camp."

The placed smelled like chili powder, cumin, and lavender scented candles. Jordan heaped ground beef into a taco shell. "Gosh, I wonder whose idea it was to send their daughter to hell on earth?" Before her father could say anything, Jordan's blue eyes snapped open, and she clapped a hand over her mouth. "I never told you what happened," she stammered.

Mark Lewis visibly cringed. His wife reached across the table and squeezed his hand.

"It's okay," I said hurriedly. "You don't have to tell me."

Without glancing at her father, Jordan dropped the serving spoon in the bowl and said, "No. I want to tell you. Are you ready?"

"As ready as I'll ever be," I admitted, then immediately regretted my choice of words.

Listening would cost me nothing. She would carry the entire burden of sharing whatever painful story she had to tell.

Jordan scowled. "Are you being an asshole? Because I hate assholes."

"Jordan!" her stepmother cried, then gave an embarrassed laugh.

"I'm sorry," I said hurriedly. "Whatever it is, I want to hear it. Really"

When I glanced over at Mark Lewis, he was staring at his plate of food and not at his daughter.

Jordan wrinkled her nose, then sniffed loudly. "Okay. Here's the short version. I did some drugs in school, and I got arrested. The cops sent me to drug court, and I could have gone to juvie and done probation, but my parents freaked out, and they cut this deal to send me to a wilderness camp. I'm not supposed to say which one because we're suing them. I was actually happy to go because I love hiking and stuff, and the other campers seemed nice, but the counselors were total assholes. Okay, except for one. When I got into a fight with them about which cabin I was supposed to sleep in, they made me do this walk around a canyon. Slippery trails and serious drops. In the dark. And I fell. Like, landed right on my back. It took them hours to get to me. And I couldn't move my legs.

They don't think it's permanent, but we won't know for a while."

"Jesus," I whispered.

Jordan smirked. "They are so screwed, and they know it. My mom says, when they pay up, I'll be able to afford to go to whichever college I want."

The baby began to cry from another room. Danielle pushed her chair back, but before she could get up, Jordan held up a hand. "I'll get him. That's one thing I can do, at least."

I watched her go, my heart twisting in my chest. That was one brave kid. And she had every right to be angry. The punishment she'd received for a first drug offense seemed excessive. Then again, what did I know? I didn't have a teenager, and at the rate I was going in my personal life, I'd be pushing sixty by the time I had one, if it happened at all.

Mark cleared his throat and forced a smile to his lips. "Do you have kids, Adam?

"No." And I probably never would the way the rest of dinner went, with the baby wailing, and the bickering between Jordan and her father, and the way kids disappeared without a trace.

Before Mark and Danielle could dish out the dessert, I made my excuses and poked my head in on Jordan. She was leaning over a cradle, patting the baby's back. When I explained I needed to get going, she pouted.

I hurried back toward my cottage, shivering in the damp night air. The fog had invaded, and I shook my phone to activate the flashlight, doubling back to Christina's cottage. She was home. Lights glowed behind the closed blinds. When I walked up the steps, I heard voices. One male. I wondered who it was, what they were talking about, and felt something I hadn't in a long time. The hot turmoil of jealousy. So, I backed down the stairs and retraced my steps.

At home, I climbed the ladder into the loft, grabbed the custom-made stash box Vic had given me for my birthday, opened the glass jar of the strongest weed I owned, then rolled a joint on the hardwood tray. Not that I made a regular habit of getting stoned, which explained why it hit me so hard. I skipped past my usual two hits and went for four. Suddenly thirsty, I went into the kitchen and poured a Jack Daniel's, my dad's old favorite, and felt the familiar burn as the first sip hit my throat. And then I poured another. When I could hardly stand, I flopped on the couch and stared down at my feet. They looked weird by the lamplight, bony and ugly, sand still between my toes. That's when I remembered I hadn't showered off at The Hook.

My eyelids closed. First because I forced them shut, then because the room spun around when I cracked them open.

I was high and more than a little drunk, and I'd dropped off.

In the distance, I heard scrabbling on a hard surface.

Sharp claws on the dock, trying to pull itself up, and then a steady thump thump thump. The distinct hollow sound feet made on planks elevated above the water.

Dreaming. You're just dreaming. That's what I told myself.

I stood up, swaying, willing my mind and body to sober up. Because something was out there in the night, and I had to see it.

As I wobbled across the room, the cold floorboards pressed against my feet. I stopped in front of the door, staring at the latch. I was barefoot and unarmed. And stoned. Not exactly the optimal condition for a fight. I crept into the mudroom behind the kitchen and rooted around in boxes until I found what I was looking for—a hammer and a flare gun.

I tucked the flare gun in the waistband of my pants and clutched the hammer, preparing to swing it if anything busted through the door. The alcohol had dulled my fear, and the pot had left me disoriented. A bad combination if ever there was.

Strange sounds drifted from the direction of the water. Chittering. A series of low growls. Not the usual noise of the wildlife which lived along the slough.

Stupidly, I'd left the flashlights and emergency lanterns intended for the house in a box still in the garage. So much for basic survival skills. Each waterfront facing cottage had a dock but no lighting fixtures, and even if I turned on the porch light and the fog was still out there—which it was sure to be—its glow would reach the path but not much farther.

What I needed was a plan, but that required a brain in full working order. Anxiety tugged my chest like a bungee cord. I crept toward the door, one hand still gripping the hammer, ears straining, tripped over a footstool, and went sprawling. The hammer flew from my hand, skittering across the hardwood floor. I landed on all fours, hard, my head just missing the coffee table. My fall must have made a terrible racket because, when I finally managed to pull myself upright, all had gone quiet outside.

The moments seemed to stretch on forever. All my muscles tensed while I debated what to do. Stay hidden inside, safe. Open the door, see.

The new vinyl windows still squeaked, so I ruled that out, congratulating myself for remembering such a detail. Maybe I wasn't in such bad shape after all. A third possibility edged around the corners of my booze-alcohol-adrenalin fueled mind. Ambush. If I left the safety of my house, whatever was out there could take me by surprise, and it wouldn't take much in my condition.

Action won out. As an expert on bushcraft, I had a bias toward action. Sitting around, twiddling thumbs, rarely achieved the desired outcome. But that was no excuse for stupidity. I turned on the porch light, unlatched the door as quietly as I could, cracked it open, and poked my head out. My skin went cold and clammy in the moist air. A pounding paranoia took over, and I was sure I'd just made a terrible mistake. Stepping out could mean death. Or worse.

The porch light spilled out onto the steps and the path below but fell short of the strip of land covered in coastal grass. A thick white mist shrouded the docks.

My eyes strained as I looked all around at the cottages on either side, the peaked roofs barely visible—to make sure nothing lurked up there—and then a sound drew my attention to a boulder. They were scattered around the complex with other landscaping features—water fountains, over-sized pots, and the occasional statue.

A figure crouched on top of the boulder. It was completely still, radiating a menace which closed the distance between us. If it stood, I knew it would be tall, taller than most men. And there was something off about its proportions. Although it seemed to have arms and legs, the head was too small and misshapen. My heart thudded in my chest and roared in my ears. I'd seen it before, in the video shot from my pontoon boat by the German tourist. But this close, it was terrifying. More disturbing. Its eyes gleamed yellow in the night. I gawked, mesmerized, fascination fighting disbelief.

It moved. My reflexes took over, and I pulled the flare gun from my waistband, pointed it above the head of the creature, and pulled the trigger. The hammer hit the detonating cap, shooting a blinding red flare into the whiteness. The crouching figure swiveled on the rock, extended hideously elongated arms outward, and the rest of its body followed, vanishing into the fog.

Without waiting around to see what happened next, I jumped back, slammed the door, and locked it, panting. I grabbed my cell phone. My trembling index finger stabbed 911, when I remembered. Even if I figured out what to say—hello dispatcher, I just saw the Slough Devil—I didn't have a signal. None of us did. And besides, I was high. And drunk. I threw the phone on the couch in disgust.

On high alert, I collapsed into my new chair which was supposed to relieve stress, nursing a Jack Daniel's until the sun came up.

Chapter 10

Adam

Fists on the front door startled me awake. Too much Jack had left me with a pounding headache. Too much pot, combined with booze, made my mouth feel like it was lined with sandpaper, and when I tried to swallow, a coughing fit made my aching head throb even more. Lurching toward the door, cursing, I tripped over the footstool, again, but that time managed to avoid falling.

Christina stood there, dressed for work, wearing heels. Hair done. Red lipstick. More put together and sexier than she had a right to be so early in the day. She grimaced as she looked me up and down.

"Ooo. Fuck. Look at you."

The events of the night before came rushing back, and I looked around wildly for the creature crouching on the rock. But it wasn't there. Of course it wasn't. It was long gone. I'd shot a flare gun at it. Or I'd hallucinated the entire episode. There were other people about, more than there should have been on a weekday. Some residents milled around, arms crossed, foreheads scrunched, and somewhere on the paths behind us, raised voices.

"What's going on?" I hardly got the words out, my throat was so dry.

Christina snorted. "I guess you haven't been outside lately, huh?"

I shook my head and winced. I needed water, but it would have to wait. "No. Not yet. What time is it?"

"Eight-thirty. Someone's had a little too much fun down at the water."

I squeezed my eyes shut, trying to banish the image of that awful thing sitting on the rock.

"Show me," I said, taking her elbow.

Christina's eyebrows lifted, and she stared at my bare feet, then gave a little shrug. "Okay, nature boy, let's go."

Her heels clicked down the steps. I shuffled alongside her, across the path, through the opening in the tall grass, and down the paving stones leading to the dock. She stopped suddenly, then stepped aside.

I didn't have to go any further. Patio furniture filled the slough. Chairs. Tables. Loungers. Tiki torches. Storage boxes had opened and spilled their contents into the water. Colorful plastic glasses bobbed alongside seagulls.

"Shit." I shook my head, setting off another throbbing wave which made my eyes water.

When I'd recovered, my first thought was the figure on the rock, radiating hatred and anger. Maybe before it left, it had gone on a vandalism spree. But I hadn't heard anything. Not a sound, and I must have stayed awake for hours. If it had gone from slip to slip, tossing stuff into the water, I would have heard splashing.

It must have left some evidence behind. I'd walked right past the boulder, so I doubled back and hurried toward it, the damp, cold paving stones sending a chill up my spine.

Christina had to run to keep up. "What? What are you doing?"

I didn't explain. She'd think I was crazy. And I'd been high. Probably higher than I'd ever been in my life—at least since college. It was possible, probable, I'd imagined the whole

102

episode, triggered by Noah's disappearance and the Lorenz monster video.

The coastal grass surrounding the boulder was flattened, as was most of the grass in both directions. Shoes, mostly. Lots of them. The imprint of a sneaker had been stamped into a small patch of muddy ground. I placed my bare foot next to it, the wet dirt squishing between my toes. It belonged to someone who wore the same shoe size—eleven. Walking back and forth, circling the area, expanding my search to the dock, then the sand bank around the slip closest to the slough, I found no unusual footprints, nothing suggesting a creature with claws had traversed the area. Then again, people had trampled through, destroying any tracks it might have left behind.

Christina pointed at the footprints. "Want to know who left those?"

I turned to her in surprise. "You know?"

"I thought you'd never ask. Yeah. A bunch of idiot teenagers decided our little neighborhood hadn't had enough drama for the week, so they decided to freak everyone out. They dressed up in black, wearing monster masks, and started creeping around, looking into windows, jumping out from behind bushes. Then, as if that wasn't enough, they decided to throw all the furniture off the decks. Some people saw what was going on, but they were too scared to go outside, and they couldn't call the police because we don't have service. But then they messed with the wrong houses." Christina grinned.

The story had left me speechless. I hadn't imagined the figure crouching on the rock. It had just been one of those idiot teenagers, my perception contorted by too much weed, and then I'd fallen asleep and hadn't heard a thing.

I ran my hand over my face, and it came away, slick with sweat. I hated to think what I looked like. "What do you mean, wrong houses?"

"Paul Ashlock and Ruth Burke. They both came out, locked and loaded, and they scared the shit out of those kids. Some of them ran, but Paul and Ruth are in good shape, and they caught a few. Ruth says they ratted out their buddies, and the police rounded up a dozen guys." She stopped, eyes questioning. "You didn't hear all the commotion?"

My attention wandered back to the boulder. No marks by a creature which had hauled itself out of the slough, and thump thump thumped across my deck. "Not really, no. Did you?"

A shadow came over her face. "I went to sleep early. And I had kind of a bad night. It's possible I drank too much wine."

The night before, I'd heard a man's voice in her living room. There were other reasons besides wine which would explain why a beautiful woman like Christina wouldn't hear strange noises, and just the thought of it made my jaw clench. Probably some guy who didn't screw up his chances by asking a woman who hated the water to go kayaking.

"I hit the Jack a little too hard," I admitted. "And some other stuff too."

"Is this a day off, or do you have a tour or a book signing to get to?"

I groaned, struggling to recall my schedule. It was full, I knew, but I couldn't remember the time of the first tour. Ten, probably, which gave me time enough to gulp down a sports drink, shower, and eat something. "I'm working."

Christina gave a sympathetic nod. "Well, I have something that may help. Dunno. Depends on how you feel. How about if I meet you at your place in a few minutes?"

When I walked into my cottage, I coughed. It reeked like I'd intentionally hotboxed it. I threw open the windows, turned on the overhead fan, shoved the evidence of my debauchery back into its storage box, and kicked it under the couch. Then, I snatched up the empty bottle of Jack Daniel's and dropped it into the recycling bin. I'd had more to drink than I'd thought, which explained my still-pounding headache. It only took a few minutes to tidy up, so it looked decent when Christina showed up, holding a small white paper bag, which she shoved at me, nose wrinkled.

"Wow. Smells like a Slightly Stoopid concert in here." She waved a hand in front of her nose.

I opened the bag so I didn't have to meet her curious gaze. "What's this?"

Christina tapped the side of the bag with a long nail painted gray. Different, but nice. A random thought popped into my head. I'd gone out with women who painted their toenails, but never their fingernails.

"Best burritos you'll ever have," she said. "On the small side, but tasty. I hate those giant, sloppy ones that fall apart when you bite into them. These are from my favorite place. El Charrito in Salinas." She paused and cleared her throat. "I actually meant to bring them over last night. With a bottle of wine, to see if you were okay. You know, after that whole thing with Cathy Baggio. But then, I don't know. I was feeling sort of wiped out and kind of in a bad mood, so I thought it better if I didn't come. Drag you down." She cocked her head to the side. "You all right?"

I scraped a hand through my hair. It felt greasy, like I hadn't washed it in days. But suddenly, I didn't much care. She'd said the words I needed to hear. She'd thought of me, enough to buy burritos. Maybe some guy had dropped by, uninvited, and hijacked her good intentions. At least that's what I hoped. My knees suddenly felt like rubber.

I clutched the paper bag to my chest. "Thank you. Thank you so much. That's so nice of you. Really. I mean, you have no idea. Seriously."

A faint smile played around her full lips, but she looked pleased. "They're just burritos, Adam." She paused. "I hope you feel better. Hangovers suck."

For a woman wearing heels, she could move fast. She was halfway down the steps before I knew it.

"Maybe we can have some wine later?" I called after her.

She whirled around and smiled. "That would be nice. Why don't you come over? Give your place a chance to air out."

Then she was gone, leaving me to stare at the boulder where my hallucination had squatted.

Chapter 11

Christina

Adam prowled around my place, restless like a cat at night. He inspected the bookshelf filled with mystery novels and my collection of Mexican American history and literature, then poked his head into my office. Everything was still in boxes in there. I hadn't gotten around to unpacking my desktop computer. What was the point without an internet connection?

"These two-bedroom units are nice," he said.

My bedroom was upstairs, and he hadn't made it that far, but I knew what he meant.

"They're only a couple hundred square feet larger than the one bedrooms, but yeah. The extra space is nice. If I knew I wouldn't be able to work from home, I wouldn't have spent the extra money on a two bedroom though."

"Hopefully that'll be fixed soon," he said, but not as if he really believed it.

After standing in front of the west-facing window, watching the light fade, he pulled down the blind, then lowered himself into the same easy chair Tommy Garcia had sat in the night before. Adam was a lot easier to look at. He'd made a remarkable recovery from his hangover. I asked him if he had any special tricks I should know about.

He chuckled. "Surfing. Does it every time. No matter how bad I feel, I make myself go out, even if it's only for an hour. It's like magic. Clears my head."

"Sounds terrible. When I'm hungover, I just want to eat greasy food and sleep it off."

We laughed, then I went to the refrigerator and pulled out the plate of charcuterie I'd picked up in Monterey. I unwrapped the wedge of blue cheese and inhaled the sharp, tangy aroma. By some miracle, the building where I spent most of my day—stuck inside, attending a marathon meeting—was next door to a small butcher shop which sold hand-cut meats. The tray had cost a fortune. Adam sat staring at it with a slight frown, and my heart sank. He had the kind of lean body usually belonging to men who believed in the benefits of a plant-based diet.

"Anything wrong?" I asked. I hoped not because I had nothing else in the house to give him.

He patted the side of his face. "No, everything looks so amazing, I can't decide what to try first."

I felt my shoulders relax. "Whew. For a second there, I thought you might be vegan."

Adam folded a piece of salami and popped it into his mouth, then chewed thoughtfully. "Me? No. No way. I mean, I tried it once, but I got bored. And I'm not a good enough cook to pull that off. And by the way, I can't thank you enough for those burritos. They saved my life this morning."

After we finished a bottle of wine, by mutual agreement we switched to club soda with lime. Adam said he'd heard from a neighbor a group of residents had stormed the property management company, demanding a security guard in the wake of teenagers vandalizing the complex, and were told we didn't have the budget to pay for it, but the sheriff's department had agreed to send out a patrol car to check the property occasionally. Like that would do any good.

Our conversation shifted to the get-to-know-you stage—favorite foods, restaurants, bands, and places. We hadn't reached the inevitable embarrassing stories phase, but we did

108

discover we both loved the Forest of Nicene Marks in Aptos and exploring the tiny town of San Juan Bautista. Since the San Andreas fault ran through it, we started talking about earthquakes—when we expected the "big one," and what we'd done to prepare for it. At first, his answer surprised me.

"You don't have an earthquake kit?" I asked, hand patting my heart, as if the news had made it flutter.

He laughed. "I don't need a special kit. I've got a garage full of stuff I could use. Canned goods. Camping gear. Battery lanterns. My dad's old lanterns. Kerosene. Fuel. Rope. Lots of rope. Tarps."

"You sound like a prepper. I know whose house I'm going to if anything bad happens." Even to my own ears, it sounded flirty. Beyond flirty. I might as well have climbed the steps to my bedroom and called, "Come on up," over my shoulder.

To his credit, Adam just said, "I'll be sure to open the door then." Which was slightly disappointing. A hint of lechery would have been nice.

All of that led to our not having cell or internet service, and the latest bombshell, which I hadn't heard about because, again, I hadn't checked my personal email at work—the installation of telephone land lines had been pushed back by several weeks, and the technology which was supposed to bring us the internet and video streaming was still a way off.

"But why weren't the phone lines installed before we moved in?"

Adam shook his head. "I don't know. Somebody screwed up, big time."

"It's unbelievable. If anything happens, we're really cut off out here."

Talk about a mood killer.

The next thing I knew, Adam got up, mumbling something about having to get up early for work the next day. I grabbed my keys and followed him outside. The usual cold breeze blew in from the harbor, and beyond it, the ocean. It was so quiet I could hear the distant roar of the surf. Adam hesitated on the porch, peering into the darkness. Night seemed to fall more quickly at Roy's Cottages.

I grabbed a sweater from a hook in the entryway and joined him.

Adam turned in surprise. "Where are you going?"

"Car. I forgot my laptop, and I've got some work to do."

"You shouldn't be walking alone at night. I'll go with you to your car."

I stopped. "You're kidding? The parking lot is, like, right there. I'll be fine."

He shrugged. The silver strands in his black hair sparkled under the white glow of an overhead light. "Can't be too careful."

It took a few minutes to find my laptop because it had slid under the passenger seat and into the back. When I straightened up, Adam was rocking back and forth on his heels, hands shoved into the pockets of his jeans, looking around.

Nervously, I thought.

Chapter 12

Christina

While driving through the parking lot the next morning, I spotted Adam outside an open garage which didn't belong to him. I was about to stop when I noticed a woman surrounded by boxes. She was tall, thin but not skinny, long dirty blonde hair.

Adam stood with his feet planted wide and his arms folded across his chest, nodding, like he was fascinated by whatever she was saying. And why wouldn't he be? Even from that distance, I could see she was beautiful, in that effortless, no-make-up way some girls have. The type who wears faded jeans with holes and a slouchy sweater but looks gorgeous and knows it. I hadn't seen her around before, but that wasn't surprising. New people were moving in all the time. Every day, in fact. By the concerned look on her face, and the way she was waving her cell phone around, Adam had probably just explained why she didn't have service. I would have felt sorry for her if I hadn't been so busy trying to regain control of my breathing. The muscles in my face had gone tight.

I didn't trust myself to stop and say hello, to be polite, normal. Not in the company of all the head tossing and hair flicking going on. So, I drove off, and when I looked in the rearview mirror, Adam had stepped out into the lane and was staring after my car. I didn't bother waving because I was still too annoyed.

Annoyed with myself for getting too interested, too fast.

At work, I couldn't stop thinking of Adam and New Girl. She looked the type to kayak, probably loved the water and surfing. Shared all his same interests, even camping. With my luck, they were probably in his bed, screwing after a couple of hours out on the water.

When I got back, Adam's Land Cruiser was nowhere to be seen, and my heart felt like someone had just thrown it on the grill. Hot and nasty. He'd probably taken New Girl out for dinner. I speed-walked past New Girl's garage, forcing my eyes on the lane ahead. I was so intent on not looking around for either of them—or both, together—I nearly collided with Liliana Garcia on a path. She gave a startled cry and dropped the bag she was carrying.

I scooped it up and handed it to her. Blue with a hospital logo on the side. "Oh no. Are you okay?"

It was obvious the woman was far from fine. Her clothes were rumpled, and her short silver hair was mashed flat.

"I'm fine. We're just getting back from the hospital." She lowered her voice, clutching the bag to her chest. "He had one of his bad episodes."

"He came to see me the night before last," I blurted out. "He said he hadn't been feeling like himself."

Technically, Tommy Garcia hadn't asked for my confidentiality. He might have just assumed I'd keep my mouth shut and not blab to his wife. But even if he didn't trust her, I did. Something was off about the man.

Liliana gasped. "Is that where he went? I couldn't find him. He was supposed to be taking a nap, and when I went to check on him, he wasn't in the bedroom. I looked everywhere for him. I was half out of my mind with worry." She paused. "What did he want? I hope he didn't bother you."

I shook my head and rushed to reassure her. "No, no, it was fine. He just stopped over to apologize. For what, I'm not sure. He did say he'd been seeing things that scared him and talked about all the medication he's on."

Liliana stiffened. "So, he told you? What the doctor said? Now, that's really something, because he made me promise not to tell anyone, and here I've been keeping it all to myself, bottled up inside. Now, isn't that just like him. I know he's sick. He's a sick man. But it's so unfair. That man is going to be the death of me."

I half expected her to raise a fist in the air and utter a curse.

"Liliana, he didn't share any details, if that's what you're thinking. He mostly complained about the doctors and all the pills he has to take. Is there a chance he's being overmedicated? It happens, you know. All the time."

Liliana crossed herself. "If only it were just that. That could be fixed. What's wrong with him can't. Now listen, Christina, if I tell you, do you promise to keep this to yourself? And whatever you do, you can't tell him you know because he'll blame me, like he does with everything these days." She pressed a knuckle against her lips as a tear trickled down her face.

My neck went all itchy, and I scratched it. "I promise."

She leaned toward me. "He's got dementia. But not Alzheimer's. The one that makes them see things and hear things too. At first, they thought he had Parkinson's Disease because of the way he started walking, all stooped-like. And he falls down a lot too because he doesn't pick up his feet like he's supposed to." She fought back a sob. "We found out right before we were supposed to move in, and the diagnosis was a big shock. I knew something was wrong, but I never imagined something like that. When I told him maybe we shouldn't move here after all, boy did he get mad. Because the minute he heard about this place, back when they were just talking about it, he was all for it. Moving here is all he ever talked about. He's always liked the water. We never had a chance to live so close to it, and now that we're here, he doesn't even appreciate it. I think the change has been too much for him. He's gotten worse. Fast. The night terrors are awful, and now he's seeing things in the daytime too."

"What do your children say?"

Liliana swiped at her eyes with the back of a hand, dragging mascara across her nose and down the side of her face. "Oh god, that's another thing. He won't tell them, and he won't let me either. Because that man is as stubborn as they come, and he's in denial to boot. Won't accept it. He calls the doctors good-for-nothing-so-and-sos. But eventually, we'll have to tell them because there won't be any hiding it anymore."

That time had passed, I thought. Tommy Garcia shouted about monsters in public and called Noah Baggio a shithead. Given what I'd just learned about his condition, it was possible he'd been suffering from it long enough to explain the incidents with his students. It also explained his early retirement. Liliana's explanation of her husband's diagnosis reminded me of something. It came to me in a flash.

"Liliana, does your husband have the same disease Robin Williams had?"

She squeezed her eyes shut and crossed herself again. "Yes. That's it. Lewy Body Dementia. It's a terrible, terrible disease. I wouldn't wish it on my worst enemy."

Liliana patted my arm, like I was the one who needed consoling, then hurried away to her nightmare of a life.

114

After eating a cheese and kosher pickle sandwich on wheat bread, I was too restless to get any work done, or even read a book. My brain kept Liliana's news on constant repeat. It was hard to imagine anything sadder. The diagnosis had come as a devastating blow to the old couple. And happening so soon after their big move seemed especially cruel.

I grabbed a sweater and went outside into the twilight. A walk was what I needed. Or at least that's what I told myself. I hurried past Adam's cottage. The Baggios' cottage was deserted. Ruth had mentioned the couple had gone to stay with relatives in San Jose for a few days, but Cathy hated being so far away from Roy's Cottages in case Noah turned up. Ruth thought there was little chance of that happening, even if she didn't have the heart to tell Cathy.

By the water, a brisk breeze ruffled my hair, and for a short time, I enjoyed the feeling of the air pushing against my face, the sound of the shrieking birds, the waves sloshing against the slips. If I'd worn a jacket, I might have lingered, but it was getting a bit too chilly, and the last of the evening light was fading fast.

After taking a path which led to the middle row of cottages, I ran into a few people I recognized from the potluck—Dawn Ashlock, out on a power walk and gripping a can of mace, and the newlyweds, Abigail and Cassie. No one had any new information about the search for Noah Baggio. We took turns expressing our disbelief that such a thing could happen where we lived.

Cassie rubbed her arms. "I don't feel comfortable here anymore. I don't feel safe."

"I don't think whoever took Noah is interested in grownups," I said. "Or women." At least, that's what Ruth had told me.

"We're thinking about moving," Cassie said.

Abigail scowled. "No, we're not. We've talked about this."

Dawn did a deep knee bend, her dark hair pulled back so tightly in a high ponytail I wondered how it didn't give her a headache. "Did you guys know that Adam Gray is an author? Paul saw his book in the window at a store down at the harbor and bought it. He's a wilderness survival expert."

"We're going to do one of his bootcamps," Abigail said. "If we ever get time off together. I volunteer at the aquarium, and I know him a little from there. If he sees any animals or birds in distress on the slough or in the harbor, he calls us, and we send a truck to pick them up. Once, he even found a beached white shark that was in such bad shape he brought it to us on his boat. It would have died otherwise."

"You're kidding?" I asked. "A great white?"

Abigail grinned. "It was a juvenile, but still. Whenever the word gets out that he's bringing in a rescue, it's amazing how many women find an excuse to be there. And a few guys too."

Dawn pursed her lips. "He's fit, for sure, but he could be buffer. And it wouldn't hurt him to have a protein shake once in a while. Okay, ladies, I gotta get moving." She winked.

"Stay safe out there. Don't let the Slough Devil get you." She power-walked away, arms swinging.

After completing three circuits around the complex, the cold air urged me home, and I was almost there, when Jordan Lewis appeared out of nowhere on her stealth wheelchair.

She stopped under a lamp post. The ends of her hair had been dyed electric blue. "Are you coming with us on Saturday?"

It's impossible to hear that kind of question without feeling there's a party going on you're not invited to. "Where? Who's us?"

"Kayaking. Adam said it's perfect for me because all I have to do is paddle, and I've never tried it before. It was just going to be the two of us, but now a bunch of people are going. I told him I wanted you to go, but he said you hated the water." She stared at me accusingly. "Is that true?"

I nodded. "As weird as it sounds, it's true."

"You have to go. Especially now." She mushed her lips together and wrinkled her nose.

"And why would that be?"

"Because this random woman invited herself, but she only wants to go because of Adam. She was all about Adam, being really nosy, asking me stuff about him, pretending like she was just being friendly." She exhaled noisily. "And I really, really don't like her."

That made two of us. But I couldn't afford to be so open about it. "I don't think I've met her. What's her name?"

"Rae. With an e. It's so pretentious."

I couldn't help but laugh at Jordan's outraged expression. "She can't help her name."

Jordan snorted. "It's probably a made-up name. She seems the type. She just opened a flower shop in Monterey. Wild Rae Floral Design. I remember it because she only mentioned it a hundred times. She's all over Instagram. I looked her up." Jordan batted her eyes and pulled a pout. "Here's my latest headshot. Aren't I beautiful? Here's me setting up for a wedding. And here's me wearing practically nothing, holding a bunch of flowers."

"Wow, you really don't like her. Any chance you're feeling the tiniest bit jealous?"

Jordan's mouth dropped open. "No! He's practically, like, a brother. Ew." Her blue eyes flashed with indignation. "But I thought. You know. You two." She was sputtering now, which was very un-Jordan like.

"What gave you that idea?"

Jordan screwed up her face. "I don't know. A vibe maybe. I mean, I know he likes you. I can tell. And I thought you liked him, and you're not annoying. So, if he's going to go out with anyone, it should be you and not her because, if that happens, it will wreck everything because she's not the type to share. I can tell."

The girl had added two and two and come up with seven, but I understood. Or thought I did. Adam had said she was only living at Roy's Cottages temporarily, and there weren't any other teenagers around. She was obviously bored and lonely, and her father and stepmother had their hands full with a new baby. Adam was one of the few people to take an interest, and after he'd delivered the fancy new wheelchair which could go anywhere, he'd achieved hero status. It wasn't surprising she'd become a bit territorial. It was flattering Jordan had chosen "Team Christina," but it was only because she sensed, of the two of us women, I would mess up the status quo the least.

Jordan grabbed the levers of her wheelchair and shook them. "Christina! You've got to come. You can't just let her…hog him!"

"Maybe he wants to be hogged," I said stiffly.

118

"Then he's stupid." She grabbed my sweater and tugged. "Oh, come on, you have to come. Please. It'll be fun, I swear. Adam says there's a bunch of sea otter babies. Who doesn't want to see those?"

Me. at least not in the wild, and not in a kayak which could tip over and dump my ass in the water. I preferred to see them behind glass at The Monterey Bay Aquarium, followed by a cappuccino at the cafe. But with the way Jordan was going on, saying no would be impossible. She wasn't the type to give up.

If Adam and Rae weren't a done deal yet, I'd be an idiot to throw the game in her favor. Rae might be taller with longer legs, but I had curves one horndog viewer once called "dangerous" in front of my co-workers during a station tour. It was awkward at the time, but it reminded me I wasn't without assets of my own.

"Okay. I'll go," I said.

As I walked a jubilant Jordan back to her place, I hoped to hell I hadn't made the wrong choice.

Chapter 13

Christina

We set out just after eight o'clock in the morning, paddling in and out of pockets of mist Adam promised would burn off. The group was larger than I expected. Rae, in Daisy Dukes and a Harvard sweatshirt. Dawn, the personal trainer, and her husband Paul, the firefighter. Abigail paddled up, saying her wife had gone into work to fill a shift. A half dozen others, who I vaguely recognized from the potluck, came along too.

Before we set out, Adam asked that we stick to the middle of the slough and away from the banks, where we could get stuck in the mud. Staying upright in the kayak was easier than I'd thought, but paddling was tougher, and my arms ached. Rae said I was doing it all wrong and was making a classic beginner's mistake—locking my shoulders and paddling with my arms instead of my torso. Adam overheard and doubled back to check on my form, while Rae shouted tips in the distance. If she'd been closer, I would have been tempted to smack her with the paddle.

After a while, I got the hang of things and was able to keep up. Sort of. Water dripped down my paddles and onto my lap until Abigail pointed out the drip guards had slid out of position and showed me how to fix them. That solved that, but my bottom stayed cold and wet. My kayak seemed to find every patch of black water filled with swirling sea grass, and the sound of it brushing against the plastic under my feet filled me with unease, making me paddle faster.

A dark shadow darted by, just below the surface, and my heart nearly stopped. A bat ray. Then another. Beautiful. Graceful. I watched, holding my breath, while they glided effortlessly through the water. I hoped they weren't a bad omen. Noah Baggio had been out looking for them when he disappeared. Then I scolded myself for being silly, superstitious even.

Up ahead, Jordan held her own in a battle for Adam's attention, and I was glad to see him doing the right thing, focusing on Jordan. After all, that's how the whole trip started, Adam promising to give her a tour of the slough. The rest of us were just tagging along.

Occasionally, Adam shouted at someone who was getting too close to shore. We'd gone some distance from where the marsh was so wide you had to squint to see the other side to a narrower stretch lined with shrubs and twisted trees.

A dairy farm loomed ahead, and soon we could see cows grazing on a pretty knoll. There was nothing but the sound of sea birds, cows mooing, and paddles dipping into the water. Stretched before us was a picturesque view of an old Victorian house with peeling white paint, a few dilapidated barns, and a green, scummy pond. It looked deserted, but Adam assured us it wasn't and said the owners made the best cheese on the Central Coast. When Rae spotted a dock, she wanted everyone to stop so we could troop up the hill and buy some. Adam shook his head and said something to her I couldn't hear, but I didn't have to. That would mean Jordan couldn't join us. Rae clapped a hand over her mouth.

Adam doubled back to check on me. "You hanging in there?"

"I'm not that lame," I said, sitting straighter in the kayak.

"Of course, you're not. I meant, are you okay out here on the water? You said you hated it."

I forced a smile. "It's actually pretty out here. I'm glad I came. And Jordan's having a great time. That's the most important thing."

As if on cue, Jordan shrieked.

Adam's back was to her. His face drained of color, and his mouth opened. It was almost like he was afraid to turn around.

And then Jordan was shouting, "Adam, look! Otters. A raft of otters!"

He closed his eyes and exhaled. It was obvious she'd given him a scare. I watched him paddle away, wondering at his rather extreme reaction.

It seemed like someone shouted about something every few minutes.

"Seal!"

"Heron!"

"Look at those pelicans! They're huge!"

Adam warned us to give the otters plenty of space, which was challenging because the slough had narrowed again. The bottom of my kayak scraped on mud, and Adam had to come over and drag me out of the muck. The shore reeked of rotten eggs, and the foul smell made me gag.

"What's that stench?"

Adam laughed. "Just the usual wetland gasses. Sulfur and methane. Don't worry. It's just natural decay, not a sewage leak or anything."

As soon as we'd cleared the shallows, he said, "Okay Christina, you owe me a beer." When my kayak rammed into a sand bank I hadn't noticed, Adam said, "You're gonna owe me a six pack by the time we're done."

123

Rae swiveled in her seat and stared. Then, she paddled off toward Dawn and started talking to her. They were too far ahead for me to hear what they were saying.

A few moments later, Rae shouted, "We're tired of waiting for you guys. We're going ahead. See what's there."

Then, they were off. The two women seemed to be in a friendly competition to see who could get there first.

Adam shouted after them. "Stop! It's too far."

The women ignored him.

Paul paddled up to Adam. By that time, I'd managed to get a bit closer.

"That's my wife for you. She loves pushing people, and even more than that, she loves being first. I've got my money on Dawn."

I did too. Dawn's back formed a perfect V-shape, thanks to all that weightlifting she did to work out her lats.

Abigail rubbed sun lotion on her freckled face without bothering to rub it in, then held out the tube. I shook my head, distracted by the sight of Adam hurrying after the two women.

"We need to stay together," he shouted after them.

I didn't know what the big deal was, or why he seemed so panicked. They could knock themselves out, for all I cared, and they were grown women comfortable on the water.

"He's probably worried because they're not wearing life vests," Abigail said.

Adam had made me put one on, and Jordan too, before we'd set out, but everyone else had refused, Rae the loudest, saying she'd been a lifeguard and didn't need one.

Jordan came up, nose wrinkled. "They're just showing off." She caught my eye. "And I think we know why."

124

Abigail glanced up from rubbing lotion into her knees. "What do you mean?" Then her mouth formed a perfect O, followed by, "Ohhhh! I get it."

The three of us watched in silence as Rae and Dawn rounded a bend in the slough. Trees clinging to the side of the banks drooped over the water, forming a canopy. Squealing, the women ducked their heads and disappeared into the gap. Adam was struggling to catch up, still yelling at them to turn around.

Jordan held a hand over her eyes even though the sun was behind her. "He's really freaking out."

From ahead, beyond the bend in the slough, came a scream, then another, higher and shriller. Dawn. It sounded like Dawn.

Jordan gasped.

"What's going on up there, baby?" Paul shouted. Without waiting for a reply, he shot forward in the water, paddling like a demon, his muscles working under his tight pullover.

Over their voices came the sound of splashing. Thrashing. Someone struggling in the water. The sound was straight out of a documentary I once saw about an orca in captivity. It turned on its trainer, throwing her into the air, then pulled her under. The woman would pop up again, and the orca would take her in its jaws, shaking her like a rag doll, body slamming into the water, dragging her along the cement sides of the pool. But there were no killer whales in the slough. Whatever was up there sounded too big to be an otter or a bat ray.

"No, no, no," screamed another voice. That time, it was Rae.

"What the fuck?" Jordan said beside me.

Adam shot out of sight, around the bend, swallowed by the canopy of foliage. The wet thrashing sounds continued, and then a howl. Human. Definitely human. A howl of disbelief, terror. And then, silence.

The three of us stayed in our kayaks, as if frozen there. The rest of the group had fallen way behind. The last we'd seen them, they'd stopped to take photos of seals sunning themselves on the shore.

We waited for what seemed like an eternity before Rae appeared, alone. She was paddling in jerky, uncoordinated movements. I thought she'd stop when she reached us, but she kept going.

"Let's get out of here now," she yelled over her shoulder. When we didn't move, she shrieked, "Let's go, now, now, now."

"What happened?" Abigail called after her.

Rae didn't answer. My heart was pounding so hard that, if she had, I might not have heard her.

Jordan stared after Rae, blinking. "Maybe we should go help the guys."

"No," Abigail said firmly. "Let's let Adam and Paul handle it. We need to get back and go for help."

We trailed Rae, and only when we'd reached the farm did she slow down. Rae turned toward us in her kayak. Blood trickled down the side of her face.

"Something took Dawn," she gasped. "It came out of the water."

"What do you mean, something?" Abigail cried. "You must have seen it."

Rae squeezed her eyes shut and shook her head. Blood plastered a lock of hair to the side of her face. "Just for a second. I don't know. I don't know what I saw. But she's gone."

When asked how she'd hurt her head, Rae explained she'd run into a tree branch. Abigail inspected the bloody gouge and announced she needed stitches. After some debate, we decided Abigail, as a nurse and faster paddler, would return to the cottages, drive Rae to the hospital, and call for help, while Jordan and I remained to wait for Adam and Paul.

"Adam," Rae stammered. "Adam…He wants everybody to stay away. Made me promise to tell you."

Abigail gave a curt nod. "Okay. When we see the others, we'll tell them to go back."

Jordan and I waited in the middle of a wide part of the slough, far from any overgrowth which could hide something, alert to every sound. A clacking sound nearly gave us a heart attack, and then we saw an otter in the distance, laying on its back, knocking two shells together to get at the meat inside. A few moments later, a shiny black triangle of a head popped up out of the water several yards away. A seal. I hadn't realized seals swam that far up the slough, but there it was. Its dark eyes studied us for a moment, then it disappeared beneath the water. Kayaks bobbing, we waited for what seemed an eternity for Adam and Paul to appear. I had no hope of seeing Dawn. Not after what Rae had said.

Eventually, we heard sirens, and then voices in the distance.

When Adam finally emerged from the canopy of trees, I felt a sob of relief rise in my throat. Paul had stayed behind.

When we got back to Roy's Cottages, Adam had to haul me onto the dock because my legs had turned to rubber. I didn't care what he thought, or anybody else. I threw my arms around his neck because I hadn't lost him.

Chapter 14

Adam

When I told Christina I planned to kayak back up the slough to where Dawn had gone missing—correction, to where she had been taken—to help with the search, she threw herself in front of the door and shouted, "No!"

We'd stumbled back to her place after dropping Jordan off at her house and explaining the situation to her stepmother. Jordan had wanted to come with us, but Christina kindly but firmly said we needed some time alone. To talk.

As I paced Christina's living room, she poured tequila shots with a hand shaking so badly the amber liquid sloshed over the sides.

Christina sagged against the kitchen island, her oval face pale, her head and neck streaked with mud. After she took a few sips of her drink, she said, "Jesus H Christ. Did you see what happened?"

"A little," I said dully. "Enough." I tossed down my shot. It had a strong, earthy flavor and an even stronger kick.

Her dark eyes raked my face. "Tell me. You have to tell me. Please."

I stared into my glass for a long time before I could say anything. "All right. When I got there, Dawn was in the water. She was splashing around, panicked. She was in the shallows, close to the bank. There were some trees hanging over, and the trees were moving, but I was too busy paddling, trying to get to her, and then something, like someone hanging upside down, grabbed her by the hair and yanked her up. It was like she was, I don't know, flying in the air. And then it let her go, and she fell into the water, way ahead of us. She came up, sputtering, coughing. There was a little sand bank nearby, so she started swimming toward it. And she got there. She made it. She even managed to stand up, and I was trying to get to her, but I could tell something was wrong because the shallows were churning, like something was in the water. And there was. Something crawled out. It looked like that thing in the video. And I'm thinking, no. No, that's not possible. And then Rae started screaming, and when I looked over, her hair was tangled in a branch, and for a second, I thought something had got her too, and she was closer, so I didn't know who to help, and when I looked back at Dawn, that thing was dragging her into the water, and she was fighting like hell. And then she was gone."

Christina drained her tequila and set down the glass. "Then it's real. That monster in the video is real. What the hell is going on?"

I shook my head, unwilling to believe the impossible, even though I'd seen it with my own eyes.

"Adam, I believe you. You need to believe yourself. We don't have a lot of time. What are we going to tell people? We have to say...something."

I looked at Christina in amazement. She'd gone from petrified to practical in seconds. It didn't matter she was shaking all over, her dark eyes wide with fright.

"How can you believe something like that?"

"I don't know," she whispered. "But I do. Maybe it's because I grew up with all those stories my grandparents used to tell us. The cucuy. The Llorona, the crying lady. My grandfather from Texas told one that used to scare me and my sister to death. La Lechuza, a witch who could turn into an owl. He used to swear he saw it when he was a kid. And one of my grandmothers believed in curses, things to bring good luck, and don't get me started on the powers of amuletos. Charms. Then, there's transferring worries to trouble dolls. Whenever my grandmother got sick, we had to drive her to a healer, even though she'd just come from the doctor's office." She shrugged. "I never thought about it like this before, but I grew up hearing about the supernatural, about monsters, so it doesn't seem so crazy to me."

I stared at her for a long time, thinking about what she'd just said, and found it oddly comforting.

Christina pushed a finger into her temple. Her eyes snapped open. "Adam, what did you see the other night? The night you were high?"

My mind jolted back to that night. Christ. I'd forgotten about it. "I thought I was seeing things. You know, because I'd had too much weed. I heard footsteps on the dock, and when I looked outside, there was someone crouched on that big rock, the one across from my place next to the path. When you told me about the teenagers they caught trying to scare people, I thought it was one of them. That my mind was playing tricks on me."

"But it wasn't," Christina said flatly.

"No. It was the same as the thing I saw today. The thing that took Dawn." I couldn't bring myself to say monster. Or creature. Or Slough Devil.

Rae lay on the couch in her living room, staring up at the ceiling, one hand over her bandaged forehead, one bare and scratched leg touching the floor in a classic fainting pose. Abigail shoved a pile of clothes from an easy chair and collapsed into it with a grunt. She looked worn out, the pale

131

skin under her eyes a grayish purple. I'd carried Jordan inside, and she sat on a loveseat, her head on Christina's shoulder. Christina absently stroked her hair while staring at Rae. A potent odor filled the room. A vase on a small dining table held white waxy flowers, a bunch of them, their scent so sweet and cloying I had to resist the urge to take them outside.

All the furniture in Rae's place was the color of oatmeal, all the pillows white or off-white. A series of abstract prints in various shades of green covered the walls. It was relaxing, like a spa, but also oddly stark for a home.

"We need to talk about this," Christina said, in that blunt way of hers.

Rae didn't reply. Her eyes fluttered closed.

"They gave her something at the urgent care," Abigail said. "She was in shock."

Christina lifted her eyebrows. "What did you tell them? At the harbormaster's office?"

Abigail sighed. "I made Rae stay in the car, so technically, she didn't tell them anything because, by the time we got there, she was talking about monsters. I didn't want them to think we were crazy, or that we were pranking them or something. We needed them to take us seriously and go look for Dawn. I said she had fallen out of her kayak without a life vest and went under, and we couldn't find her." She grimaced. "I may have said she didn't know how to swim."

"Makes sense," I said.

It was probably the best explanation she could have provided, given the bizarre circumstances. There was nothing like a person who didn't know how to swim to mobilize search and rescue. My hands hurt, and when I looked down at them, my palms were red and irritated. My frantic paddling had given me blisters.

Christina got up and perched on the edge of the couch next to Rae. "Rae, I know this is a lot to handle right now, but we need to know. What exactly did you see?"

Rae turned her face to the wall, her shoulders shaking. Christina patted her on the shoulder.

"Hey, I know this is hard, but I need you to sit up for a few minutes. Just a few minutes, okay? And then we'll leave you alone, I promise."

Jordan leaned forward, her pointy chin all angles. "We're all traumatized. Not just you. Get over yourself already. Christina's asking you a question. Everyone is going to find out something happened out there, and besides Adam, you're the only one who saw it. So why don't you put your big girl pants on and tell us."

Any other time, a sixteen-year-old scolding someone nearly twice her age would have made me laugh. Instead, I felt grateful for her words, as sharp as they were.

Rae's legs kicked, and a fist pounded the couch. "All right," she cried. She rolled over so fast she knocked Christina to the floor.

She'd changed out of her wet clothes, so she was wearing sweats and a tank top. Her body began to shake. Christina reached over and draped a striped throw over her.

"I didn't get a good look at it," she said, a bitter edge to her voice. "One second, we were just having fun, and the next, her kayak was on its side, and she was being dragged into the water, and whatever it was had fucked up hands, or paws. And long claws. Big ones. Really big."

"You didn't see more of it? Like a head, or a tail?" Christina asked.

Rae bit her lip. "Maybe. I don't know. It moved so fast it was all a blur. And everything was so confusing because Dawn

133

was all over the place in the water. Because something was dragging her." She hesitated. "But maybe I saw a head. And then my hair got caught on a branch, and I thought I was being attacked too, and then Adam got there." She patted her bandage, as if to make sure it was still there. "But I can tell you this. It was not an animal. Not a normal one." She hesitated. "But it had a human shape. Two legs. Two arms."

Abigail cleared her throat. "Is it possible it was someone in a wet suit? Or a costume. You know, trying to scare us. Like those kids the other night?"

"No way," Jordan muttered.

"Maybe," Rae whispered. "It's possible. I guess."

"Why would someone go through all that trouble?" Christina asked.

Abigail gave a little shrug. "Those teenagers went through a lot of trouble, driving all the way over here, at night, to scare us. Maybe whoever did it this time is more serious." She pointed at Christina. "You used to work in the news business, right? I remember seeing all those stories about the environmentalists who protested when they started building this place. One of those people called it an abomination and said they'd never give up trying to shut it down. So, what if they haven't?"

Jordan pressed her palms against the sides of her head. "You're saying someone dressed up as a monster, then waited around in the slough to kill someone? That's insane."

"What happened out there was insane," Rae cried. "You didn't see it. I did. And it was covered in fur, for fuck's sake." Rae paled and teetered on the couch.

For a moment, I thought she was going to pitch forward, but Christina's hand shot out and steadied her. Rae's head swiveled toward me. Her eyes were red and pooled with tears.

134

"Whatever it was, Dawn's dead. What do you think it was?"

My throat had gone so dry the words didn't want to come out. "I'm not sure. Like you said, things happened so fast."

Rae threw off the blanket and cast a scorching glance in my direction. "Liar. The least you can do is tell the truth. That's what Jordan wanted me to do. You can at least do the same. Or are we playing by different rules?" Her words tumbled out, slightly slurred from whatever they'd given her at the hospital.

Christina got to her feet with a loud sigh. "You two aren't that far apart on this, you know. It's simple really. Say you saw something, but with everything that was going on, you're not sure exactly what."

"That's what I just said," Rae snapped. "I'm sorry, but I don't understand what's happening here. Do you want me to say something? Not say something? Because I'm totally confused."

Christina stepped to the center of the room, hands on her hips. "Let me spell it out so we're all on the same page. Are you and Adam ready to say you saw a monster with claws come out of the water and kill Dawn? That means telling everyone, including the police and whatever authorities show up, our neighbors, the media, and the entire world. Because that's what we're talking about. As soon as we say that word, monster, there's going to be a shit storm. And here's something you might not have thought about—we were all together. Someone, somewhere, is going to pit us against each other. Gee, Christina, do you really believe Adam and Rae? How well do you really know them? And pretty soon, we're all dragged into this. Some of us have jobs and reputations, and talking about monsters is serious business that we probably want to think about a little more carefully." She shrugged. "You know. Let's really think this through."

Abigail's eyes widened. "I didn't see anything."

Rae blinked. "I could lose customers. I just booked some really big weddings and events. I'm doing all the flowers."

"We need to be careful, that's all," Christina said quietly. "But now that we know something is out there, we can't be stupid either."

Chapter 15

Adam

Christina stayed with Rae, Jordan, and Abigail while I drove to the spot where the teams would begin their search.

There weren't many places to launch, and the spot I was thinking of was close to where Dawn went missing. Christina hadn't wanted me to go, but I had to. I worried we'd sent search crews into danger, not telling them the whole truth about that thing, or things, in the water.

When I pulled up, a fleet of emergency vehicles awaited, and men and women in a variety of uniforms were swarming the area. Even from where I parked on the side of the road, I could hear voices coming from the slough. They were already in the water, searching.

"Safety in numbers," I muttered. To reassure myself.

The harbormaster greeted me. She was a striking, broad-shouldered woman with long, straight iron-gray hair. Darlene Woodward had grown up on Devil's Landing and worked as a lawyer before switching careers.

"You guys have had some bad luck," she said dryly. "First the boy, now this. The husband is out on the water. I didn't have the heart to tell him it's search and recovery, but he's a firefighter, so I'm sure he knows that already, and this is just his process. The poor guy. And newlyweds, I hear. Sad."

Darlene knew sad. Working on the water was dangerous business, and over the years, she'd seen boat wrecks, dock mishaps, floating bodies—dead and barely alive—lost skiffs, and burning trawlers. All that made her matter of fact about such tragedies. Even so, she radiated empathy and confidence.

"No sign of her," Darlene continued, leaning against her truck. "I heard you saw her go in."

I nodded, toes clenching in my sneakers. "Yes. But I couldn't get to her in time."

Darlene frowned. "I don't understand, Adam. Her husband said she knew how to swim, and the slough's not that deep. And she was fit, he said. So, where's her body?"

I'd known Darlene all my life. She'd known my parents. The expression on her face betrayed her suspicion and bewilderment.

When I didn't reply, she said. "Something's not right, Adam. You want to tell me what it is?"

Christina hadn't accounted for Darlene Woodward, and in my befuddled state, neither had I.

When I didn't answer right away, Darlene slapped her hand against the hood. "What is it you want to tell me, Adam?"

"I don't want to, is the problem," I said.

Darlene had this way about her. She was the ultimate authority figure, so I stood there, fidgeting, my palms sweaty and tingling.

I stammered out an answer. "I saw something. I don't know what it was. An animal maybe. It was big though."

"You mean, like a mountain lion?" Darlene asked voice rising. "I thought she fell into the water, so excuse me if I'm a little confused here."

I looked down at my feet, feeling like a kid trapped telling a lie. "It was a little chaotic, Darlene."

The harbormaster blinked. "I'm sure it was. But which was it? Dawn Ashlock fell out of the kayak and somehow disappeared, or an animal got her?" Her obsidian eyes narrowed. "So, what kind of animal might that be, Adam? It sure would be helpful to know what you think, especially with your expertise and educational background and all. Because right now, all our efforts are focused on the water. Are you telling me we need to start a land search as well?"

"It wasn't a mountain lion," I stammered. "And not a boar. I only saw it for a few seconds."

Darlene held up a hand. "Did it come out of the water? Or was it on the shore?"

"Both maybe?"

My thoughts whirled as I tried to remember. Darlene was right. There had to have been more than one. It's just that they moved so fast. So impossibly fast.

"So, you're saying there were two of them, or more?"

"Maybe."

"I see," she said, shoving her hands into her pockets. "No, actually. I don't. You're not making any sense, Adam, and if I didn't know you better, I'd think you were in shock. Or hiding something. But this isn't your first rodeo, so what do you say you just tell me what's going on?"

Darlene's eyes raked across my face. I felt my neck go hot. When I didn't reply, she cocked her head, then her mouth went slack.

"You saw the Slough Devil, didn't you?"

Even though it was still cool out, I could feel sweat beading on my forehead. "Maybe."

Darlene grabbed my arm and squeezed it, hard. "Good. At least I'm not the only one. I thought I was losing my mind." She gave a bitter laugh. "Which is a real concern at my age."

I was so stunned by this unexpected confession, I leaned against the truck and took a few deep breaths.

"What are we going to do?"

Her face had a pinched look. "I don't know, Adam. This is a new one on me."

139

Chapter 16

Adam

The Slough Devil existed.

I was having a hard time believing it, even though I'd seen it. As had Rae and Tommy Garcia. And now, harbormaster Darlene Woodward—someone I knew and respected—admitted she'd seen it too. Briefly.

It happened about a year ago on a Mother's Day kayak excursion with her adult children. They'd been at the far eastern end of the slough. Her kids had just turned around and were facing west, but a movement in the trees caught her eye, a dark shape among the green.

At first, she'd thought it was a man, but the shape was wrong, the head a bit too round, a little too small. Then, the figure had scaled the branches and disappeared into the thick canopy. She could feel it watching her, and she'd paddled away as fast as she could. Later, she watched the Lorenz video clip, comparing the creature caught on film to what she'd seen, and concluded they'd been the same. But she told no one.

"Who would believe me?" she'd said. "It's hard enough being a woman harbormaster. Can you imagine the reaction I'd get if I went around telling people I saw the Slough Devil? I'd be laughed out of my job. The fishermen like telling that story, but they don't really believe it. And you know how they are. They'd say I was hysterical, that they were right after all, that a woman had no business holding this job."

The search for Dawn Ashlock continued until the sun went down and resumed the next day and the day after that. Dawn's body was not recovered. Rae and I were asked to write and sign statements, explaining our versions of events. With the harbormaster's help, we coordinated our responses. Neither of us saw her fall into the water, but something—we didn't know what—appeared to drag her under. No mention of hands—or paws—with claws. No mention of an oddly shaped head.

Marine biologists were consulted, and I was asked to ferry a team of them up and down the slough, answering their questions. Dodging their questions, to be more accurate. A scientist with a questionable reputation made the media rounds, speculating a great white shark had made its way up the salt marsh, and that's how Dawn had met her tragic end.

Darlene said she thought it was absolutely ridiculous, but she was grateful for the diversion, so she just shrugged and told reporters, "I don't know. I'm not a shark expert."

Most people came to believe two things—a shark had killed Dawn Ashlock, and a pedophile kidnapper had snatched Noah Baggio.

It didn't matter search crews hadn't found blood in the water or a severed limb, and authorities hadn't located the dirty white van which supposedly whisked Noah away. The stories, and their connection to Roy's Cottages, dominated the news cycle for days until they finally faded away.

But my neighbors didn't forget.

It was all they could talk about. Suddenly, they feared the slough, too afraid to sit on the docks and enjoy the fresh sea air. Too nervous to walk on the paths meandering next to the marsh, like a shark could sprout legs and chomp after them.

If they'd seen what I had, they'd be terrified.

Christina insisted I stay at her place, which was further away from the water, and I readily agreed. She helped me move my things. We didn't talk about what that meant between the

142

two of us. To our surprise, Rae moved in with a red-bearded surfer guy who worked in tech. He lived in a cottage on the west side of the complex, near the park. I'd only met him briefly when he'd hauled Rae's kayak to the dock on the day Dawn died.

Christina was more surprised than I was. She'd been convinced Rae had set her sights on me, but she hadn't seen what I had. Rae was a flirt, and when no one was looking, I saw her flash her tits at the surfer guy, then laugh.

When I told Christina, she'd rolled her eyes. "They were probably meant for you, you dummy."

Maybe. But at that point, all I cared about was Christina.

The residents of Roy's Cottages demanded a community meeting and insisted on representatives from the property management company and law enforcement. Leading the charge was Abigail and her wife, Cassie, the two nurses. They asked Christina to write a press release to media outlets so there would be some accountability. Just what we needed. More media coverage.

Darlene Woodward agreed to host the meeting, which I admit was a clever move. The harbormaster's office was small and cramped, so we met in the community room, which inexplicably stank of fish, and since it lacked insulation or heat, the temperature began to drop the moment the sun went down.

Darlene took me aside and whispered, "I could have put in a heater, but this way it keeps meetings short."

She had come prepared, wearing a parka, and seemed to get a kick from selling Devil's Landing sweatshirts and beanies

143

to those who'd come unprepared for the cold. TV news crews came from as far away as San Francisco and San Jose. The local stations were there too, along with a reporter I recognized from the public radio station.

Gary, the property manager, stood next to the sheriff. They both wore grim expressions. The TV camera operators set up at the side of the room while people continued to pour in. Darlene sent an assistant to fetch more folding chairs and when the double doors finally closed behind us, I counted seventy-five people. Rae and her boyfriend sat behind us, holding hands.

Rae leaned forward. "I'm not saying anything," she whispered. "For the record."

That made two of us. Three, including Darlene. Three people who'd seen the creature, but who'd agreed staying silent was the wisest course of action. Luckily, Liliana Garcia and her husband had stayed home. That was the last thing we needed. The old man standing up, shouting about seeing the slough monster. It was clear now he hadn't been hallucinating, nor was I the night I smoked too much weed.

Rich and Cathy Baggio sat in the front row, along with Paul Ashlock and Ruth. He still had the same dazed expression he'd worn since his wife, Dawn, vanished in the marsh.

Sheriff Lucas, a tall bald man with rimless glasses, introduced himself and got right to it. "I know this has been a very traumatic couple of weeks for the residents of Roy's Cottages, especially the families of Noah Baggio and Dawn Ashlock, and our agency is aware of their concerns. And the concerns of the community there too." He hesitated. "There's no other way to say this but in the most forthright way. These are two unconnected events. An abduction and an accident on

144

the water, which may or may not have involved a shark or some other animal…"

"Where's her body then?" Paul thundered. "That's the part I can't understand. It doesn't make sense."

Sheriff Lucas cleared his throat. "Out of precaution, the slough will remain closed for the next three days while teams continue their search. And to let the marine biologists have a little more time to look for any signs of predators not normally found in the marsh. We advise everyone living at the cottages to be a bit more vigilant, be aware of their surroundings, and let us know if you see any unusual activity."

Christina jabbed my side. "Oh, oh. Here we go."

The room erupted. "You've got to be fucking kidding me," someone shouted from the back of the room.

"We have no cell service!" Abigail cried.

"We don't even have land lines," Cassie shouted.

"Oh, come on, people," a familiar voice boomed from somewhere off to my right. It was Sig, the fisherman. "Give the sheriff a break. He doesn't owe you a damn thing. You decided to move here. There's never been this many people living up the slough. It's rural out here. Always has been, and instead of you adjusting to the way things are, you want to turn it into something it's not. Now you're complaining you don't have this, and you don't have that, and you want somebody to fix it. Maybe you should have paid a little more attention to what you were signing up for."

Another fisherman, a small wiry man with a hooked nose, stood up. "Sig's got a point, you know. Those extra patrols you've been asking for are going to cost money. Taxpayer money. All so's you feel safe because you're not used to living the quiet life, and it scares you. Accidents happen all the time in the water, and you're living right next to it. And as much as I

145

hate to say it—and my apologies to the parents of that little boy—but kids go missing every day. I watch the news. It's a horrible, terrible fact of life. The police can't be there around the clock like your own personal bodyguards. And here's another thing. I attended all those meetings about that place you're living in. Every single one. I was dead set against it from the beginning." He pinned his gaze on me and pointed. "Isn't that right, Adam? You were there too. Before you switched sides." His finger swept from one side of the room to the other. "But I don't remember a single one of you sitting here, acting all high and mighty, showing up to any of those meetings. If you had, you might have learned a thing or too, like how there aren't phone lines out there. Like how Sand Road sometimes floods so bad there's no getting across for days at a time. I bet you don't even know that." He lifted his chin and surveyed the room, which had fallen into shocked silence.

"You're kidding?" Christina said.

I sighed. "No. Sometimes in high surf or heavy rains, the mouth of Roy's River gets clogged and floods the road. It seems to happen every few years. It's one of the reasons I got those big tires on my truck."

As the room erupted—again—Gary the property manager repeated his favorite line. "All right, everyone, it seems like this is coming as a surprise to you, but the flooding issues were well documented in the disclosures."

Christina groaned. "Jesus. What else is in there?"

I shrugged. "Besides being in a flood plain? We're on the edge of a fire zone, and we're next to the Monterey Bay. The San Gregorio fault line runs through it."

Christina gave a little moan. "I'm an idiot," she said, dropping her head onto my shoulder.

It wasn't a big deal. Just the usual expression of affection between two people. But to me, it meant more. A sign the self-reliant, confident woman felt vulnerable, out of her element. A reminder I had someone else to think about besides myself. I swallowed and put an arm around her, breathing in the scent of her shampoo. A hint of sandalwood. Subtle, but nice.

Talk of the flooding had one upside. It changed the focus of the meeting. While everyone was genuinely upset Noah Baggio had been snatched from Roy's Cottages and Dawn Ashlock had presumably died on the slough, the news that flooding was inevitable made everyone forget the original agenda.

Sheriff Lucas and Gary were more than happy to step aside and let Darlene Woodward take over the meeting. She answered the onslaught of questions with ease. "Well, we're talking about Mother Nature here, and there's only so much we can do to mitigate her impacts. Public Works has installed gauges, and the engineers do a good job keeping an eye on them. When the river reaches a certain stage, the crews go out and clear the riverbed, but that's not always enough. Sometimes, the water level gets too high, too fast, and the road floods. When that happens, you just have to wait until things dry out. Over the years, they've talked about raising the road, but that would cost tens of millions of dollars, and there's just not enough money in the budget, not with all the other improvements needed around the county."

Cassie shot to her feet. "Are you saying we could be...cut off out there?"

"That's exactly what I'm saying," Darlene said. "If you're at the cottages, you'll be stuck there, unless you have the right kind of vehicle that can clear the water. But if the flooding is bad enough, you'll be stuck. And if you're on the other side of it, you won't be able to get back home."

"When that happens, the Inn at Roy's Harbor offers discounts to the locals," Sig offered helpfully. "But I don't know how that's going to work, with so many of you living out there now."

"But some of us have jobs," Cassie sputtered. "I'm an essential worker. I can't just miss a shift because of flooding,"

Gary stepped forward. "Well, when you bought your place—which is in a unique location—you bought into that lifestyle, and occasionally, it's going to come with some inconveniences. Like being stranded temporarily." He forced a smile to his face.

With skin stretching over jutting cheekbones, wearing a voluminous black coat, he had the appearance of a harbinger of doom, trying but failing to put a positive spin on the bleakest of news.

Chapter 17

Christina

When Adam came back from his morning run, he said he saw Paul Ashlock kayaking in the slough. Paul had joined the search team still looking for Dawn, or the remains of Dawn.

A feeling of unreality had set in. That we had the horrible luck of having a murderous creature for a neighbor defied belief, but it explained everything. The German tourist's video. Tommy Garcia's warning the day Noah Baggio went missing. The scratched-up dock. The figure Adam had seen crouched on a rock, staring at him. A ten-year-old boy simply vanishing, and not long after that, a woman, a strong swimmer, disappearing in six feet of water. And how dozens of people looking for her had found nothing.

"I hope Paul's okay out there," I said. "I hope they're all okay out there."

Adam looked up from stacking the dishwasher. Correction. Re-stacking. He said the way I did it was all wrong, and there was a strategy to it. I didn't bother arguing. He was right about that. I gave things a quick rinse and shoved them in any old which way. If he wanted to stack the dishwasher, I was more than happy to sit back, drink my coffee, and admire his tight butt from afar.

"He'll be fine," Adam said. "They're concentrating on the lower part of the slough today, near Devil's Landing." He stood up, rubbing his lower back. "I don't think those things go down that far."

149

That's how we'd come to talk about the slough monster. They. It. Those. Vague terms which helped us avoid giving voice to the nightmare invading our lives.

I stared into my coffee. It was black. Adam said I'd fallen into the bad habit of adding too much cream and sugar. Without them though, my French roast tasted sad. I got up and grabbed the carton of milk. It was one percent, so I had to add a lot.

"They made it down this far, Adam. I don't know. I've been thinking. Maybe I was wrong. Maybe we should tell people. I don't know what we'd say, exactly, that wouldn't make us sound crazy."

Adam plucked the sugar bowl from the counter and placed it in front of me. "Then what would you say?"

I added a teaspoon of sugar and stirred it in. "I don't know. Maybe you can make up some bullshit story about a predator on the loose. Or predators. Like climate change is driving mountain lions out of the mountains, and sharks are swimming up the slough because the ocean is screwed up, or polluted, or something. They'd believe you."

Adam frowned as he thought it over. He'd lost weight in the last several days. His thighs looked thinner in his jeans. "I could, but the problem is, I'm not a marine biologist. Plus, that would just reignite the story. As it is, if nothing else happens, everybody will forget and just go back to their usual habits. And besides, what do we really hope to achieve? Hey, everybody, we think we've moved into Slough Devil territory, so we should all leave now? Put up a perimeter fence?"

"I don't know," I admitted. "But I'm worried."

He sighed, running a hand through his black hair. It was glorious, with all those silver highlights against his tan skin. "I'm worried too." He grabbed his backpack from a chair and

150

swung it over his shoulder. "I'm going to Vic's. I need to make some calls and rebook some tours." He groaned. "It's going to take forever. Jordan's going to come with me. We're taking her for lunch at the wharf. Vic's going too."

"How she doing with all this?" I asked, getting my stuff together to head into work.

"Fine. But she has a plan she's trying to talk me into. She wants us to tell Ruth and Paul. Everything. And then, she wants them to hand out their guns to all our neighbors and teach them to shoot, so if a monster shows up, people can kill it."

Jordan was no typical teenager, that was for damn sure. I was impressed, and horrified. The first unusual sound, and there was bound to be an accidental shooting.

"Jesus," I said. "She's not threatening to tell Ruth and Paul, is she?"

"Not yet," Adam said. "But she's already pestering me for a gun. Says she doesn't feel safe in the wheelchair, even with the air horn."

"Maybe she should go home to L.A."

"I tried telling her that, and she said her mom is still looking for a place. But I talked to Jordan's stepmom, and she says the real story is Jordan's mom is having too much fun living with her new boyfriend and isn't in a big hurry. And the stepmom and dad aren't in a big hurry for her to leave either because she's a big help with the new baby."

We walked the short distance to the car, the sky gray and overcast.

It was eight fifteen and the parking lot was mostly empty. The cottages had come with an open-air space and garage, which most everyone used for storage. Rae's car was gone. So were Cassie's and Abigail's. Adam waited until I was behind

151

the wheel, then stuck his head through the window and kissed me.

"Maybe we can do a bit more of that later," I said wistfully.

The last few nights we'd spent staring up at the ceiling, listening for strange sounds. More than once, I found him prowling around, peering out the windows, clutching a flare gun.

His kiss lingered, and when he started rubbing the back of my neck, I was half tempted to text my boss I was running late and haul Adam back inside for a quickie. And then his eyes snapped open, and he looked up. A giant rain drop hit his cheek, and then another.

After last night's meeting, and all that talk of storm-induced flooding, the possibility of rain had taken on ominous overtones. My scalp prickled. It often rained this time of year on the Central Coast, but I'd never depended on a road that got washed out. If that happened while I was at work, Adam would be on one side, and I'd be on the other. Without phones, there was no way to check in unless he happened to be in signal range.

"I guess we don't know what the forecast is, do we?" I asked. Living without an internet connection or mobile service was getting old.

Adam shook his head. "No, but I don't think we have anything to worry about. I always check the long-range forecasts because of the tours, and I don't remember seeing any rain predicted." He paused. "But with everything going on, I haven't been thinking straight, so I haven't checked recently."

"The meteorologist I used to work with said ten-day forecasts are only right about half the time," I said, starting the car.

When I waved goodbye, Adam looked as gloomy as the darkening skies.

I drove west, waited forever to turn left onto Highway 1, then headed toward Sixty-Eight. My first meeting of the day was in an office park near the Monterey Airport. By the time I was done, the pavement was damp, and a half-hearted drizzle had begun. Back at the office, I checked the weather forecast online and didn't like what I saw. A storm was gathering over the San Francisco Bay Area, and there was a chance it was headed our way. A fifty percent chance.

Not just any storm—an atmospheric river, the kind which dumps a lot of water.

The last time one of those hit, I was working at the TV station and all hell broke loose. Road closures. Accidents. Mudslides and, of course, flooding. At the time, it was just a news story. Personally, I wasn't affected. This time, it was different.

If an atmospheric river was going to point its hose at us at Roy's Cottages, I wanted to know about it in advance.

Before I got stuck on a long conference call with new clients, I decided to have a chat with my former TV station's meteorologist. I called Miles Dorcas, who went around calling himself "The Dork" before anybody else could. We'd spent three years together on air, five nights a week. He was the closest thing I had to a work husband.

He picked up right away. "What? I'm not talking to you since you bailed on my last game night."

I glanced out the window. Clouds the color of steel wool hunkered in the sky. "You know I hate charades. Miles, you know that atmospheric river they're talking about in San Francisco?"

Miles sniffed. "Yes. Because, you know, I'm a meteorologist."

I laughed. "Are those online degrees even legit?"

"Yessss," he hissed. "I paid a lot of money for that thing."

"Seriously, Miles. What's the chance it's going to hit us?"

I must have sounded nervous because, suddenly, I could hear him tapping away at a keyboard.

"Let me check. I'm putting the phone down and putting you on speaker, so what do you say you avoid the salty language for once." Miles was from the South and only swore when drunk. "Okay. It looks like it's going to hit the Santa Cruz mountains, and that won't be fun. They still have the burn scar to worry about from the last fire, so they're already issuing alerts for the area. Highway Seventeen is going to get clobbered. So what else is new. Let's see." More tapping. I could imagine him behind his array of computers, his "I Love Milo" mug on his desk, next to the framed photo of him tornado chasing in Kansas. "Okay, well Watsonville is going to get some of it too, but it's likely to move over the bay and skip the peninsula. Maybe brush by Pacific Grove and Pebble Beach, if it doesn't blow past them too."

I flopped back in my chair. "Thank God. Are you sure?"

"The radar doesn't lie, my dear," Miles said.

"Are you sure you know the difference between all the colors on the screen?"

"Okay, that's it. You are officially dis-invited to my Easter Mimosa brunch." He paused, tapping. "Just a second. The National Weather Service just updated and...let's see. Okay, they're saying what I'm saying if that makes you feel any better." Miles took me off speaker. "Hey, you never texted me back," he said, lowering his voice. "It's like your new place is

154

cursed or something. That little boy who was kidnapped, in front of his own home, and then that poor woman who drowned. That's awful. Are you nervous?"

I bolted upright in my chair. "About what?" Had Miles heard something?

"About living in a place where people go missing. Or die." He snapped his fingers, and I winced at the sharp sound. "And come on, we must have played that monster video dozens of times. I know we thought it was a fake, but wouldn't it be crazy if it were true?" Miles gave a maniacal laugh and hummed the theme from the Twilight Zone.

"Actually, I was just worried about the road to our development flooding."

That got Mile's attention. "Oh God, is that where your place is? Mmmm. Oh wait, that's right. You weren't at the station the last time the river hit flood stage. We were all over the story, but they hadn't built any homes yet, so mostly, some farms lost their crops and a few cars in the lot at Devil's Landing went for a swim." He gave a low whistle. "I get why you're worried now. I tell you what, if anything changes on the radar, I'll text you, okay?"

I explained our pathetic lack of phone service and our equally pathetic lack of internet service, then listened to Mile's expressions of disbelief.

It ended with, "And you didn't know that when you bought the place?"

I would have. If I'd read the disclosures.

Chapter 18

Christina

We went from sprinkles to heavy rain in twenty-four hours. Then, it rained nonstop for two days. The potholes on Sand Road filled with water, but it hadn't flooded. Yet.

The search for Dawn Ashlock's body had been called off, and there were no plans to continue. We invited Paul to have dinner with us, but he politely refused. He was often down by the slough, gazing at the water.

Rae seemed to be avoiding us. Or maybe it was just me. When I asked Adam about it, he said I made Rae nervous, that she felt I'd been too hard on her.

Cassie and Abigail came over for wine, and we all had a little too much to drink. Abigail had warned us in advance not to say anything to her wife about Adam seeing a creature in the slough because Cassie was nervous enough as it was and would insist on selling their place. Cassie kept pressing Adam for details about what he saw when he responded to those first screams on the kayaking trip down the marsh, but he stuck to the script. He saw something, an animal maybe, but it all happened too quick, so he wasn't sure what kind of animal. I could tell she was suspicious though, by the way she squinted at him while he told his edited version of the story.

The next day, I checked on the Garcias. Liliana came to the door, freshly showered, neatly dressed, and perkier than when I last saw her.

"Oh, he's been sleeping a lot. I don't know if it's the new medication, or what, but he's been sleeping through the night, thank goodness." She jerked her head toward the bedroom. "I hate to say it, but I can use any break I can get. I heard about the meeting the other day. Do you think the road will flood? I'm not too worried. We're on higher ground where we are, not like those other cottages next to the water. And I had some groceries delivered, so we've got plenty to eat if it comes to that."

I took her hand and gave it a reassuring squeeze. It felt warmer than the last time. "We should be okay," I said.

If my friend, the meteorologist, wasn't wrong.

Adam drove to see Darlene Woodward. She said the gauges showed the river was still well below flood stage, so she didn't think we had much to worry about. They met for a drink at a harbor dive bar. Over his second beer, he admitted he thought he'd seen the slough monster outside his cottage. Darlene had nearly choked.

"Darlene said we ought to keep our eyes open and be careful. I think she's beginning to worry," Adam told me when he got back.

Not what I wanted to hear, but what did I expect? The harbormaster was in the same predicament. It was one thing to alert the public about a serial killer, a swarm of sharks, or a natural disaster looming, but it was another when the danger was the Slough Devil. Who wanted to go on record with something like that? Not Darlene, not Rae, not Adam, and certainly not me, with a new job, nor Abigail, who'd just got a promotion at the hospital. Jordan said if she told anyone, her father wouldn't believe her, and he'd find a way to put her on a seventy-two-hour psychiatric hold. Jordan was still pushing to tell Ruth and Paul so they could hand out their guns to the neighbors like candy at Halloween.

When another morning rolled around and we could still hear rain drumming on the roof, I could tell Adam was worried. The wind had kicked up during the night. It sounded like someone was standing outside, throwing buckets of water at our west-facing windows.

"I forgot to tell you," Adam said, pulling on his sneakers. "I called Gary at the property management company for an update on our phone situation. He said he's still working on it, but he got us a satellite phone for emergencies. He's going to drop it by today before the rain gets any worse."

I looked up from my computer. "Just one?"

He shrugged. "They're expensive. We'll have to share it. He's going to put it in the mailroom so anyone who needs it can use it. It's better than nothing."

I knew next to nothing about satellite phones, just that they were supposed to work where cell phones didn't.

"Are they able to connect to the satellites in rain? Through clouds?"

"They're supposed to. And you can text on them too."

I watched him as he shrugged into a rain jacket. "What are you up to today?"

Adam's eyes darted away from me, and my stomach fluttered.

"I'm going with Paul." His voice was just loud enough for me to hear. "To Devil's Landing. He thinks it's possible Dawn's body ended up in the salt ponds."

"What do you think?"

He shrugged. "Not likely, but anything is possible."

Three hours after arriving at work, my cell phone came to life, vibrating in my hand and blaring an emergency alert. The

159

screech repeated through the building, along with a chorus of cries of alarm.

A coastal flood watch is in effect for the next 24-hours.

I scanned the list of areas, and my heart thumped when I saw it included Sand Road and Devil's Landing.

I was trying to remember the difference between a watch and a warning, when my phone blasted out another alert, and this time the screen held another ominous message.

A storm surge watch is in effect for Devil's Landing and Sand Road.

What the hell did that mean? Flooding, I understood. It had been spelled out clearly enough at the community meeting, but storm surge? We were miles east of the harbor and the ocean. Would a surge be powerful enough to reach us at Roy's Cottages? And if so, what did that mean?

My phone rang. Miles, not Adam, as I'd hoped, but I answered it with a flash of relief anyway. Miles would have answers.

"Hey, we're about to do cut-ins, and it's going to get crazy, but I wanted to call you first." Miles sounded breathless, excited. Meteorologists lived for extreme weather, and it didn't happen that often in California. "If I were you, I'd get the hell out of there. Evacuate. Things are looking worse, fast, and it's just a matter of time before that watch is upgraded to a warning, which in case you forget, means bad things are going to happen."

I pressed the phone to my ear, hard. "Miles, that surge warning. What's it mean?"

"It means this storm has wind, and it's going to push the water toward the shore, and that's not good for the river where you guys are." Miles paused long enough to shout, "All right, I'm coming," and continued. "Christina, now's not the time for

160

you to play investigative reporter. You just gotta trust me. If I were you, I'd stay off that damn road and book a room in Salinas and stay there until this is over."

That was the smart thing to do. But Miles wasn't me. I had a boyfriend who was probably home and had no way of knowing about the emergency alert. I also had neighbors. Good people. Liliana and Tommy, one of them very vulnerable. Cassie and Abigail had the day off, they'd said, and were planning on assembling a bookcase and watching movies. Jordan was probably babysitting her baby brother. If that was the case, we might have to take them with us. There was plenty of room in Adam's truck for the two of them if we could figure out the baby's car seat.

Hopefully, Darlene Woodward would remember we were without cell service at Roy's Cottages and would send someone to warn the residents, or go herself. Or the sheriff would dispatch a deputy.

But I couldn't be sure. I couldn't chance it.

My boss popped his head into my office while I was shoving my laptop into my tote bag. "Hey. If you need a place to stay for a few nights, you can borrow the corporate rental in Corral de Tierra. It's empty for the next week, so it's no problem."

I glanced up in surprise. Such acts of generosity were rare in the TV world where I came from. "Really? Are you sure?"

"Of course. And if you need it longer, and somebody's coming, we can always put them up at a hotel." He pulled out his phone and started tapping, and a moment later, I received his text. "That's the address and the code to get in. The keypad is on the side door. The hot tub is under an awning, so you should be able to use it even if it's raining." He winked.

161

A soak in a hot tub sounded great. Some alone time, relaxing with Adam away from the prospect of creatures lurking somewhere along the slough sounded amazing. Suddenly, I couldn't wait to get there. I didn't care how much Adam protested. I was dragging him along with me and, if necessary, Jordan and the baby too.

The ride home played out like a video game. Visibility was horrible, the wind constantly blew things across the road, and the potholes had become massive. I tuned into the public radio station to see if they were doing any news cut-ins, but they were still running NPR programming. The sound of rain hitting the car was so loud I had trouble hearing, so I turned it off. I needed to focus anyway.

When I turned onto Sand Road, wind battered my Honda Civic, and I tightened my grip on the steering wheel. Mine was the only car as far as I could see, and for good reason. Electrical wires drooped all over the road, in one place tangled up with a tree which had toppled sideways. Branches and fronds were scattered across the pavement. Water overflowed the deep ditch running along the right side and streamed onto the uneven pavement, creating small pools in addition to the countless number of potholes.

About a quarter of a mile in, I encountered a small mudslide, then a larger one further on. A few trucks rumbled past, splashing the windshield with brown slush, making me flinch and temporarily blinding me.

I cursed up a storm to match the one raging outside. "Fuck! Fuckity fuck fuck."

When I swung into the parking lot at Roy's Cottages, I saw people scurrying through the downpour, hoods pulled low over their faces, pulling suitcases and carrying bags to their cars.

Operation evacuation was underway, thank God.

I was so tense my neck and shoulders ached, and I practically had to pry my fingers off the steering wheel. When I got out, the wind whipped my hair and blew rain into my face, making it hard to see. A vehicle pulled up, blocking mine.

Adam's old Land Cruiser. I'd never been so glad to see it, or him.

He jumped out and gave me a quick hug. "I thought you'd never get here. Okay, let's get your things and get out of here. Jordan's at your place. I'm sure her parents have heard the news by now, but we can't wait around forever. She'll just have to come with us."

"So, you know? About the flood watch?" I shouted while we ran toward my cottage.

"Some deputies came by and went door to door. Some people are refusing to leave though. Not many, but enough."

"Jesus! Like who?"

"Paul. And the Garcias. I know you like them, so I stopped by to see what their plan was. Tommy had a bad night, so Liliana gave him something to help him sleep, and now she can't wake him up, but she said she's not worried because their place is up on a knoll and not next to the slough. I tried telling her that's not the concern. Or at least not the major one, but she wouldn't listen."

I wanted to know everyone's plans, but there wasn't time for that. If the deputies had done a door to door, the residents had received fair warning, and what they did was up to them. Still, I was worried about Liliana. She was under a lot of stress and could use a push in the right direction. I vowed to stop by and see if I could talk some sense into her before it was too late.

163

When we made it to my place, I saw Jordan's two wheelchairs on the porch. Adam grabbed the small one and ran off with it to the truck. Inside, Jordan sat on the couch.

She bit her lip. "My stepmom took the baby to the doctor. He has a cold or something. I don't know where my dad is. He must have heard by now."

"He's probably on his way," I said.

Jordan sighed. "Maybe." She threw her head back and stared up at the ceiling, blinking. "I'm glad we're leaving. This monster thing has really been getting to me."

"Me too," I admitted.

Jordan leaned forward, pressing her hands into her knees. "Where's Adam? What's taking him so long?"

I folded a sweater, stuffed it into a tote bag, and went to the front porch. The rain was coming down sideways. Cassie dashed by, clutching a box, Abigail not far behind, shopping bags dangling from each hand. "We're going to stay with friends in Marina," Abigail shouted.

I gave them a thumbs-up, relieved to see them going.

There was still no sign of Adam. Maybe he was trying to talk sense into the holdouts. The neighbors looked up to him as an expert. I told myself not to worry. The parking lot wasn't far, and there were plenty of people around.

After five minutes, he still hadn't returned. Then ten minutes passed. Then fifteen, and I began to pace.

When Jordan mumbled, "Where is he?" I couldn't stand it anymore. I was putting on my coat to go look for him when I heard his footsteps pounding up the porch.

Water streamed off his jacket, the whites of his eyes nearly glowing under his black hood. His breath was coming out in shallow spurts, like he'd seen something which scared the hell out of him.

My stomach felt like it was ten stories tall, with an elevator dropping past each floor.

"What?" I asked him. "What?"

I heard the distant cries of people.

Adam leaned against the door, panting. A puddle of water collected at our feet.

"The river. The levee must have breached. We watched the water pour in. The road is flooded."

Chapter 19

Adam

A small crowd gathered in the downpour outside Christina's cottage, asking questions, begging for reassurance. I didn't know for a fact the levee had breached, but it was a good guess. Water had come pouring over the hills and fields to the north of us where Roy's River paralleled the slough, and since Sand Road was lower than the land surrounding it on both sides, it was basically a long, wide trench waiting for something to fill it. Within minutes, it seemed, Sand Road had transformed into a channel.

Roy's Cottages was now surrounded by water. Anybody who wanted to come or go would need a boat.

As far as I could tell, our houses weren't in any danger of flooding. At least not yet. Instead of slab foundations, the developer had built the elevated cottages resting on piers, reinforced for earthquakes. The developer had made a big deal about this during the planning phase, touting their experience building homes in unique coastal environments like ours. In other words, areas vulnerable to climate change. And flooding.

As the rain continued to fall around us, I did my best to explain what I'd seen.

"We're not in any immediate danger," I reassured my neighbors. "I'm sure we'll get help soon."

Rae and her new boyfriend huddled together under an umbrella. The bandage over her forehead was gone, but not the sickened look in her eyes. "But when?" Rae cried. "When will they come?"

I knew what scared her. It scared me too. My mind struggled to accept what my eyes had seen. Twice.

"Soon," I said. 'I hope."

Mutters rippled through the drenched crowd. They continued to stand there, shuffling, expecting me to say something more. To guide them.

If only they knew how uneasy I felt about our situation.

"What should we do?" a woman shouted. It was Cathy Baggio.

I'd heard she and her husband had decided to move. Then, I recalled seeing a U-Haul truck at the far end of the parking lot.

"We picked the worst time to come back and pack up." Her voice was sharp with bitterness.

"Can't seem to get a break," Rich said.

My neighbors just wanted answers. Answers I couldn't give them. My experience in wilderness survival training didn't help me deal with everything facing us now. Mostly because we weren't in the wilderness. Just cut off from communication.

And then I remembered the sat phone. The property manager had promised to drop it off in the mailroom earlier in the day, and with any luck, he'd done it. I could make some calls, get some information.

But there was no point getting everyone's hopes up or, worse, triggering a stampede for the sat phone, so I said, as calmly as I could, "Okay, listen up. If you haven't already, make sure you're ready to go in case help shows up. Small bags, not big ones. You want to be ready to go quickly. Remember to grab your valuables, including passports if you have them. And it looks like this storm doesn't plan on easing up anytime soon, so we'll probably lose power at some point. Gather all your flashlights, find batteries. If you've got lanterns or any other camping equipment that might come in handy, get them out."

A man with a long beard shot a hand into the air. "I've got a generator in my garage."

"So do I," Paul Ashlock said.

I hadn't noticed him, standing at the back of the crowd. Cassie and Abigail flanked him.

Ruth Burke, the former police chief, pushed forward. "Me too. I've got two small portables and a big one too." When people turned to stare at her, she gave a little shrug and said, "They're part of my earthquake kit."

I raised my palms to the sky and said, "That's the ticket, thank you. Anybody else? Who else has a generator?"

"We do," Rich Baggio said. "But we'll need it for ourselves."

"Us too," someone else said.

Abigail darted forward and stood between me and the crowd. "Oh, come on, people. Really? That's how it's going to be?"

"We'll let them do them," Ruth said, raising her voice louder against the pelting rain. "I'm happy to share my generators. And if we lose power and you've got stuff in the fridge, I've got an empty refrigerator in my garage I can hook up."

Abigail thumped her chest and mouthed, Thank you.

The Baggios hurried away, and after a few awkward moments, so did everyone else.

Before Paul could leave, I grabbed him by the elbow. "Hey, you worked in emergency services. Why don't you come with me?"

If the satellite phone wasn't in the mailroom, I'd need his help. On the day Dawn went missing, he'd held up under the enormous stress of looking for his own wife, joining the search team without getting in their way.

He nodded and jogged after me. "Where we going?"

"Mailroom. There may or may not be a sat phone in there."

He stopped for a moment, eyes going wide in surprise, then he gave a tight nod. He didn't ask questions. We headed for the middle of the complex. When we arrived at the mailroom, Paul already had his key out. Within moments, we were inside.

The room wasn't insulated, and it had an industrial style corrugated roof. The sound of the rain hitting the metal was almost deafening, but at least it was dry. Paul spotted the sat phone before I did, perched on a shelf above the mail slots. I wondered why the property manager hadn't left it on the sorting table in the middle of the room, until I spotted the cord running from the black phone into the wall. He'd left it charging.

Paul snatched up the phone and stared at it. "They got a good model at least. This is the one we use on back country fires and whatnot. And it's got an eight-hour battery life."

"Just tell me it works in weather like this," I said, eyeing the ceiling.

"It's made for it. Sleet and snow and fog and all that. Who we calling? Sheriff's office?"

I shook my head and consulted my phone. It didn't work, but at least it was good for one thing. It held all my telephone numbers. "Darlene, the harbormaster. She'll know what's up."

Paul handed over the sat phone, and I punched in the number. She picked up immediately and snapped, "This better not be a telemarketer, not at a time like this."

"It's me. Adam."

A long silence followed. Finally, she cleared her throat. "Where are you?"

"At Roy's Cottages. I'm calling from a sat phone. What happened at the river?"

A loud exhale met my ear. She talked in a loud enough voice for Paul to hear, and he nodded along as she spoke. "It breached in two places. It was a storm surge, just like they warned us about, except this time, it happened. I usually count on those weather people to be wrong half the time, but this time, we weren't so lucky. I don't know how it was up where you are, but the wind was howling down here, and I heard on the radio they hit cyclone force speed. They caused a storm surge from hell, and we saw waves cresting over the levee. It was really something to behold. This area's not called Devil's Landing for nothing."

Paul cleared his throat and made a circular hand gesture, the one which signals, wrap it up.

"Jesus," I said. "Hey Darlene, so what's the plan for us out here. We're kind of....stuck."

Darlene didn't hesitate. "The plan is, Adam, for all of you to sit tight because, right now, you're not a priority. Roy's Cottages isn't in imminent danger, and we only have so many resources to go around."

The answer made me dizzy. "But Darlene..."

"Don't Darlene me, Adam, not at a time like this. You have no idea what we're dealing with out here. We're evacuating farm workers from those crappy-ass apartments near the river. Some of them are still on the roof waiting for help, and we've got an entire assisted living facility that's taking on water like a sinking boat. Half those people are on oxygen, and the other half can't walk without assistance. It's a

171

nightmare. You're just going to have to be patient, Adam. That's all I can tell you."

Her words had the opposite effect. I only felt rising panic, the kind which made me want to scream, *No listen to me. You don't understand.* And of course, she couldn't understand because I wasn't telling her the whole truth. The flood water didn't scare me. What might be in the water did.

I should have said I understood she was doing her best in a terrible situation, but I was silent.

She snapped, "You should know how this goes, Adam. It's basic triage. And what's happening now is what we were afraid of. The district is pushed to the limits as it is, and adding all those people up where you are just put more strain on the system. Not a single agency has received an additional penny in funding to do what we do, so it's more with less." She took a deep breath. "I guess I should get off my soap box and get back to work. Now, I don't want to give you the impression we're not monitoring the situation out there, Adam. We are. And we'll send folks as soon as we can, but once again, I want to be honest with you, it probably won't be until tomorrow."

"I appreciate that, Darlene," I said. My voice sounded hoarse, weak to my own ears.

Paul grimaced. "She has a point."

I handed the phone to Paul and watched as he plugged it into the charger. "I still don't like it. I hate being cut off like this."

For reasons I couldn't fully understand—instinct maybe—it felt like the storm had made us more vulnerable to the monsters lurking at the far end of the slough. I was fairly certain I'd seen one outside my cottage at night. I was nearly positive a creature, not a kidnapper, had made off with Noah Baggio, and I'd seen enough to know one had pulled Paul's

172

wife into the water in roughly the same area as the Lorenz video. The Slough Devils were getting bolder. The good, clear weather and the bustle of the slough had probably been a deterrent for a long time, and then we'd come along, invading the periphery of their territory.

I didn't know what they were exactly, but I knew a predator when I saw one. Those things knew where to hide and how to stalk. And we were their prey.

The rising water and the isolation left us open to attack. As the storm raged around us, it didn't seem so far-fetched. I wanted to confide in Paul, desperately, but I couldn't bring myself to tell him all I'd witnessed, all I feared.

"We can't kayak out. It's too windy," Paul said. "And most people couldn't make it that far on a good day. How about your boat?"

I'd been thinking about my pontoon boat. It only sat fifteen people, and I didn't dare take more, not in this weather. But I could ferry people out in stages, provided I could talk them into leaving. The trouble was, the boat was docked at the harbor nearly five miles away. We'd have to get to it first.

"Are you up for a miserable walk?" I asked.

Paul lifted his sandy eyebrows. "Yeah, sure, but the road's flooded. How we going to get there?"

"There's an old tow path that runs along the slough. Back in the day, farmers used it to pull barges down to the harbor. Hard-core runners use it as a trail now."

"Let's go," Paul said, crossing the mailroom toward the door.

While he locked it, I noticed several laminated signs in the area I'd missed on our way in.

SATELLITE PHONE IN MAILROOM FOR
EMERGENCY COMMUNAL USE.
LEAVE PHONE ON CHARGER!
DO NOT REMOVE.
Thank you, Central Coast HOA Managers

The signs were everywhere.

While Paul went to his place to change into hiking shoes, I ran to Christina's cottage to tell her and Jordan about the plan. Jordan was stretched out on the couch, her legs across Christina's lap, and she struggled into a sitting position when she heard me come in.

"My dad never came," Jordan said, holding a pillow against her stomach. "I can't believe it, but I'm not really surprised. What's going on?"

"I'm going to get the boat. It'll be a while, but get some stuff together, and be ready, and be prepared to get wet. We'll have to go without the canopy. I won't be able to put it up in this wind, and the rain will just blow it sideways. Christina, do you think you can start talking to people? See who wants to go?"

Christina set down her mug on the coffee table. "Of course. Please tell me you're not going alone."

I shook my head. "Paul's coming with me. We'll be as fast as we can."

Christina held out a hand, and I pulled her to her feet and out onto the porch. Rain drops bounced off the railings of the steps. I drew her to me, her body warm against mine, and only let her go when I heard Paul's boots thudding up on the path. We jumped apart, like we'd been caught doing something we shouldn't. But it was only our guilt that we were together, and Paul was alone.

Heart thudding so hard I could hear it in my ears, we left.

Our boots squished into the mud as we followed the tow path west to Devil's Landing. There was no chance of getting lost. All we needed to do was follow the marsh. The water was higher than I'd ever seen it. In some places along the opposite embankment, trees rose out of the water. Wind pushed the rain into our faces, the damp cold making it a miserable slog while we trudged toward our destination.

We'd gone about a half mile when I heard something.

It was coming from the slough. Chittering. Low growls. The same noises I'd heard the night that thing crouched on the rock outside my cottage. My skin prickled. I stopped abruptly, grabbing the back of Paul's jacket to keep him from going any farther.

He whirled around. "What...," then his voice trailed off as he heard it too.

Paul turned toward it, his entire body going rigid. The wind created waves in the slough, and our necks strained forward. We searched the water, but I knew. I sensed them there. My instinct told me to run, to back away from the water, but I couldn't move. To keep the hair out of my face, I'd pulled it onto the top of my head in a knot. The hairs on the back of my neck lifted.

The slough churned with slick black heads.

Paul didn't take his eyes off the water. "Are they seals?"

I clutched his elbow, like parents do to keep their children away from danger. "No." I backed up a little, pulling him so gently I hoped he wouldn't notice.

"Okay," he said after a moment. "That's weird."

175

The water seemed to heave and boil. The dark shapes moved in a mass toward us, and my legs and knees went weak. I took several deep breaths to force air into my lungs. My eyes scanned the water, and I saw strange shapes further down the marsh to the west, where we were headed. I wondered, briefly, if they'd been tracking us all along. Two lone men walking near the water. There was no telling how many there were. I saw what just one could do to a strong woman taken unawares. We were outnumbered. And those things were strong.

There was no time to explain what they were to Paul, or the danger we were in. But I didn't need to.

He tugged my sleeve. "Maybe we should go."

I considered what I knew about the creatures. They could swim. And climb. They had claws. Long ones, by the look of the gouges on the side of the dock. I could only hope the claws would slow them down on land. Unless they were retractable.

"Yeah, forget the tow path," I said. "It's too close to the water. Move up the embankment, and when we get there, run like hell."

Paul didn't need me to say it a second time. We sprinted up the slope and had just made it to the top when we heard splashing behind us.

Chapter 20

Adam

Paul came to a sudden stop when we finally huffed up to the outskirts of the complex. "You want to tell me what those things were?"

I kept running, pulling him along with me. "Not outside. Let's go to your place."

The slough next to Roy's Cottages had risen since we'd left, the water now level with the docks. The sight was enough to make me break into a sweat.

If those things in the water wanted to come ashore, all they had to do was belly up to the slips. No claws required to haul themselves up over the sides.

It wouldn't be long before the docks themselves were under water. I wasn't worried about the cottages flooding. Even those closest to the marsh were situated high enough, and each house sat on an elevated platform.

The water level changed everything. It gave the monsters easy access—an on-ramp, to us.

At Paul's cottage, we entered through the back door and hung our wet jackets and took off our boots in the mud room. Every cottage had one. He had a one bedroom like mine with the same layout. Any similarity stopped there.

Over-the-top beach cottage décor—sea-foam green walls, nautical ropes, framed watercolors of seashells, and lots of light wood. Paul headed straight for the refrigerator and pulled out two beers, then gestured to a stool.

He took a swig, then leaned his elbows on the counter and stared at me expectantly.

I cleared my throat. "I haven't told you everything."

"I guessed that."

All that running made me thirsty. I drained half the bottle while I thought of what to say. If it weren't for his dead wife, I might have done it sooner. In the short time I'd known him, I'd come to like and respect the firefighter.

I put down my beer. "I got a better look at what pulled Dawn into the water than I said."

His eyes snapped open, and I held up a warning hand. I was determined to get it out without interruption before I chickened out.

"It wasn't a shark or a mountain lion or anything like that. I can't tell you what it was exactly, because I don't know. But it looked like that thing in the video that went viral, the one the German guy shot from my boat. Look, I thought it was fake. Because how could it be anything else? I only saw it myself for a few seconds, but it was enough. It's tall and ugly, with a small round head and long arms. It can swim and climb trees. I don't know what else it can do. I've seen it three times. Once on that day we went kayaking, and once outside my place, but that second time, I was high, so I thought I was just seeing things. And then today. What we saw in the water."

Paul straightened. Like my place, his cottage had an open floor plan. He crossed the room and peered out the large front window, shoulders up around his neck. Even though the house was positioned in the middle row, it was angled in such a way it had an uninterrupted view of the slough.

"I don't see anything," he reported. "Yet."

The rain had let up just a bit. The fierce downpour had turned into a steady rain.

Paul grabbed two more beers from the refrigerator and slid one toward me. With a thumb, he pushed off the cap. "So, you didn't tell me because you didn't think I'd believe you."

"That's right. I'm sorry."

He dipped his head. "It probably would have pissed me off. To hear you talking about monsters while we were looking for my wife. But I saw those…things in the water. And seeing is believing." When he looked up, he blinked slowly, like he was trying to wake up. "What are they? Where did they come from?"

I shook my head. "I don't know. When my dad ran the tours, the monsters were part of his shtick. He said they lived at the end of the slough, that no one had seen them for a long time. When I was a kid, my mom used to tell me about a boy who went missing more than a hundred years ago. She said a monster came out of the water and took him, but I thought she'd made it up to keep me from wandering around and falling into the water." I hesitated. There was no point in over-complicating things by sharing too many stories, but I wanted to tell him. Needed to tell him. "Once, my dad told me about a circus that came to the harbor, just before the big earthquake in San Francisco. The circus was from another country. It had an unusual act. Some strange animals that no one had ever seen before. But when the earthquake hit, they got out of their cages, ran up the slough, and were never seen again."

Paul exhaled and tapped the beer cap against the counter. "Since those things can swim, maybe whatever escaped from the circus bred with otters or something."

My ears started ringing, and I suddenly felt light-headed.

I must have looked stunned, because Paul said, "What? What's wrong?"

179

He had just proposed a horrifying theory. And he had no idea how truly horrifying it was.

Most people thought otters were cute and playful. In fact, they were dangerous wild animals with a powerful bite, and they were known to menace other species. A scientific paper's revelations about the sea otter were so shocking tabloids picked up on it with headlines calling them evil killers and rapists.

I couldn't tell Paul about the documented cases of otters raping baby seals until they killed them. Or about male otters biting females during copulation, sometimes killing them in the process.

That a hybrid creature could exist was unbelievable. That it might possess the worst traits of the wild otter was terrifying.

When I didn't respond, Paul got up and disappeared into the bedroom. Something metal banged against a wall. I could guess what he was up to.

When he returned a few moments later holding a rifle, he said, "If one of those things got my wife, it's time to go hunting."

We stared at each other for a long time, Paul standing tall and straight as a sentinel.

"I'm not sure that's such a good idea," I finally said. "Think about it. It sounds like a cliché, but we don't know what we're dealing with yet. You go out there? Start shooting at the water? Who knows what's going to happen. Maybe it'll be like that old movie, where the creatures start multiplying. Or maybe they've got built-in armor, like the giant sloths used to have, and bullets aren't going to work, or worse, they ricochet and kill you." I pointed at the rifle. "And those things make a lot of noise. For all you know, you could be summoning them from all over the place. And just you standing out there alone?

180

Could you handle twenty or thirty of those things?" I held out my hand for the rifle. "Come on. Before we go commando, we need to think this through."

Paul's mouth stretched into an angry straight line. "Fuck you."

Whatever energy I had left seemed to drain from my body. My legs and arms felt heavy. I fumbled out the words. "I'm sorry, man. But I need you. We need you. I can't have you going out there and getting yourself killed."

Paul stared at the rifle, and his shoulders slumped. "Those fucking things killed my wife." His eyes welled with tears.

It was the first time I'd seen him cry.

We sat in silence for a while.

When we finished our second beers, I said, "How many guns do you have?"

"Two rifles, twelve handguns. Ten if you don't count the twenty-twos."

"That's a lot," I said.

Just knowing they were in the next room made me feel slightly better. We were cut off, stranded, with monsters swimming in the slough, but at least we weren't without resources.

Paul rubbed a flannel-covered sleeve across his eyes and sniffed. "That's not a lot where I come from. I've got friends in Wyoming who have dozens. Dawn talked me into selling most of my collection before I moved out here." He groaned. "I wish to God I'd hung onto them." He straightened. "Ruth has guns. At least that's what Dawn said. Does Ruth know? About the creatures? Come to think of it, who else knows?"

"Just a few people," I said cautiously. "Rae, because she'd been with Dawn and wasn't sure what she'd seen that day either. Jordan and Christina. And Abigail. But it wasn't a conspiracy. We just didn't know what to tell people."

Paul gave a curt nod. "I get that." He paused, eyes darting to the window. "What do we do now?"

I stood and rubbed the back of my neck. "I'm going to call Darlene Woodward again and tell her what we just saw. Then I'm going to hand the phone to you, and you're going to tell her I haven't lost my mind, and in your professional opinion as an emergency responder, they need to get us out of here before it gets dark."

Paul looked over at a wall clock made of painted driftwood. "Sunset is in three-and-a-half hours. That doesn't give them a lot of time."

We put on our jackets and boots and left.

In the mailroom, the satellite phone was gone. We searched everywhere, thinking someone had forgotten to plug it back in.

But it was missing.

"Are you kidding me?" Paul exploded. "Who would do that?"

The floor was covered in muddy footprints. Ours. I opened the door and scanned both directions. My heart sank.

There would be no tracking footsteps to find the asshole who'd taken the phone.

There were none, except for those we'd left ourselves.

Chapter 21

Adam

We weren't in the right frame of mind to go house-to-house, looking for the missing satellite phone. For all we knew, the monsters were swimming around in the slough, getting ready to swarm us. We knew next to nothing about them. Their numbers. Their intelligence. Intentions. Ability to communicate.

Our ignorance fueled our anxiety. The simple question, "Do you have the sat phone?" came off as an accusation. Not all our neighbors answered the door, and the ones who did responded defensively, sometimes angrily.

The balding vice principal whose name I could never remember snapped, "Why would you think I have it? I didn't even know it was there."

An older man with a mustache and goatee crossed his arms in front of his chest and scowled. "No, I don't have it. I read the signs. It said, clearly, to leave the phone where it was."

Liliana Garcia, her husband hovering like a shadow in the background, sucked in her cheeks. "You know something? I am not in the mood today to tolerate any pendejadas, and you have a lot of nerve coming to my house, accusing me of stealing."

My cheeks burned. "I'm not, Mrs. Garcia. I'm checking with everyone to see if they took it. Accidentally."

"I wouldn't even know how to use such a thing," she said, then slammed the door.

I spotted Paul on the former police chief's porch. It looked like he'd told Ruth about the creatures because she was clutching the door frame with her mouth slightly open, staring at the marsh in the distance. I pounded up the steps, water cascading from the rain gutter onto the top of my hood, falling in a sheet in front of my face.

Ruth glared at me. "Are you guys messing with me, or what?"

"I wouldn't do that, Ruth," I said.

Paul grimaced. "That's what I've been trying to tell her."

Ruth was dressed, ready to evacuate. Jeans. Sweatshirt. Thick-soled sneakers. I could see a rain jacket draped across the back of a chair and a backpack sitting on a table.

"Monsters, Adam. Really?"

I shoved my hands in my pockets. "I know. It sounds insane. I mean, maybe it's something we've never seen before. Like a...new species or something."

"A new species," she echoed. "Well, you know what? Why don't you just show me what you two are talking about? Paul says they're in the water. Let's go take a look." She stomped into the house and came out wearing her jacket and a grim expression. Ruth pulled up her hood and pushed past us.

She strode down a path which ran between two houses toward the slough. Paul ran after her and tried to grab her elbow, but she pulled away.

"Oh no. You said there's something in the water, and now I want to see it."

Ruth hurried toward the edge of the marsh. She stopped when she saw the docks underwater.

In both directions, the slips had vanished. Rain drops bounced on the water. The wind was picking up again, like it usually did in the afternoon.

Paul kept a safe distance, as did I. I could feel Paul tensing beside me.

"I should have brought my rifle," he muttered. "Don't get too close," he called after her.

Ruth flapped an impatient hand while she scanned the slough, first left, then right. She stood at the edge of a sand bank, several yards from the water. My heart jack hammered in my chest.

Paul cleared his throat. "See anything?"

My eyes hurt from squinting, trying to see through the rain. "No."

Several agonizing minutes passed, and then a shadow sped between a gap in the trees across the slough, followed by the sound of a distant splash. Another dark figure shimmied down a tree and loped toward the water. It was tall and had to stoop to avoid the branches overhead. The same small head, long arms, and misshapen body I'd seen crouched on the rock outside my cottage. It shot into the water. Two dark heads bobbed in the waves, making straight for us. Then more. Not as many as we'd seen further down the slough, but enough to make my body go cold with terror.

Paul had seen them too because he said, "Shit."

Ruth's back was to us. Her hands lifted to the side of her head in a caricature of disbelief. Paul and I watched her take a few unsteady steps back, fell, then scrabbled backwards. We shot forward, grabbed her elbows, and pulled her up. She stood between us, one hand pressed against her mouth. The middle of the slough had begun to churn, black heads just barely visible above the water.

Ruth exhaled. "How fast can those things move? Anybody know?"

"Fast," I said. "But we don't know how they do on land. They've got claws, I think, so that might slow them down."

Ruth nodded. Never taking her eyes off the things in the water, she reached into her jacket, pulled out a gun, and handed it to Paul. "Here. I'm going to need a few minutes to adjust." Her hand was shaking.

Paul stared at it like he'd never seen a pistol before.

Ruth nudged Paul. "Take the shot."

Memories of every nasty, contentious meeting over the development of Roy's Cottages came flooding back, and I heard myself gasp. "Wait. What if they're assholes in wet suits? Trying to scare us?"

It wasn't so far-fetched. Wet suits seemed to exaggerate certain body types. Maybe they were wearing the style with hoods, the kind made for winter surfing, along with a face covering.

Paul froze.

"Doesn't matter," Ruth said. "They're still a credible threat. Whatever they are, I think we're looking at whoever is responsible for attacking Dawn and taking Noah. Now take the shot, Paul. I've got your back, and if it makes you feel any better, shoot to injure and not to kill."

For a man who was all for monster hunting a short time ago, Paul seemed reluctant to fire away now he had the chance. Jaw working, he aimed at the roiling water but didn't pull the trigger.

"Any day now," Ruth muttered.

Something moved on the shore off to our right. And then a voice called my name. When I saw who it was, I think I screamed.

Christina stood close to the shore, waving her hands over her head. She'd taken the path running next to my cottage to get to the slough, and in a flash, I understood why. Paul and I had been gone a long time, so she must have been worried and went down to the water to find us.

I heard furious splashing in the slough. Paul and Ruth did too because they started shouting at Christina to get away from the water. I stumbled toward her on legs made of rubber across the wet, sucking sand, motioning for her to go. With the hood of her rain jacket covering her ears, and the drum of the rain, she didn't hear our warnings.

She was close enough I could see her mouth open to say something, but before she could, a dark figure slithered out of the water, staying low, and grabbed her ankle. One moment, she was standing, and the next, she was on the ground. And then, she was being dragged toward the lapping waves of the marsh.

Behind me, Ruth was yelling at Paul. "Shoot! Shoot it!" but the creature's movements were too erratic. Paul wasn't far behind me, probably trying to get closer before he fired.

The figure hunched over Christina. With one hand, it pushed her head into the shallows, and with another, it was clawing at her clothes, trying to rip them off. It didn't seem to be as tall as the other creatures, so my mind registered it a juvenile. My brain tried to make sense of what it was doing.

It swung a leg over her and squatted. In a flash, I understood.

The damn thing appeared desperate to mate. With my girlfriend. My insides twisted.

I whirled around and shouted, "Shoot!"

But instead of taking aim, Paul came to a stop, and his mouth fell open. Someone was screaming, and it wasn't Christina because she was still face down in the water, struggling.

Shrieks pierced the sound of my heart hammering in my ears. When I turned around, something bright blue was whizzing down a path and then across the sand. Jordan, in her dune buggy wheelchair. The teenager was closing the distance between her and Christina.

I could see Christina's bare legs now. The beast had managed to drag her pants down around her ankles and was attempting to mount her while she continued to violently thrash. Shock must have slowed me down because Paul had pulled ahead.

Jordan got to Christina first.

There was something in her hand, long and dark. An umbrella. The wheelchair stopped so abruptly Jordan was nearly catapulted from it. The creature was so hell-bent on Christina it didn't notice it had company, and then Jordan was jabbing at it with the sharp end of the umbrella. It reared into a standing position, radiating fury at the interruption. Grabbing the umbrella, it gave a mighty yank, pulling Jordan onto the ground. Something shiny flew onto the sand.

Christina managed to pull herself to a kneeling position, choking and sputtering.

The creature hurled the umbrella aside and swiped at Jordan with long black claws. It caught her on the side of the face. Jordan roared in pain but quickly recovered. She rolled toward the object she'd dropped, grabbed it, and slashed at the monster's ankles.

A knife. Jordan had brought a knife.

The creature snarled. It either hadn't registered the pain or it hadn't been much of a cut. It opened its mouth and bared sharp teeth at Jordan, who cowered, then it turned back to Christina, who was standing, just barely, hands on her knees. She stared at the creature with glazed, unfocused eyes.

An ear-splitting bang as a gun fired.

The Slough Devil staggered but did not fall. I watched as Paul fired again, this time missing. Ruth had finally reached us and was trying to wrest the gun from Paul's hands, but he shook her off and tried again, this time striking the beast on the shoulder. The force of the forty-five spun it around.

From the water came the ominous sounds of sloshing. Three round heads popped out of the marsh, followed by uneven shoulders and then long strange torsos. They darted past Christina and Jordan, hissing, arms reaching out to the smaller juvenile, and pulled it back toward the water. It lunged at Christina while she struggled to pull up her pants, and a larger one unleashed a raspy growl which caused the juvenile to go limp. Then, they slipped below the water and were gone.

All of that happened in a matter of seconds.

When I reached Christina, she burst into tears. I pulled her into my arms. Felt her shuddering against me.

Jordan propped herself up on an elbow. "Can someone fucking help me up?"

Paul rushed toward her.

Ruth gazed at the water, fists pressed into her forehead.

Chapter 22

Christina

Jordan sat huddled on the couch, shivering, and sipped a cup of instant hot chocolate Ruth made for all of us. We'd stumbled into my cottage, numb with shock.

When I caught a glimpse of myself in the hallway mirror, I hardly recognized the dirty and bedraggled woman staring back at me. Blood mixed with mud in my hair. That thing, that monster, had used its hands to pin me down, and I'd felt its claws pierce my scalp, my skin. Ruth fetched towels and tended to Jordan while Adam helped me into the bathroom upstairs. Paul stood watch at the front window, holding the rifle he'd brought over from his place. Adam had refused to leave my side, and I hadn't protested.

Adam lowered the lid on the toilet and sat, biting his nails, while I took a long shower, feeling the nearly scalding water rinse away the filth clinging to my body. Mud had managed to push its way inside my private parts, and I had to lift my leg to get it all out. Swirls of blood circled the drain.

That thing had tried to rape me.

At first, I hadn't understood. I thought it meant to drown me, until I realized that wasn't its goal. I could hear it huffing behind me, tearing at my clothes. I could feel its cold, wet body pressing into mine, and then I felt something hard against my bare buttocks. A penis. Larger and harder than a man's.

It couldn't be happening, I'd thought, out in the open, in daylight. Not with Adam and Paul running toward me. When I'd managed to lift my head above water, I'd spotted the gun. It was just a matter of time—a few more seconds—before Paul shot the fucker, but the monster's icy rod continued to grind into my lower back, seeking entrance. The adrenalin shooting from my body saved me from passing out, and it lingered still in my system, keeping me upright in the shower, my mind churning, remembering the feeling of the monster straddling my body.

When I finally stepped out of the shower, wrapped in the largest bath towel I owned, Adam made me sit on the toilet while he inspected my scalp, then smeared antibacterial ointment into the wounds, which stung. He did the same on my lower back, and by the hissing sound he made, I knew it was bad back there.

When he was done, he followed me into the bedroom and watched as I pulled on sweatpants and an old, soft flannel shirt. My sick-day uniform. I felt sick to my stomach and sick in my heart. Everything felt wrong.

Adam broke the silence. "I have something to tell you. But only when you're ready."

My fingers weren't working properly. They couldn't quite get the hang of buttoning my shirt. "Who knows how much time we have," I said bitterly. "You might as well tell me now, ready or not."

Adam winced, then crossed the room to stand next to me. He took my hand in his and kissed my fingers. His lips were soft and gentle. "Have I told you recently how much I love that you're so practical? Even at a time like this?"

I leaned my head on his shoulder. Adam had a way of saying just the right thing with the fewest words.

"No, but thank you."

His lips brushed my hair. "So, about what happened."

A sour taste filled my mouth. Whatever he was about to say made me want to put my hands over my ears and think about something else.

"Okay."

Adam pulled me toward a chair and pushed me gently into it. He stared down at me and cleared his throat. "Paul's telling the others so we're all on the same page. But he doesn't know everything because…" His voice trailed off. "Well, you'll understand." He rubbed the side of his face. He looked exhausted. The circles under his eyes nearly matched the gray of his irises. "My dad told me a story once when I was a kid. A circus came to Devil's Landing a long time ago. In 1906 to be exact. It had an act, he said, with some strange animals that scared the audience, and then the big earthquake happened, and the animals broke free, attacked the circus operator, and ran up the slough. To tell you the truth, I forgot about the story until recently. I mean, I didn't even think to tell you because, even if I had remembered it, I wouldn't have thought it was important. But Paul and I got to talking, and I told him. He wondered if maybe those animals had bred with another animal, like maybe otters…"

My brain struggled to keep up. I didn't know much about otters, but I had seen them at the aquarium and up close on the day of the kayaking incident. Looking back on those awful moments at the water's edge, I thought I could see a faint resemblance to the thing which had assaulted me in full view of Adam and the others. I pulled my knees to my chest.

"Jesus."

Adam continued. "So, here's the thing about otters. They may look cute, but they've been known to rape baby seals until they're dead, and when they mate with females, it's a violent business. The males bite them on the back of the neck and nose, and researchers use the scar patterns to identify the females."

I gripped the sides of my chair. "Is it possible? Those things are part otter?"

Adam shrugged. "I'm not sure what those animals were that escaped from the circus, and it's rare for two different species to produce offspring, but it's not unheard of. Donkeys and horses, lions and tigers. Sometimes it happens when territories overlap, like with polar bears and grizzlies. So, we could be talking about a hybrid we haven't encountered yet because they've been hiding out at the east end of the slough. Honestly, it's a big area, and the brush grows so thick, who knows what's in there. And who the hell knows what those circus animals were."

"And then we came along," I said.

"Exactly."

When I shifted in my chair, my backside scraped against the nubby fabric, and I flinched from the pain. The creature's claws had done that, but that's not what my mind kept coming back to.

"How much do you know about otters?" I asked.

Adam frowned. "A bit. I know a scientist who rescues them. Why?"

I cleared my throat. "Is there anything…," I searched for the right words, "special about their anatomy. You know. Down there."

Adam winced, then took a breath and recovered. "Male otters have a penis bone. A baculum. But that's not unusual in mammals. Apes and monkeys have them. So do dogs, bears, sea lions. If I remember right, hoofed animals don't have them. Nor do humans, of course."

"Thank god," I said.

Adam managed a weak smile, then his eyes widened. "Why? Why are you asking that?" His voice rose. "Are you saying…"

I pushed to my feet, my lower back aching from the bruises beginning to form. In a day or two, the skin would turn purple. "Yeah, I am. I felt it. That fucker had a penis bone."

Adam went a pasty white. His eyes had a faraway look, and I had to shake his arm to snap him out of it. My chest tightened while I waited for him to explain.

Finally, he said, "I read about some weird stuff in college. Like the case of an orangutan raping a woman at a research camp, but in that case, it had been raised in captivity, so the animal was habituated to humans. Since some animals engage in forced copulation, it's not considered rape as we understand it. I remember seeing a video from Ireland where a horse tried to mount a policeman at a fair. And there are some videos of people on vacation, swimming with dolphins, when a dolphin humped a woman."

Adam squeezed his eyes shut. I knew what he was thinking because my thoughts had gone there too.

"We can't tell Paul," I said.

"No," he said, voice flat. "There's no point. There's nothing he could do about it. And we don't know that's what happened to Dawn. We don't know what's going on with their troop. Or whatever you call a group of things like that. It could be there aren't enough females to go around, or maybe it was a way for a juvenile to prove itself to the older males, or show its dominance over our territory."

I shivered, recalling its frantic thrusting. "It didn't seem that way to me."

Adam pulled me to my feet, put a protective arm around my shoulders, and squeezed. "We need to make sure they don't

195

get close to anyone again. And at least we were able to get them to back off. That's got to be a good sign."

His words did nothing to reassure me. The prospect of those things going on a rape spree, in addition to whatever else they had planned, made my head throb, and I felt dizzy.

"We need to warn people."

Adam gave a grim nod. We talked through what we would say to the others, deciding to mention nothing of penis bones or forced copulation. Just sticking to what little we knew, or thought we did, which included that we might be dealing with an unidentified hybrid creature. When we went downstairs, I could tell by the way everyone looked at me that they knew what had happened. Or at least they suspected. Even Paul. It didn't need saying, but it hung in the air like a bad smell no one wanted to mention.

A monster had sexually assaulted me and would have succeeded if not for Paul with a gun and Jordan in a wheelchair.

Which reminded me.

I turned to her and said, "When I left, you were on the couch. How did you get down the steps and into the chair?"

Jordan's lower lip quivered. Ruth had bandaged her cheek where the creature had swiped at her with its claws. I was reminded she was just a kid. A brave one. She could have gotten herself killed out there.

"I was mad you left when I told you not to because Adam told us to stay inside. I didn't want to be left alone, and I wanted to know what happened, so I opened a window and started yelling. Some man heard me and carried me to my chair. He wasn't too happy about it though."

After some discussion, we decided to break into two groups and go door to door to warn our neighbors, but before we did, I insisted we agree on a script and stick to it. The last thing we needed was to sow confusion on top of fear. After some debate, we decided on, "Adam and Paul saw something in the water. Not sure what, but it could be dangerous." It sounded vague, but any mention of monsters would have just made people panic. Or think we were crazy.

Adam, Jordan, and I formed one group. Paul and Ruth the other. Adam, Ruth, and Paul carried guns. Ruth offered one to me, but I'd never used one, and there wasn't time to teach me. Besides, my head was still fuzzy, and I was jumpy, so I'd probably shoot myself or someone else.

We set out in the rain and began knocking on doors.

Chapter 23

Christina

There were twenty-one cottages, and most of the residents were home. Anyone who'd been at work had received the county's alert and rushed back. Except for Jordan's parents. Which just confirmed her dad cared more about his new wife and baby than her. I had to bite my lip to keep from saying, "Screw 'em," because she didn't need to hear me say what she was obviously thinking. It was sometimes easy to forget she was only sixteen because she acted so mature. Mostly.

When we warned the owners, reactions followed a typical pattern. Surprise. Disbelief.

"What do you mean something is in the water? Like what?" When we couldn't answer, they became suspicious. Some came right out with it and said, "What is this really about?"

Others seemed to misunderstand. We weren't warning the slough might flood, but that something dangerous lurked in the marsh. But they took it the wrong way and thought we were worried about the rising water level.

As we approached the Garcias' house, we heard shouting inside. I knocked anyway.

Liliana Garcia opened the door, her eyes red. Tommy shuffled up behind her.

"What the hell do you want?" he snapped. "My wife already said she didn't take that phone."

Before Adam could say anything, I said, "We just came to see how you're holding up. With the storm and everything."

Liliana shot a withering look at her husband before replying. "That's awfully nice of you. There's not much we can do about it, and we weren't going anywhere anyway." She lowered her voice. "Tommy's been acting up something awful. Said he heard gun shots."

From the bottom of the steps, I heard Jordan cough. Liliana glanced at her and frowned.

"That poor girl shouldn't be out in the rain like that. She could catch a cold."

I didn't bother arguing. My grandmother, while she was alive, was convinced people could get sick from being exposed to the cold, and no matter how many times we told her about viruses, she never believed us.

Liliana had enough to worry about. She didn't need to hear our story of something scary in the water, so I merely said, "Adam thinks the storm is going to worsen, so you're better off staying inside."

"You can come hang out at our place," Jordan called. "We're at Christina's."

Liliana made a clucking sound. "That is so thoughtful, young lady, and I do appreciate it. But I think we're better off staying here." She turned to her husband, who was holding on to the edge of the entry table and swaying slightly. "Isn't that right, Tommy? We're fine exactly where we are."

Tommy groaned. "Oh brother. Of course, we're fine here. We don't need to go gallivanting around in this weather, do we?"

We made our excuses, left, and were cutting through the parking lot when we ran into Rae and her boyfriend, Kyle, getting out of his truck. The wheels were covered in mud. We scurried under one of the few carports to get out of the rain.

"Did you try driving out?" Adam asked. His voice was tinged with hope.

Kyle's shoulder-length red hair was wet and plastered to his head, his hoodie soaked. I wondered if he didn't own a rain jacket, then remembered Jordan saying he was from Los Angeles, so that explained that.

He slammed the door. "Yeah, I thought it was worth a try, but we didn't get far. I tried sticking to the side of the road, but we almost got stuck, and the banks are so steep we almost rolled over. It was a bitch getting back." He shook his head in disgust. "I don't advise it, Adam. Even with the lifts on your Cruiser."

"Wasn't planning on it," Adam said.

Rae blinked in the wind. "Why are you guys outside?"

"Oh, we're out telling people to stay away from the water," Jordan offered. "We were down by the slough, and a monster came out and almost got Christina. It tried to fuck her, but Paul shot it. Which was a good thing because it paid no attention to me when I stabbed it."

"What?" Rae cried.

Adam's head snapped back. "Jesus, Jordan."

The teenager lifted her pointy chin and aimed her blue eyes at Adam. "What? That's what happened. I mean, we're not telling everyone that because, you know, they'd freak. But they know about the monster. Rae saw it. They have a right to know."

Kyle pulled Adam aside. "What's this about a monster attacking Christina?" he said, but loud enough we could all hear.

Rae doubled over, hands on her knees, and began to hyperventilate. Kyle sprung to her side and began rubbing her back, glaring at Jordan, who muttered, "It didn't happen to her. It happened to Christina, and she's fine."

No. No, I wasn't fine. Just hearing those words aloud reminded me of my head under the water, holding my breath, praying I wouldn't drown while feeling the weight of the creature pushing my pelvis into the sand, its knobby furry knee trying to shove my legs apart. My stomach churned, and I staggered to a corner of the carport and dry heaved. A delayed reaction.

After Adam explained what happened at the marsh, as briefly as he could, Kyle and Rae followed us back to my place. Both wanted a gun.

"Do you even know how to use one?" Jordan asked Rae when we got inside.

Rae slid an elastic off her wrist and tied up her long hair. "No. But how hard is it? You point and shoot. It's that simple."

Jordan snorted. When Adam gave Jordan's hair a little tug, she glanced up and mouthed, She is so dumb.

Terrified was more like it. As Rae stared at the array of guns on the coffee table, she began shaking all over, and her face turned ashen.

"This is a nightmare," she whispered to no one in particular. "I just want to get out of here. I just want to leave."

Kyle pocketed two guns and steered Rae across the living room. She moved like a sleepwalker. Adam pointed a warning finger at Jordan to keep quiet, and Jordan's face crumpled. She hated being scolded by her hero.

We walked them out onto the porch.

"Why don't you guys stay with us?" I said.

The wind drove the rain into our faces.

Kyle stopped at the top step and peered at the stormy sky, his rugged face in profile. "Thanks, but I've got the generators hooked up. At the rate we're going, I wouldn't be surprised if we lost power." He patted his jacket pocket. "And we should be fine with these. Besides, my place isn't anywhere near the water."

When they were gone, the rest of us stood for a few moments. The wind felt good on my face, reminding me I was alive. Adam's hand twitched on my shoulder, and he cocked his head.

"Do you hear that?"

My heart gave a thump of alarm. "No. What is it?"

"Listen."

Time froze. I strained to hear something other than the relentless rain. And then, from the distance, came the sounds of screams and the unmistakable pop of a gunshot. Adam bolted down the steps before I could stop him.

A few yards down the path, he whirled around and shouted, "Stay there. Get a gun. Give one to Jordan," and then he was gone.

"Don't you leave me again, Christina," Jordan called.

If she hadn't sounded so panicked, I might have followed Adam. And then I came to my senses, aware of what my body was telling me. After what happened, I was in no shape to go tearing across the sprawling complex. My hands shook, my knees wobbled, and despite the cold wind, I'd broken out in a sweat.

We hurried back to my place. It was a struggle to get Jordan inside, but I finally managed it. Mercifully, she didn't weigh much. Jordan sat in her wheelchair, inspecting a gun.

"I wish we had the internet so I could watch a video on how to use this thing." Words of bravado. She looked scared, her pixie face strained and pale.

I eyed the guns on the coffee table. Once my hands calmed down, I'd choose the smallest one with a longer barrel. Earlier, Paul and Ruth had loaded them all, and Ruth said the twenty-two pistol was easiest to handle.

Jordan had scoffed. "That nine-millimeter Paul used didn't kill that fucking monster. I want something that's going to stop them, not just piss them off."

Throwing open the window, I kneeled on a chair and listened. The screams had stopped. No more gunfire. No way of knowing if that was good, bad, or beyond whatever I could imagine. I heard myself say, "Please, please, please," but what I meant was, "Please, let Adam be okay. Please, let Adam come back to me."

And ten agonizing minutes later, he did, along with Ruth and Paul. They looked even more worn out than before, haggard to the point of appearing sick. None of them spoke. Adam collapsed onto the loveseat, pulled me onto it with him, and rested a hand on my knee. It felt like he'd had it in a freezer. The cold from his fingers seeped through my joggers. I wiggled to find a comfortable position. The scrapes on my rear end stung, and my back ached from the beating it had received when the monster had straddled me. Adam stared up at the ceiling, blinking, trying to catch his breath.

"Aren't you going to tell us what happened?" Jordan burst out.

Ruth nodded. "That gentleman who lives near the little park, the university professor..."

"The cranky know-it-all," Paul interrupted.

Ruth cleared her throat. "Well, he's dead now, so I think we can forgive him. We knocked on his door and said there was something in the water, and it was a good idea to stay inside. He wanted to know what was in the water, and we said we didn't know, but we thought it was a dangerous animal that posed a risk to the community. But he wanted to see it for himself. He marched straight down to the water, and you can guess what happened next."

"How many?" I asked.

Paul stood up and began pacing. "Three." He stopped long enough to point at me. "No sign of your friend though, so maybe I killed him after all."

"I hope so," I said, leaning into Adam. Despite his attempts to comfort me, I didn't feel any safer. Not with those things roaming around.

The noise of the attack on the professor and the gunshot had brought out a small group of people demanding to know what happened. Paul tried telling the truth, but that hadn't gone well. Someone called him a right-wing nut job. Someone else said grief had messed with his head, and he needed to see a shrink. Most ignored what Ruth had to say.

"But you're a former police chief," I said. "Why wouldn't they believe you?"

She shrugged. "I'm a woman. A black woman. And I'm no longer wearing a uniform."

"That's so wrong," Jordan muttered. "So, what do those idiots think happened to the professor?"

Ruth got to her feet and rubbed the back of her neck. "I don't think anyone is thinking logically. They're focused on the road closure and how long we'll be stranded. It sounds like the professor was a bit of a recluse. His neighbors barely knew him, so he wasn't close to anyone." Her shoulders drooped.

"We should all stick together. Sleep here tonight. Out of all our places, this one is situated the best, farthest from the water. It'll be night soon, and if those things are half as smart as I think they are, they'll be back for more."

Chapter 24

Christina

Adam talked me into taking a nap. But when I closed my eyes, the memory—the feeling—of that thing crushing me into the wet sand came flooding back. It took some time, but eventually I fell asleep. When I woke, I felt groggy, like I'd downed some serious pain medication.

Downstairs, I poured myself a ginger ale and mixed in a splash of grenadine. The sugary fizz brought me back to life.

The rain had slowed, but the wind had intensified. Gusts made the west-facing windows thrum. Adam and Paul sat on the floor in the living room, surrounded by flashlights and lanterns, making sure the batteries worked. Ruth had brought over bags of groceries, and she and Jordan were deciding what to make for dinner.

"Carbs," Jordan said. "We need carbs."

"Macaroni and cheese?" Adam said over his shoulder.

So that's what we made. Homemade mac 'n cheese, with onions and Ruth's secret bread crumb topping. On the side, we had grilled spicy chicken sausages and a baby heirloom tomato salad with arugula because I always had plenty of both. Despite everything happening, we devoured our food. Not with enjoyment, but with determination, more like we knew we needed the fuel for whatever was to come. For dessert, I busted out three small tubs of fancy ice cream, and we polished those off too.

The alcohol stayed in the cupboard. We needed clear heads.

After all that food, Jordan got so sleepy we insisted she take a nap. I pulled out the sofa bed in my office and made it up with fresh sheets, and Adam carried her from the wheelchair and tucked her in like she was five years old. She was so tired she didn't protest, and she was asleep before we left the room.

While we cleaned up, the conversation turned to the storm. Outside, the wind had begun to howl.

"If this keeps up, we'll lose power for sure," Paul said.

That's when they realized, in the hubbub following the slough monster attacks, they'd forgotten to retrieve the generators from Ruth's place. Adam, Paul, and Ruth hurried off, armed, and I went upstairs to tidy up. My bedroom was stuffy and smelled like menthol cough drops. Adam had smeared some sinus-clearing muscle balm on my sore back, avoiding the scraped spots, and the room reeked. I threw open a window and felt the wind rush in, lifting my hair.

I went into the bathroom. It was a disaster—blood streaks in the bathtub, red splotches on the floor and in the sink. I grabbed a rag and some foamy cleanser from a cupboard and set to work. When I bent over the tub, my back spasmed, reminding me to take it easy.

The bathroom wasn't very big, and it only took a few minutes.

I heard a noise in the bedroom.

A thud.

At first, I thought the wind had knocked down a lamp. But something was moving across the hardwood floor. And then I heard a faint rumble, like a low growl. My heart froze.

I was alone, vulnerable, far from guns and knives.

Reaching behind me, I slid open a drawer and plucked a pair of eyebrow scissors from a tray. They were ridiculously small, but they were sharp.

The smart thing to do would be to lock the door and stay in the bathroom. But would a flimsy bathroom door keep that thing out? And Jordan was downstairs, sleeping, even more vulnerable than me.

I had to act.

A dark figure stood in the far corner of the room, lurking in the shadows. I couldn't see it clearly, but I knew by its size and shape it was the one that came after me earlier.

It shifted from foot to foot, staring. Water pooled on the floor at his feet. It stank. Like wet dog mixed with the rotten-egg stench from the mucky parts of the slough. I could see the long, terrible claws. The ones that had pierced my scalp and raked across my back. While it was taller than me, the size of the room seemed to put it into a new perspective, diminishing it somehow. It was thin, with a strangely small head, long-limbed, and covered in dark bristly hair. Its face was a blur of features. It chittered, radiating a menacing excitement which made my blood run cold.

I watched, not understanding at first what I was seeing. Just above his legs was a vertical strip of fur darker than the rest, nearly black. It was raised, like a scar. Slowly, it widened and something protruded. Something long and hard.

I fought a wave of terror, the urge to scream, to run, to crumple to the ground in a useless heap. But then it would be on top of me, and it would finish what it started on the beach. That's why it had come back. I could feel its desperation.

Something clicked inside me.

No.

That was not going to happen. Not without a fight. The thought of falling victim to that thing for a second time in the same day, and in my own house, filled me with a burning-hot rage. It might be a monster, some bizarre hybrid creature. Dangerous. But an animal. And I was going to treat it like one.

I tried to remember what they said you're supposed to do if you found yourself alone with a wild animal. Hold your ground. Stay calm. Backing away slowly wasn't an option. It would pounce. I made myself as big as possible, lifting my arms. It took a step toward me, snarling. Make noise. That I could do. I yelled, like stopping a charging dog.

"You stay right there, fucker," I yelled.

It froze.

I yelled some more. "I'll kill you. I'll kill you until you're fucking dead." Then I laughed, a harsh, barking laugh which made me sound deranged. When it continued to stare at me, I shouted, "Yeah, that's right, you fucking fucker. That's what's going to happen to you. I'm going to take these cute little scissors and cut your dick off."

I kept screaming, and it hunched its shoulders and snarled, revealing sharp teeth which seemed to glow in the dark corner, but it stayed put. Maybe I could keep it there until Adam got back. They had to return soon. How long had they been gone? How long had the monster and I been engaged in this horrible standoff? Seconds? Minutes? A half hour?

"Christina?" a voice called from below.

It was Jordan at the bottom of the stairs. The creature's head swiveled.

It angled its body in the direction of the door. I had to do something, and quick. Maybe I'd put up just enough resistance it was in search of a new, more vulnerable target. Maybe it remembered Jordan, how easy she was to pull to the ground.

A wet towel lay draped across the back of a chair next to me. I'd used it to dry my hair. It was thin and frayed at the ends, a typical cheap gym towel, nubby with a blue stripe. The kind my sister and I used to snap at each other when we were teenagers.

I snatched the towel. It wasn't dripping wet. That would have been ideal. But it was wet enough. Normally, I would have laid it on a flat surface and rolled it, but there was no time for that, so I twirled it a few times, wrapped one end around my wrist, holding the strike end with my other hand. I side-stepped toward the creature, leaned in with my shoulder, and flicked my wrist hard.

Crack.

The towel snapped about a foot from its face. The creature reared back, slamming against the wall. Its lips pulled back, revealing a row of ugly sharp teeth the color of dirty cement.

"Oh, you like that, do you fucker?" I muttered.

"Oh my god, Christina," Jordan screamed.

"Stop making noise," I yelled. "And you better have a gun pointing at those stairs." Wheels swiveled on the hardwood, and I could imagine Jordan racing for the coffee table.

I cracked the towel again, and again, each time ending with a satisfying snap. Closer each time to the monster's face. It cowered in the corner, its arms raised in defense. It had been oblivious to Jordan jabbing it with an umbrella, then slashing its ankles with a knife, and minutes later, gunshots, which it obviously survived. But a simple towel snap made it back off.

My right arm was getting tired, but I ignored the ache, and I was repeating the same crazy phrases, but it didn't matter. It was reacting to the tone of my voice—loud and commanding—and I didn't dare stop. Something else had

211

retreated too. Its monstrous erection. I barked out another laugh.

"I guess you don't like it rough," I shouted, aiming the end of the towel at its genital area.

It yelped. Good. That's what it deserved. I hoped its skin would split open.

"You fucker. That's what you get." I cracked the towel again, feeling bolder, and this time striking it on the leg. "This is what bad monsters get when they try to drown the shit out of me."

Below, the front door banged open, footsteps pounded across the living room, and Jordan screamed, "It's upstairs!"

Then, Adam was calling my name. In the cacophony, my attention shifted—the towel dangling from my hand—just long enough for the monster to twist its body and spring sideways, something I'd never seen any person or animal do before. It scrabbled out the window, claws rasping against the sill.

Adam moved so fast he flew into the room and collided with the bed. I felt lightheaded, giddy with relief, and I laughed.

"Christina!" His stern voice made me laugh even harder. "Christina, you could have been killed. Why did you come up here by yourself without a gun?"

"I know, it was stupid. I should have brought a gun. But I had something better." I collapsed into a chair and held up the towel. "This."

Chapter 25

Adam

I was furious at myself for leaving Christina and Jordan at home alone while we fetched the generators. Paul and Ruth could have handled it between the two of them.

Christina assured me she was fine. More than fine. After she'd managed to beat back the creature, she seemed more like herself. The incident down at the slough had not only terrified her, but it had also eroded her resilience, the confidence which made Christina so unique. Her eyes seemed clearer, her shoulders straighter. She no longer had the appearance of a dazed sleepwalker. She was still scared, like the rest of us, but she had fought and won.

Listening to the storm rage outside, we huddled in Christina's living room, loaded guns on the coffee table.

Paul and Ruth were fascinated by Christina's story and asked her to repeat it several times. Jordan demanded Christina demonstrate her towel flicking maneuvers, and when she did, the teenager clapped her hands and said it sounded exactly like a whip.

Paul winced. "It feels like one too if its wet. I hated going swimming with my brother because he'd get me every time."

Ruth nodded. "Oh, my brothers got up to that too, but my mother would have killed them if they'd ever tried that on me."

Jordan wheeled herself to the kitchen, then called Paul to help her fill a bowl with water. She spent the next half hour practicing towel flicks until she got bored. Ruth made hot chocolate for everyone. I cradled my mug in my hands, its warmth easing the stiffness in my fingers.

We wondered if the creature's reaction was instinctive, somehow connected to their circus animal roots. Maybe trainers had used whips on the animals to scare and intimidate them, and that fear had become a part of their DNA. Inherited trauma.

Ruth tapped her gun. "Y'all can use towels if you want, but I'm sticking with my Glock, thank you very much."

"Speaking of guns," I said. "Do one of you want to come with me to see what's going on with the slough? I'm wondering how much it's risen."

"No," Christina said.

"Bad things seem to happen when you leave," Jordan snapped. "Or haven't you noticed? I mean, you're like every bad scene in a scary movie where somebody has a stupid idea and people go, oh yeah, let's do that stupid thing."

Paul frowned. "Are you really worried it might flood, or do you just want to see what's going on with those things?"

My imagination had kicked into overdrive. I pictured the creatures swinging out of the trees at the far end of the slough and swimming toward us, amassing on the opposite bank. An army ready to invade. Angry we'd invaded their territory, thirsty for retribution, ready to strike when we were vulnerable. I felt a desperate need to see it for myself. But the others were right, of course. The water was the most dangerous place to be, and I had no business down there.

"Doesn't matter," Ruth said. "No one's going anywhere. We're staying put, and that's final."

A gust of wind rattled the windows, and seconds later, the lights went out.

214

We reached for our flashlights and scrambled to our feet. Outside, there was nothing but inky darkness. Not a single light anywhere.

Paul's face pressed against the window. "It looks like the entire complex is out."

"What could have caused that?" Jordan asked. She leaned closer to Ruth, who gave her knee a reassuring pat.

"The wind probably knocked a tree into a power pole and brought the whole thing down," Paul said. "Happens all the time. How about we fire up those generators? The power company isn't going to send anyone out for repairs, not with the weather like this."

Even with our flashlights, the corners of the room remained dark, the beams casting eerie shadows. I'd done a fair bit of rough camping on U.S. Forest Service land where the only light came from lanterns and the canopy of stars overhead. But none of those experiences prepared me for the panic I felt when the lights went out at Roy's Cottages—the outage brought out a primitive fear of what darkness might bring.

Christina's hand found mine. Her fingers were cold. I rubbed her hands to warm them, then helped Paul and Ruth plug cords into the generators. Within minutes, we had the refrigerator and three lamps in the living room connected, and the false comfort of light was ours again. We sat for a few moments, listening.

We could hear voices outside, neighbors talking about the outage.

Paul went to the front door and stuck his head out. Leaves blew in. The wind howled around the rooftops and whistled through the coastal grass. It had to be in the fifty mile per hour range out there. He slammed the door and turned to face us, jaw clenched.

"We warned people, did we not, that the power might go out and to get ready?"

"Yeah, we did," I said.

Christina got to her feet with a wince. My toes curled, thinking of the unspeakable thing that monster tried to do to her earlier in the day. It felt like a year ago.

"It's like earthquake kits," she said. "People know they should have them, but they don't. When I was working in news, we did a story about how most Americans are not prepared for a disaster. As in, not even having any extra food or water."

Paul fumed. "But we told them, and they're out there acting as if it's a complete surprise. Same kind of stupid behavior I see on the job. Oh, was I supposed to clear the brush from my house? Is that why the wildfire destroyed my house? Oh, was I supposed to change the batteries on the smoke alarm? Don't get me started."

Ruth gave a grim laugh. "We don't need to. You're doing fine on your own." She stopped, eyes widening. "Oh shoot. Didn't I tell people they could come to my place to bring over food to my extra refrigerator?"

"Yeah, you did," I said, raising a hand. "But that was before…" My voice drifted off. It didn't need explaining. The memories were burned into our brains.

"Fuck 'em," Jordan said. "Let them figure it out."

Ruth got to her feet with a sigh. "It's not that simple, Jordan. I made the offer, now I need to live up to it."

"But you can't go," Jordan exploded. "You saw what's out there. It's dark, and they could be hiding. Fuck that. They're probably hiding, waiting. What's wrong with you people? You're supposed to be the adults." She rattled the armrests of her wheelchair. "And Ruth, you're the shooting expert, and I'm stuck in this thing."

Paul and I registered our protests at the same time. "Hey. Whoa."

Jordan flopped back in her chair. "I'm sorry. You guys are great and everything." She pointed at Ruth. "But she was, like, the head of the police." Jordan turned to Christina. "Tell her she can't go, Chris. Tell her."

Christina grimaced. "She's got a point, Ruth. Just a few seconds ago, you didn't want the guys to check the water, and now you're saying you want to walk in the dark all the way to your garage so people don't lose all the cheap food they bought from Costco? Come on. It is a little ridiculous."

Ruth's mouth opened, then shut. Her shoulders slumped. "You're right," she said quietly. "Of course, you're right. I'll be honest, I'm not thinking straight."

"None of us are," I said firmly. "We've had a hell of a day." Looking over at Paul, I added. "And a hell of a week."

Paul dipped his head. The firefighter was so stoic it was easy to forget he'd lost his wife in the slough. The attempted rape of Christina had to have cast an even darker pall on the tragic fate of his wife. I wondered if he had dared to contemplate it.

Voices moved closer to the house. Two people arguing, by the sound of it, followed by tentative footsteps on the porch.

Jordan pointed at Ruth. "Just. Say. No."

Paul opened the door, a lantern swinging from one hand. Liliana Garcia stood there, dressed in a long-hooded parka. She flicked off her flashlight. Her husband remained on the path, clutching the banister, one foot on the bottom step.

217

"Hurry up, god dammit," he barked. "I'm freezing my ass off out here."

When Christina heard Tommy's voice, she hurried to the door. "Come in, come in," she said, waving them inside.

"And hurry the fuck up about it," Jordan muttered. She shot me a pleading look. Her face was tight with anxiety.

Mrs. Garcia shook her head. "No, no. That's all right. We won't come in. We've got some lanterns at home, and we plan on going to bed early. There's nothing else to do."

Jordan made a wind-it-up gesture with her hand. I went over to Christina, put my arm over her shoulder, and gave it a squeeze. Beyond Tommy Garcia, I could just make out the second row of cottages. A path running all the way down to the slough began several yards from where Tommy stood. My eyes scanned the darkness for any movement. I didn't like it that the door was open. I didn't like it those two old people were out at night.

I was about to order them inside, when Liliana looked directly at me and said, "I've been feeling terrible ever since you came by. About the satellite phone. I took it. I was worried Tommy would have one of his episodes, and he's got heart problems too, and if something happened to him, I didn't like the idea of having to walk all the way to the mailroom at night to get it. I should have told you, but I was...you know, ashamed. So, we've brought it back." She turned around. "Haven't we Tommy?"

Mr. Garcia scowled. "We need it more than they do. They're young and in good health. Not like us." He fumbled in his pocket and held up the phone. "And you haven't seen what I've seen. Those damn things sneaking around. What's going to happen if they show up? How are we going to call for help, that's what I want to know?" The old man lifted his foot off the step and nearly fell over. When he'd regained his balance, he said. "You know what? To hell with you. I'm keeping it."

Tears came to Liliana's eyes as she clapped a hand over her mouth. She recovered quickly though. Putting her hands on her hips, she shouted after her husband, "Oh no you're not, mister. We're—"

Whatever she was about to say was interrupted by chittering from the darkened path. I swept my flashlight across the area. Its beam caught several pairs of yellow eyes floating in the air. My brain filled in the rest of the image. Tall, misshapen bodies, half-crouched, waiting to pounce. By the way Paul and Christina stiffened, they'd seen them too.

Moments later, they erupted out of the dark and rushed at Tommy, their grunts and growls blunted by the savage wind. The beam of my flashlight captured Tommy's open mouth, the bulging eyes—a parody of horror. A creature shot into the beam of my light and shoved Tommy so hard he went flying, landing face down on the wet ground.

Paul grabbed the sleeve of Liliana's coat and tried to yank her inside, but she wriggled out of it, and he was left holding the parka as she lurched down the steps, shrieking her husband's name.

Behind us, Jordan cried, "Shut the door!"

Ruth pushed past us, gun raised. Three creatures surrounded Tommy, heads cocked to the side, studying him, clawed feet scraping the pavement. Uglier than my worst nightmare. I shoved Christina back into the house. If the juvenile male was hiding somewhere, I didn't want him to see her.

"Steady that light, Adam," Ruth yelled into my ear, the muzzle of her gun poised mid-air.

219

Feet planted wide, I held the flashlight with both hands. Liliana, in the chaos, had fallen and was sprawled at the base of the steps, whimpering. The creatures hunkered down and began to drag Tommy away.

He managed to raise his head, the satellite phone still clutched in one hand. "Thank you, Lord," he screamed. "Your will be done."

The gun went off. The bullet missed and struck the nearest cottage.

We watched as Liliana crawled after her husband. A figure darted out, catching a bullet on the arm. With a malevolent snarl of defiance, it pulled the screaming woman into the night.

Chapter 26

Adam

We blamed ourselves for what happened, but our guilt was half-hearted. We were sickened by the loss of the Garcias, but we knew—even if we didn't say it—none of us could have done anything differently and survived.

Trying to go after them would have cost a life. Or lives. We'd made the worst sort of risk calculation. And we were alive.

Christina sat in stunned silence, her head in her hands. Ruth and Paul patrolled the windows and door, peering out between the blinds, talking quietly among themselves. Jordan eyed Ruth and Paul nervously, biting her nails.

"What should we do?" she asked after a while. "What's going to happen tonight?"

"I don't know," I said quietly. "No one does."

She threw back her head and groaned. "Why? Why did I get stuck here? Why didn't my dad come back when he got the weather alert? Uh."

I laughed, an ugly harsh sound. "That's just another thing I can't answer." I ruffled her hair, and she blinked back tears.

"They're going to come after us, aren't they?" Jordan said, her voice rising. "They're going to try and kill us all." She doubled over, her hands in her hair, and moaned. "No, no, no, no." When she straightened, her lips trembled. "What if Dawn is still alive? Maybe they're...you know." She shot a wild glance at Christina, who was breathing through gritted teeth, shaking her head. "Maybe that's what they want to do. Capture the women and make us their sex slaves."

Ruth stomped a foot. "Jordan! Think about what you're saying!" She jutted her chin in Paul's direction. The firefighter's jaw had gone slack.

Jordan clapped a hand over her mouth. "I'm sorry, Paul. I'm sorry. I'm just freaking out. I didn't mean it. Please. I'm sorry."

Everyone was too horrified to say anything. That Dawn was still alive had not occurred to me, but considering the sexual assault on Christina, it wasn't beyond the realm of possibility. Paul staggered into the office and slammed the door. A few moments later, we heard an agonized howl, then muffled sobbing.

Jordan strained forward in her wheelchair, snatched a pillow from the couch, and covered her face.

Christina moved to the sofa, fixed her eyes on mine, and patted her knees. It took me a moment to understand what she meant, but then in a flash, I got it. I scooped up Jordan and carried her to the couch. She didn't put up a fight—instead she went completely limp. I set her down next to Christina, who pulled Jordan's head onto her lap and began smoothing back her hair, whispering in her ear. Jordan closed her eyes and sniffed.

Ruth picked up another gun, then went back to the window. "It's making me crazy. Not knowing what's going on out there. It sounds like people must have gone back to their homes after what happened. And even if our phones were working, I don't have anyone's number because I hardly know anyone here. It's not like we could call and say, 'hey, remember those things in the water we tried telling you about? Well, they're here, and this time you might want to listen to us.'"

"This is a shit show," Christina said.

Ruth sighed. "You can say that again."

"This is a shit show," Jordan said, hair covering her face. At least she was talking. A silent Jordan worried me more than a talkative one.

With Paul still out of commission in the other room—silent now—I picked up a gun from the coffee table, a Beretta, and did something I should have sooner. I climbed the steps to Christina's bedroom, double-checked the latch on the window, and peered outside. The rain had slowed to a steady drizzle, but the wind was louder up there. The walls were taking quite a buffeting in the wind. Most of the cottages I could see were dark, except for two, windows lit with the warm steady glow of lanterns.

The long day had taken on a nightmarish quality. Too many horrible events crammed into too short a time. Three people dead, that we knew of. Christina escaping with her life, twice, scarred forever. Paul downstairs, thinking his new wife might still be out there, somewhere, tormented by vicious hybrid creatures with a taste for human females.

And who knew what horrors the night might still deliver.

Swinging the lantern in front of the window to make sure nothing was there, I slid it open and listened. Through the Pacific-brewed squall, I thought I heard a shriek. I battled the urge to run downstairs, to be with the others, but I was the only one in a position to hear anything. I forced myself to stay and listen. Another shriek soon followed, then a silence which seemed to stretch on forever.

I was about to shut the window when I heard screams.

Coming from the water. Probably the first row of cottages closest to the slough.

The attack I'd dreaded was happening.

I had sensed it coming. Felt it. And now it had arrived, all I felt was relief. The uncertainty—the waiting—for something to happen had become unbearable.

"Let's get this over with," I said, shutting the window and locking it.

When I ran downstairs, the screams had become so loud, so prolonged, everybody could hear them. Jordan sat bolt upright, her fists pressed against her cheeks. Paul had come out of the office and stood next to Ruth a few feet from the front door, clutching his rifle. Christina paced the room, holding a twenty-two.

Footsteps pounded up the steps, then frantic knocking. We all jumped.

"Don't open it," Jordan cried.

We remembered what happened the last time, the way the creatures had appeared and dragged away the Garcias. No one moved. Fists continued to hammer on the door.

"It's Cathy Baggio," a voice shouted. "You've got to help me. Let me in. For God's sake, please."

Ruth cracked first. Before anyone could stop her, she undid the latch, flung open the door, and pulled the woman inside. Paul cursed and kicked it closed.

Chest heaving, tears streaming down her face, Noah Baggio's mother panted, struggling to catch her breath. Her dark eyes were wide and frightened. The hair band she wore around her head had slipped to her forehead, and she snatched it off.

Ruth touched her arm and said, "What happened?"

"He's gone," Cathy burst out. "He didn't come back. I don't know where he is, and then I heard screaming. And I saw somebody. It was dragging our neighbor out of the house, and there was somebody else on the roof, and then a body came flying out of the upstairs window. It was her husband. So, I just ran, and I saw your light."

At that, Paul and I exchanged glances. Our light. Our comfort. Our betrayer. We might as well have beat a drum and announced, "We're home. Come and get us."

I didn't know what light might signal to those creatures out there, but it's something I should have thought of. We extinguished the lanterns, flicked on our flashlights, and aimed them at the floor, forming circles on the hardwood.

Jordan groaned. "This sucks. This really, really sucks."

"Where did he go?" Ruth spoke with eerie calm.

Cathy swallowed. "To your place. To your garage. Our refrigerator went out, and we had some stuff we didn't want to spoil. Rich remembered your offer and said he'd take it over."

Ruth said nothing. Her face had turned to stone.

"Please," Cathy whispered. "You have to help me."

Stepping between them, Paul said, "Wait. Your husband said you had generators. Why didn't you plug in your refrigerator?"

Cathy wouldn't look at Paul. "The generators didn't work. They didn't have any gas." She paused, shoulders slumping. "My husband is missing."

Paul shook his head, lip curling. I knew what he was thinking. The day before, Rich Baggio admitted he had generators but made it clear they were for his family only, and now his wife stood before us, demanding our help.

Ruth cleared her throat. "I need to go." She shifted her gaze to Paul. "Can I take your rifle?"

Paul gave a curt nod and stepped aside. "This is a bad idea, Ruth."

"Probably," she said.

We watched as she zipped up her rain jacket with steady, precise movements, her jaw set hard as concrete. No one tried to talk her out of it. Not even Jordan, who contented herself with killing Cathy Baggio with her eyes. Ruth rotated the doorknob and stopped before she pushed it open.

Turning, she stared down at Cathy Baggio as if surprised to see her so close on her heels. "You're not coming."

Cathy sniffed. "The hell I'm not."

Ruth glanced around, expecting someone to object. When no one did, her nose twitched and she said, "Follow my orders, whatever you do. No matter what happens." Pointing at me she said, "Give her one of the twenty-twos."

I picked the last one up from the table and put it in the woman's hands. They were small. Child-sized. After I showed her how to take off the safety, I said, "Good luck."

Her lower lip trembled.

They left.

When I turned around, Jordan was staring at me with a blank expression. "Why did you let them go?"

"Her husband is missing," I said. "She has no one left."

Jordan threw her head back and wailed at the ceiling. "And who's fault is that? So much for personal responsibility. We told them something was in the water. We told them to stay inside. And what do they do?" She waved her hands in the air. "Oh no, our milk might go bad. Let's walk in the dark so we can have milk in the morning. What the fuck!"

I held up a hand. Jordan—not one to quiet down without a fight—opened her mouth, then her eyes widened.

A fresh wave of screams. This time closer. From the sound of it, from the middle row of cottages, the one directly in front of us. The wind—the relentless wind—had to be distorting the sound, along with the humidity from the rain, but I couldn't remember how, not with my half-working brain. Then I realized it didn't matter. The increase in volume meant the monsters were closer and on the attack, and we didn't have time. We needed to act. If only we had a plan.

Christina jumped to her feet. Her hair had escaped its ponytail, and half of it seemed to be in her face. She impatiently brushed it away. "We need to hide."

"Hide!" Paul echoed. "Where?"

Christina opened her mouth to answer, but before she could get the words out, from the cottages in front of us, we heard glass shattering, then a series of thuds and, finally, wood splintering.

"Windows," whispered Jordan.

"And doors," Paul said. "They're busting in the doors." Gripping the rifle, he turned to face Christina. "If you know of a good hiding spot, now's the time to tell us."

Christina sprinted for the mudroom and dropped to her hands and knees. Moments later she was pulling up a hatch in the floor. "A crawl space. Mine is one of the few units that has one. It's for extra storage."

I crossed the room and peered into the darkness. There was a short ladder, but that was all I could see. "Is that the only way in?"

Christina gazed up at me, nodding. "Yes. It has finished walls, and there's a handle on the inside too."

"Guys," Jordan hissed. "There's something walking on the roof."

We froze.

The pattering of feet. Heavier than a cat or a raccoon. Faster than a possum. Slough Devil feet. Then, the sound of claws scraping against the outside wall, moving up, then another thud.

There was no telling how many were up there.

If Christina hadn't scared one away earlier, they probably would have broken the glass by now. They were smart enough to exercise caution. They could have busted down the front door. Or the ground floor windows. Instead, they'd taken the harder route to the second floor. Why? My heart nearly stopped.

Christina.

The upstairs bedroom is where the juvenile male had last seen Christina. That was her habitat. That's where he'd find her again.

"Get in," I said, so harshly she flinched.

She didn't argue and disappeared down the hatch. I handed down a lantern and hoped we'd soon feel safe enough to use it. When I turned around, Paul had already scooped up Jordan.

"Get in," he barked. "I'll hand her down."

Running my tours and the survival boot camps, I was the one who usually gave the orders. But Paul's experience as a firefighter had kicked in, and he'd taken charge. A part of me balked, resisting like a teenage boy just to show he could. And the notion of hiding didn't come naturally. Not to someone who believed in taking action to solve problems. Hiding was passive. And going underground, into a crawl space with just one escape route, seemed like the worst possible idea.

I was so lost in thought, when Christina's hand shot up and tugged at my pants, my body gave a violent jerk. That shocked me back to my right mind, and I clambered down the ladder, the aluminum rungs vibrating under my weight. The crawl space was just high enough for me to stand. I held up my hands, and Paul dropped Jordan into them. When I'd set her down next to Christina, Paul peered down, and we stared at each other for a moment. Then, he straightened, picking up his rifle from the floor.

From upstairs, glass broke, raining down on a hard surface. Paul's eyes snapped open.

"Get down here, and hurry!" I said.

The ceiling thrummed. Furniture overturned. Something smashed against a wall. Chittering. Growls. A howl of frustration. I'd closed the bedroom door behind me. Maybe they weren't good with doors, at least opening them in the traditional way.

He shook his head. "No. When they come downstairs, I'm going to shoot the fuckers that killed my wife."

Before I could reply, he dropped the hatch, and I had to duck to avoid getting hit on the head. A moment later, I heard something being dragged across the floor, over the hatch. Probably the bench Christina had bought for the mudroom where she changed her shoes. We sat huddled in the darkness, too stunned to say anything. Jordan slumped over and fell into my lap, her shoulders shaking.

A door banged open. The bedroom door.

Clawed feet scraped the steps, skittered up the walls of the stairwell. Then, the gritty crackle of rifle fire. Paul had given Ruth the rifle which had a larger capacity magazine—twenty rounds—which left him with the rifle he used for deer hunting. It only had ten rounds, and he was blowing through them fast. The gun fire stopped as suddenly as it started.

"Shit," he said, loud enough I could hear him.

My mind filled in the horrifying picture above. Paul shoving more rounds in the magazine, his back against the counter. Christina gripped my arm, nails digging into my flesh.

Paul didn't scream. He grunted, as if surprised. And then a sickening smack, the kind which made my stomach flip on the boat while giving tours—the unmistakable sound of a head hitting something hard. An eruption of chittering and growls. Something thudded against a wall. Again and again.

Paul's body repeatedly striking the wall.

Jordan whimpered. Christina pressed up against me and I could feel the rapid beat of her heart. A steady scraping commenced, and a thump thump thump. Instead of taking their prize out the front door, they were dragging Paul up the stairs.

Silence.

They hadn't heard us. Or sensed us. I was sure they were gone, but I had no intention of lifting the hatch to find out. There was no sound except for breathing and Jordan sniffling. I flicked on the flashlight and swung the beam around the crawl space. Pipes. Unpainted walls. Solid, thank God.

We panted from fear, loud like dogs left in a hot car. I imagined the monsters stopping outside the cottage, heads cocking, wondering if they should come back inside to investigate. The builders hadn't scrimped on the crawl space. It was as well-insulated as the house, and without windows, we couldn't hear anything. The pandemonium raging earlier could be over, or it could still be going on, for all we knew.

Just in case, I turned off the flashlight, and we were plunged into darkness.

We sat, huddled together, on the cold hard floor for hours. After a while, my head throbbed from the smell of the chemicals evaporating off the new sheetrock, wood and other construction materials. The only sounds were my thudding heartbeat and our ragged breaths. The hours passed slowly, our bodies shaking, my muscles cramping from the prolonged tension. Our bodies exhausted, we stretched out, holding hands. The hard floor made it impossible to get comfortable. I

230

could only imagine Christina's discomfort, her back covered in scrapes and bruises, but she didn't make the slightest noise of complaint. Eventually, we fell asleep.

When I returned to consciousness, I felt like I was floating.

After an eternity, the others woke too.

"Is it morning?" Christina whispered.

"Think so," I said.

We waited several more hours, ears straining—listening for anything which might tell us what was going on outside. I crawled to the front and placed my ear against the wall. Silence. My feet were so numb I had to take it slow climbing the aluminum ladder, Christina shining the flashlight on the rungs. Jordan had both hands covering her ears, like she expected a loud noise.

I hoped not. My heart couldn't stand it.

I used both hands to push the hatch open. The bench Paul had shoved across it wasn't too heavy, and it slid to the side.

Blood whooshed in my ears when I peered out, sure a monster had remained behind as a sentinel and would leap out at me, swiping at my head with its terrible claws. But the kitchen was silent. The counters and walls were smeared with blood, the steps to the bedroom smudged red. I slowly got to my feet.

Christina's head emerged. She scanned the room with dull eyes, then gave an almost imperceptible sigh. I was too numb to go upstairs. Paul wouldn't be there anyway. The monsters had taken him through the window, I was sure. Motioning for Christina to stay where she was, I drew my gun—the weapon I'd nearly forgotten about—crept toward the front window, and pulled the blind aside.

231

No one. Nothing. The storm had stopped, and the sun had come out. Water glistened on the native grass along the path, mixing with drops of blood.

I stared out the window for a long time before finally getting the nerve to crack open the front door. From the direction of the slough, I could hear the seabirds. But no voices.

A part of me wanted to rush back into the house, push Christina into the crawl space, and pull the hatch closed behind us. Just a few hours more. A few more hours of safety. Putting off the inevitable exploration beyond the porch.

Suddenly, I had to pee, and I raced past an alarmed Christina to the small bathroom off the kitchen. When I was done, I helped Christina up the ladder, then carried out Jordan. They disappeared into the bathroom and were in there for a long time.

We emerged into the sunlight, blinking, each holding a gun, safeties off.

Our eyes never stopped roaming, taking in the busted-out windows and doors. There were signs of mayhem everywhere.

Jordan's dune buggy wheelchair was untouched, exactly where we'd left it at the bottom of the steps. I took off my flannel shirt and dried the seat as best I could. I held a finger up to my lips, then nodded in the direction of the parking lot, away from the water.

With Jordan in her silent electric chair, we passed a body sprawled across a path, and we stopped for a moment, staring at what was left of it. Cathy Baggio. Mangled. Mutilated.

I looked around for Ruth but didn't see her. A few moments later, I spotted a rifle on the ground next to a light pole. Paul's rifle. The one he'd given to Ruth.

Christina gasped beside me. With a trembling hand, she pointed at the pole. Gouges scored the black paint, revealing the silver metal underneath. Claw marks. I felt dizzy. When I squeezed my eyes shut, I imagined a creature shimmying up the pole, clinging to the top, and dropping down onto its victims. I hoped Ruth had managed to get off a few shots.

Cathy Baggio's body was the only one we saw. The only human body.

We stumbled across the juvenile male where two paths crossed—one toward the lot, the other toward the slough. Blasted full of holes. It wasn't moving. By the looks of it, Ruth's work.

Christina aimed her gun at its head, hand trembling. I shook my head, and she understood. We weren't out of danger yet. A loud sound could summon the creatures if they were still around. She kicked it with the toe of her boot, nearly falling over in the process.

The dizziness intensified. I staggered toward the parking lot, and when we saw the road, we ran toward it, Jordan racing ahead in her silent, electric wheelchair. When she reached the curb, she gave a strangled, "Yes!"

The flooding had subsided. Enough, anyway, for us to get out if I stuck to the elevated mid-section. The water formed deep pools on either side, but they would be easy enough to avoid. For one terrible moment, I thought I'd forgotten my car keys at the house, but they were in my pocket, and my knees went weak with relief. Jordan was already speeding toward the Land Cruiser.

Minutes later, we were driving away, the doors locked, Jordan's dune buggy wheelchair in the back.

Chapter 27

Adam

The three of us were the only survivors.

We hoped the women taken were dead and not enduring horrors somewhere at the east end of the slough. Investigators spent weeks at Roy's Cottages. We told them what happened, but we could see in their faces they didn't believe us. They hadn't found the dead juvenile monster. The Slough Devils must have retrieved it.

Trauma. We heard that word a lot.

And then we became victims, the only survivors of a new style of extremist. Eco-terrorists who'd worn custom costumes and staged a never-before-seen assault on the residents of a controversial housing development in an environmentally sensitive area. People who fouled a jewel on the Central Coast of California. Who those so-called terrorists were, they never made clear. If they had any proof, they never shared it. Just vague references to radical groups on social media sites. Where they came from, no one could say.

And that became the story. Or the narrative, as Christina called it.

"That's so fucked up," Jordan said.

"Then where did all the bodies go?" I asked one especially annoying investigator, with a small tight mouth like an asshole. Search teams had looked for weeks up and down the slough, at Devil's Landing, in and around the harbor, and even poked through the east end, according to the harbormaster. How hard they looked once they saw for themselves how vast and impenetrable the area was, I never knew.

"Not very hard," Darlene Woodward guessed.

The investigators didn't want us to leave the area. We were interviewed for weeks by various people from different agencies. Christina's boss let us have the company townhouse in Corral de Tierra, which suited us just fine because it was nowhere near the water. We even felt safe enough to use the hot tub at night. The house had an extra bedroom for Jordan.

She hadn't forgiven her father and stepmother for not coming to get her when they'd received the emergency weather alert, and when Christina suggested she stay with us, her father agreed. A little too quickly, I thought. Her mother visited, but Jordan was furious with her too after she'd arrived with her new, younger boyfriend, who Jordan hated on sight.

The plan was for Jordan to fly to Los Angeles when we were done being questioned, and after several weeks, we drove her to the airport and saw her off. It was then I understood how parents felt saying goodbye to their kids leaving for camp or college. A lump the size of a grapefruit appeared in my throat when we approached security, and when she made it through to the other side and waved, tears came to my eyes. I was a wreck, so Christina drove the Land Cruiser. Not very well.

There were lots of memorial services. We didn't go to most of them. Some were held in cities and states far away.

We did attend some. There was one ceremony for Abigail and Cassie in the East Bay. Another for Liliana and Tommy Garcia at a church in Salinas. We drove to Berkeley and met Ruth's family, spent the afternoon dodging awkward and painful questions.

236

Soon, accusations came flying my way when reporters at the cable channels recalled I had been opposed to the housing development.

Why did I eventually move to Roy's Cottages if I'd been so against the development at the start?

I must have been in on the eco attack from the beginning.

Maybe I was the mastermind.

Maybe I was a radical environmentalist weirdo turned mass killer.

As soon as we were allowed, Christina and I fled to the cabin in Sedona. We took long walks on red dirt trails, ate, drank too much wine, and fell asleep exhausted, only to bolt upright hours later, drenched in sweat. Sometimes, we'd compare nightmares. Sometimes, we'd be awake all night, desperate for dawn to come.

When we refused to do the final interviews on the dock outside my former place at Roy's Cottages, Tamara Rhodes went from cajoling, to pleading, to angry, all in fifteen minutes. But we weren't going back there, and when she mentioned the contract, Christina pulled it out and reread it from top to bottom, then consulted our lawyer, just in case.

"Sorry, Tamara," Christina told her over the phone. "There's nothing in the contract that obligates us to go back there. So, you'll just have to figure out another way."

Christina had put her on speaker so I could hear too.

There was a long silence, and then Tamara said, "Fine. I'll just have to shoot a stand-up or something out there myself."

Christina shot out of her chair. "That's not a good idea, Tamara," she shouted.

We tried reasoning with her, but Tamara wouldn't listen. Sometimes, she seemed to believe us—about hybrid animals, or monsters—but I came to realize it was an act she put on just for us. To get us to open up and talk. A tactic. It had become clear she believed the experts who touted the eco-terrorist theory, as ridiculous as it was. The trouble was, neither side had proof. People believed the version that made them comfortable.

Several days later, Christina got a call from an unknown number. She stared at the phone, then set it aside and went back to reading. A fantasy romance, she said, to take her mind off real life. The phone rang again, and when she didn't answer this time, whoever was calling left a message.

"Maybe it's important," I said casually.

My worry was it had something to do with Jordan. We'd been checking on her regularly, but still. Between the ordeal she'd endured at Roy's Cottages, and the life-changing injury inflicted on her at the camp for troubled teens, Jordan was still very fragile. She'd learned the nerves in her lower back might take another six months or longer to recover, and the news had come as a devastating blow.

"But he said you'll be able to walk again?" I'd asked, pacing.

"Probably!" she'd wailed. "But it's taking fucking forever."

That was one thing which hadn't changed. Jordan cursed as much as ever. Possibly more. It made me hopeful, though. If she'd stopped, I'd be worried.

With a sigh, Christina listened to the voice message. I watched in growing alarm when her face went from bored, to confused, to stunned. Her mouth fell open, and she clutched the phone to her chest.

"Christina? What is it?"

Christina didn't respond. She stared into space, blinking. I snatched the phone and listened.

"Hello, Christina. This is Sara Rafiq. I'm the associate producer who was working with Tamara Rhodes. I have some bad news, I'm afraid. It's about Tamara. I really don't want to leave a message like this, so can you please call me back at your earliest convenience?" A pause. "I wanted to prepare you. Just in case you see it on the news. It's all over the place already, I'm afraid."

I ended the message. "She went to the slough, didn't she?"

Christina rubbed her eyes. "She must have." She glanced at her laptop, half-hidden under a pile of cushions on the couch. "Should we check the news first?"

"Just call Sara."

"Okay."

Sara picked up right away. She confirmed what we suspected. Tamara Rhodes was dead. Or least that was the assumption. A sound engineer too.

"They were at Adam's dock," Sara explained. "She was standing at the edge, and they were filming the closing. Some final words. We'd worked on the script up until the last minute. The sound guy had seen something in the water, and Tam thought he was joking around. And then something came up over the side and pulled her in. The cameraman ran down the dock and kept filming." She paused. "We saw the footage. She got dragged under the water all the way across to the other side, and then she was pulled out of the water into the trees. You just see the person who did it for a few seconds, and then they're gone. The police, or whoever, are looking at the film. We're cooperating of course, and we gave them a copy."

"Jesus," Christina whispered. "What about the sound guy?"

"We don't know. The cameraman didn't see what happened to him. He was gone when the cameraman stopped shooting."

Chapter 28

Christina

We didn't have cable at the cabin, so Sara, who'd taken over as the producer of the documentary, gave us a password to watch the documentary live online, which was fine by us. Watching it on a smaller screen might reduce the impact somehow, make the events less real.

Adam and I had an early dinner at five o'clock. We'd sat outside a café with a view of Coffee Pot Rock and ordered vegetable soup and grilled cheese sandwiches. On the way back to the cabin, we stopped at a liquor store, and we bought a bottle of Jameson whiskey for Adam and some Pinot Grigio for me. There was no way we were watching that documentary sober. Five minutes before it started, Adam brought over his custom weed box and rolled us a joint. To relax us, he said.

I needed relaxing because I was filled with dread. The inside of my cheek was puffed up and sore where I chewed it, and I'd already shredded two nails.

We were the only two adult survivors. Jordan had refused to participate, even though her parents had given their permission when they'd learned about the appearance fee. A nice addition to her college fund, they'd said.

"Fuck no," she'd said. "No way."

Adam got over his belligerence, and the camera loved him. Those serious gray eyes. That streak of white hair which seemed to appear overnight. It fell next to his face, making his tanned skin glow on camera. People loved him on social media. By the time the documentary aired, thanks to all the advance publicity, he had hash tags associated with his name.

If he hadn't been sitting right next to me, our hips touching, one arm slung across my shoulder, I might have felt a bit nervous about all the competition suddenly appearing. If Adam had been into social media, and knew how to check direct messages, I'm sure he would have seen dozens of boob and dick pics.

Instead, he pressed his lips against my ear and said, "You look beautiful."

I didn't look as shitty on camera as I'd expected, with all the weight I'd lost. At least my boobs hadn't completely disappeared, and the makeup people had done a great job. My experience as an anchor kicked in, so at least I was able to string together a cohesive sentence. But if you knew the both of us, and knew what to look for, you could see we were off. That we weren't quite right. Those moments of hesitation. The way we'd stare off camera for just a second, trying to pull it together.

We had some segments together. Just a few. In one, we recounted the Garcias' visit to return the satellite phone, and Tommy Garcia's last words when he was dragged to his death. "Thank you, Lord, your will be done."

"What do you think he meant by that?" Tamara's voice asked from off-camera. They'd left her in, of course.

"He'd been recently diagnosed with Lewy Body dementia," I explained. "It's a horrible disease. He'd been suffering from hallucinations and insomnia, and it was only going to get worse. He must have been terrified, praying for an end to his suffering. So when..." I hesitated. "When they came and took him, maybe he thought his prayers had come true, and he was being spared." I shrugged. "I don't know."

The camera faded to black. For maximum impact.

And on and on it went. Adam and I talking, explaining. Tamara did a walk through the complex, showing photos of the cottages before. And after. She explained the layout of Phase I—three rows of elevated cottages, the mailroom at the center, surrounded by a grid of paths and lovely landscaping. My cottage, closest to the parking lot. Adam's cottage, closest to the water, and the rock where he'd seen "the hybrid" crouched. Woven throughout, anthropologist Patti Nelson's story of the circus from Eastern Europe, the strange and frightening animals that escaped their cages during the earthquake and vanished up the slough.

Several famous biologists shared their verdicts on whether these animals might have bred with otters to produce such a creature.

Possible, they concluded, but not likely.

"Assholes," Adam said, sounding like Jordan.

I wished she was with us, even though it wouldn't have been the healthiest choice for the teenager. But I missed her, and so did Adam.

That ended the segment about the circus, the so-called "origin story" of the Slough Devil. We kept expecting the documentary to revisit the circus fortune teller's suggestion that evil magic had made the strange creatures, and the 1906 earthquake had broken the magic spell enslaving them, but it was never mentioned again. Tamara asked Patti Nelson if she had any guesses on what the animals might have been.

The anthropologist had shrugged and said, "Some kind of ape, possibly?" The way she said it left plenty of room for doubt. It was obvious the documentary producers didn't put too much stock in the evil magic backstory, and they moved on.

243

Even if the documentary didn't talk about it, Adam and I did. Plenty. If the circus origin story was true, and the beasts had killed their cruel handlers, they had a history of striking back at those who wronged them. When we moved into Roy's Cottages, so close to the place they'd hidden from the world for decades, it was only natural they'd see us as a threat.

I shared my story about using a wet towel as a whip to fend off the juvenile male, and within half an hour, there were Photoshopped memes of me all over social media as a dominatrix, or an animal tamer in a corset. Adam and I agreed not to reveal the monster tried to rape me. Too many women had disappeared on that horrible night in April, and once I talked about it, that's all any of the families would be able to think of.

Whatever end had come to all our neighbors, I hoped it happened fast.

We made our way through our bottles, sagging against each other, heads touching. Limp.

Finally, the two hours had nearly passed. Social media documented the reactions. Nearly an even split between those believing a colony of unknown hybrids were responsible and those who believed it was of eco-terrorists.

In a somber tone, the narrator announced content warnings. "What you're about to see contains…"

Words in a stark white font over a black screen.

Then there was Tamara, in full make-up, hair done, wearing a blue zip-up jacket and black pants. Young. Smart. An Ivy League grad, I later heard. She was talking into the microphone when she twitched, looked down at her feet, and yelped. The camera bounced, and when it steadied again, she was falling, a shoulder and hip slamming into the dock. An unseen force gave a mighty tug, and her body jerked closer to

244

the edge. Another tug, and she went over the side. The camera panned wildly as the operator screamed her name.

"Oh my god," the man said.

The camera whipped around until, eventually, it pointed at the opposite shore. A dark misshapen figure dragged Tamara's limp body from the water and disappeared into a clump of trees.

The film clip was played again, more slowly this time, as several experts weighed in. Tamara's abductor, they concluded, had worn a custom wet suit and mask, intentionally distorting his shoulders.

"But what about the head?" Sara, the new producer, asked off camera. "It's small for someone that tall and large. And the arms were…were very long."

An expert shrugged. "Some people have small heads."

The experts disagreed whether Tamara had been alive when she was taken out on the opposite embankment. Once again, search teams from multiple agencies had joined forces to look for her and the sound man. They found a trail of blood, later determined to belong to the producer, but it led east through clumps of coastal grass and shrubs and ended further up the marsh, at the shore. Officials speculated a small boat had been waiting, and she was taken away.

When I looked over at Adam, he was sitting on the edge of the couch, his back straight, his hands on his knees. He was staring at a point above the computer screen, gray eyes unfocused. His lips were moving, but I couldn't make out the words. He looked like he was in a trance, and he scared me because I couldn't remember him ever looking so completely dazed.

I had to say his name three times before he looked over at me, and then he hardly seemed to see me at all.

Adrenalin shot through my body, wiping away the wine and the weed, and suddenly, I was stone cold sober.

It took him nearly five minutes to come out of his fugue state, and when it was over, he kissed my forehead and told me to stop worrying, he was fine.

"I was just shocked," he said in a tired voice.

The documentary was ending. There was a recap, a summary of the conclusions reached by all the experts who'd appeared, and then a photo montage of the victims and a reminder only three people had survived, one of whom was a minor who had yet to tell her story.

And then it was over.

"Fuck," I said.

Adam didn't say anything. When I glanced over at him, his face was shiny with sweat, and his arms were crossed against his stomach like it hurt.

"I fucked up, is more like it," he finally said.

I got to my feet and stared down at him, hardly daring to breathe. We looked at each other for a long time. What happened at Roy's Slough would connect us forever, but suddenly, I knew—felt—it could also break us.

"In what way?" I said quietly.

Adam slowly raised his eyes to my face. "I should have told people about the Slough Devil. The truth. From the beginning."

"They wouldn't have listened," I said, curling my fingers into my palms, feeling the ragged edges of my chewed-up nails dig into the flesh. "They wouldn't have believed you."

Adam shook his head. "It doesn't matter, Christina. I'm a naturalist. You heard what that fisherman said at the book signing. Remember? He asked if I'd ever seen the monster, and I said no. But if I'd stood up at the community meeting and done the right thing—told everyone what I'd seen—they would have been shocked, but I could have convinced them. Because I'm from Devil's Landing, and they know me. They trust me. If I'd spoken up that night, it's possible Darlene would have admitted she'd seen it too."

My insides felt like they were melting. I shook my head. "No. That's the idealized, magical version. If you'd started talking about seeing monsters, people might not call you crazy to your face, but they would have thought it. They'd have avoided you. Ignored you."

Adam shrugged. "Maybe. But maybe not all of them. If I'd not been so worried about people thinking I'm crazy, my reputation, more people would be alive today. Maybe all of them."

"That's what you think?" I whispered.

"That's what I think. Besides…," he murmured.

The agony in his voice cracked my heart. "Besides what?" I whispered.

Adam wound his fingers around the long white lock of hair and tugged, like he meant to pull it from his head. "I should never have stopped fighting against that damned development. I knew it didn't belong there. It's a protected area. I knew it was wrong, what they were doing. I should have fought harder. Leveraged whatever credibility I had. I should have written editorials for the major newspapers, like Vic said. But what did I do? I gave up. I gave up too soon, too easily. If I hadn't, maybe the place would never have been built."

I sank back onto the sofa and stared down at my hands. Hands I hardly recognized. Sunburned from our long walks. Nails that hadn't seen an emery board or polish in months.

"It wouldn't have worked, Adam. Not with more people for it than against it." I paused, fighting a wave of nausea, "But

Adam, I'm the one who said we shouldn't go around telling people about the Slough Devil. Me. Not you. So, what's really happening here, what you're really saying is, I'm to blame."

Adam grabbed my hand and pressed it to his lips. "No. That's not what I'm saying. You were just being cautious. You were trying to do the right thing, for all of us. But at some point, I should have stepped up. Warned people. If they didn't want to believe me, couldn't believe me, then fine. But at least I would have done the right thing. Given people information and a choice, but I didn't, and now I have to live with it the rest of my life."

Adam rose, pulled me to my feet, then placed his hands on my shoulders. His gray eyes bore into mine. "Maybe we shouldn't have watched that stupid documentary."

I wrapped my arms around his waist. He'd lost weight too, and I could feel his ribs through his thin shirt. "It's too late now."

<hr>

With hefty deposits to our bank accounts, we talked about what we'd do next.

Correction.

I talked. Adam nodded a lot and pretended to be interested, but his heart wasn't in it. He was as sweet and thoughtful as ever, but he was quiet and distracted. My sister wanted me to move closer to her in Golden, Colorado. I'd visited and liked it there. Pretty neighborhoods, restaurants, cafés, and lots of parks. I even started researching jobs. And there was plenty of outdoor stuff to do. Adam could start a new tour business or work as a ranger somewhere.

"I like Colorado," Adam said, but in a vague, non-committal way.

Some couples, I remembered reading, broke up after experiencing traumatic events, like the loss of a child. I worried that was happening to us too. Maybe I reminded him of things he'd rather forget.

My anxiety about our future as a couple became a dark cloud following me through the days. Sometimes, Adam would stroke my hair or rub my back, but in an automatic, absent way. I felt like shaking him. Talk to me, God dammit. I called my sister when he walked to the market.

"Oh my god, Christina. We're talkers. I mean, big talkers. Not everybody is like us. It sounds like he just needs some space."

So, I gave him space. I stopped talking at him. But things got worse. He moped around the cabin, rarely leaving.

When I couldn't stand it anymore, I asked him what was wrong, and he said, "I think I'm coming down with something."

Yeah right.

The next week, I got a phone call. From Sara Rafiq. I'd read the documentary was a huge success, and I thought she was going to pass along some media requests for interviews since no one knew where we were, and we weren't returning emails or messages. I put her on speaker.

"Did you hear?" she said.

I'd been washing dishes. A soapy glass slipped out of my hand and crashed to the floor. Adam was in the backyard, napping on a lounger.

"No."

"A group claimed responsibility."

I stared down at the mess on the floor. "For what?"

"For the killings. At Roy's Cottages. It happened the day before yesterday. The group hasn't been identified yet, but they're saying it was an elaborate plan to teach people a lesson about destroying protected areas."

I kicked at the largest piece of glass, and it went shooting across the red tiled floor. "That's bullshit."

Sara sighed. "There's something else. The eco-terrorist theory has really taken off since the documentary. We heard the developer that built Roy's Cottages is pushing to start phase two. Now that this group has claimed responsibility, they figure it's only a matter of time until they're caught. It looks like the rest of the project is going forward."

"But no one will want to live there!' I shouted.

"They're already getting applicants, Christina. People are desperate for affordable housing, and they think it's just a crazy story."

When we hung up, I swept up the broken glass, then went outside and told Adam.

The next day, when I woke up, I knew something was wrong.

Adam was an early riser. No matter how badly he'd slept, he was up by six o'clock. I slept in until seven or seven thirty, and when I staggered into the kitchen, there was a fresh pot of coffee waiting for me.

But on that day, no welcoming aroma, just silence. I was alone in the cabin.

Adam left a note on the table.

If no one believed those hybrids existed, nothing would be done about them, he wrote. If people moved into the cottages, they'd die. He couldn't let that happen. Not again. He loved me. He hated to leave me. Didn't want to do it. But he had no choice.

I remember screaming. Running out the front door, crying his name. His old Land Cruiser was still in the driveway, so he'd walked. He didn't pick up his phone. Didn't respond to my messages. I found the key to the truck and drove like a mad woman all the way to the Phoenix Airport, but it was too late. He'd gone.

The following day, I learned the harbormaster was reported missing, along with the contents of her gun safe.

Chapter 29

Christina

I flew into the Monterey Airport and headed straight to the sheriff's department where I reported Adam missing. I shared my suspicions he'd gone off with Darlene Woodward to hunt for the hybrids at the east end of the slough. The officer who took my report recognized me from the documentary. He treated me kindly and assured me they'd begin a search as soon as possible, left me sitting at his desk while he went off to talk to Sheriff Lucas.

As I left the building, holding back tears, I passed a small group of uniformed officers talking.

Suicide.

Double suicide.

No one had seen Adam or Darlene, alone or together. Their bodies were never found. They never returned home.

Adam's friend Vic somehow tracked me down. We met at a coffee shop off Highway 68.

"Did you know he'd come back here?" I asked.

Vic stared into his cappuccino. "No. If he had, if he'd have told me, I would have talked him out of it. Or tried to. Adam could be stubborn as hell. We talked a few times though. I believed him, by the way. About those things."

And Vic didn't believe it was suicide, either.

"No way," he said. "No way."

Maybe not. But it was a suicide mission. At least, that's what I thought at the time.

People moved into Roy's Cottages, cameras rolling. A week passed. Then a month. A year. No monsters appeared. No eco-terrorists in elaborate costumes.

If Adam were alive, he'd come back to me. But he didn't. I knew he was dead. Felt it in every bone of my body. I hoped he and Darlene had killed every last one of those fucking things, and after a few years, I came to believe they had.

Sometimes, I thought about visiting Patti Nelson, the anthropologist interviewed in the documentary who'd done the research about the circus from Eastern Europe and the animals that escaped up the marsh. Maybe she'd found out more. Maybe I could learn about what they were, to help me understand what they eventually became. And then I thought, what was the point? It wouldn't bring back all those people. It wouldn't bring back Adam. Besides, in an instant, my life had changed, and I had to refocus. So, I did the only thing I could. I moved on, as best I could.

With the money I had from the sale of the cottage and the fee I'd earned telling the truth to a world unequipped to hear it, I found a bungalow in Golden, Colorado around the block from my sister, brother-in-law, and nephews. For once, my sister didn't judge me or scold me, and I was welcomed into their lives. I found a corporate communications job with a brewery start-up called Clear Monster Beer, named after Clear Creek which runs through downtown Golden and along part of the front range.

It didn't matter if people thought I was a publicity stunt. It paid well, and they weren't into clock punching. My hours were erratic, but they didn't care. Everyone returned my messages at first because they were curious about me. Later because the expanding brewery had carved out a unique niche that was easy to pitch.

Miles, the meteorologist I'd worked with on the Central Coast, got a job at one of the TV stations in Denver and ended up buying a place in my neighborhood.

Not long after that, I got a call from Vic saying he'd taken a job in Denver too, and within three weeks, I was able to call him a neighbor. Sort of. He bought a penthouse overlooking Clear Creek. When he asked for my help decorating the place, I agreed, and we went furniture shopping together, but when he invited me over for lunch, I took one look at the children splashing in the shallow waters below and left.

He became a regular visitor to my place after that. We always talked about Adam. They'd met in college, I learned. Liked the same girls, he admitted once, when he'd had a bit too much to drink, but Adam always won, even if he never got around to asking them out.

Since we were both new to Golden and we were both grieving Adam, each in our own way, we started hanging out together. Vic showed up one day with an enormous TV and installed it in the living room. A gift, he said. We quickly discovered we both liked fantasy movies, the more epic the better, but we watched a few and noticed, as if for the first time, there was no avoiding monsters, so we switched to murder mysteries and thrillers.

Against my protests, Vic finished my basement, built a pergola in the back yard, and installed a radon pump.

When I first met Vic, he was what my sister called, "cute but kind of chubby," but fitness-obsessed Colorado had a way of rubbing off on people. He joined a gym and started running the Clear Creek Trail, and when I invited him to go with me to my nephew's birthday party, my sister didn't recognize him.

She jabbed me in the ribs and said, "Look who's a hottie now."

"Is he?" I remember asking, peering out the window to watch him tossing a football with my nephew.

He was. He'd probably dropped twenty pounds, shaved the scruff, and found a barber who knew how to cut his thick curly hair. I felt a hot flash of guilt.

Adam's best friend.

When I admitted that to my sister, she took my face in her hands and said, more gently and carefully than I would have thought possible, "But Adam's not here, is he? Vic is."

I locked myself in the bathroom and had a long cry. And when I came out, I poured two sangrias into frosted glasses, pushed through the backdoor, and handed one to Vic. When he slipped an arm around my waist, I leaned in.

Two years after the documentary aired, I got a call from Jordan. Not a text message, an actual phone call.

"Guess what?" she screamed into the phone.

My heart lurched. I knew she'd recovered function in her spine, and she'd begun to walk again, though not as fast as she'd expected. But her voice was too excited for it to be bad news.

"You got a white streak?" I guessed.

She'd been threatening it for a while, an homage to her hero, Adam.

"No! I got into the College of Mines."

I think I cried because I was so proud of her. And I missed her. Fiercely. Colorado School of Mines was just blocks away. We could…have pizza. Whenever we wanted.

I helped Jordan move into the dorms and, later, a small apartment she shared with two other girls. She was walking again and no longer needed a wheelchair, but that didn't stop her from using the dune buggy wheelchair Vic had built her. Jordan didn't have a car, but in that thing, she didn't need one.

And it worked just as well in the snow as it had on sand.

Seventy degrees in Golden Colorado felt more like eighty, and since it was a Saturday, we were free to enjoy the summery weather. Vic helped me make sandwiches in the kitchen, the windows open to the backyard. It was noisy out there, like it usually was when Jordan was around.

She sat in one of the new wooden deck chairs next to the little plastic pool wearing shorts, flip flops, and a bright blue tank top which matched the color of her eyes. She'd grown her hair out so it reached to the middle of her back, and she'd talked me into giving her bangs, which looked adorable on her.

"Oh no, you don't," she said.

The sound of furious splashing followed, then giggles.

Jordan's hand slapped the armrest. "Hey! You've got me all wet."

A rubber ducky flew across the air and struck her on the forehead, and she sputtered, or pretended to.

More giggles from the pool.

I watched, my breath catching in my throat, as Jordan pushed herself to a standing position. Taking slow and careful steps, she picked her way across the lawn.

Halfway to the pool she said, "Okay, Ad-duhm. Now you're going to be sorry." Her hands flew up in front of her face to ward off another rubber ducky.

257

"Jor-duhn," shouted the small voice from the pool. He stamped his feet and kicked water at her.

Jordan laughed. She laughed at everything he did, which, of course, delighted and encouraged him. "Okay, little man. Get over here. You need more sunscreen."

Adam did what he always did when the pool was involved. He threw himself down, clung to the sides, and began kicking,

Vic looked up and laughed. "Oh, oh. Looks like it's intervention time." Without waiting for me to ask, he charged out the door and galloped across the lawn.

Adam rolled to his feet and began pelting him with rubber duckies. The only reason we had so many—in rainbow colors no less—was Vic had bought a bucket of them and brought them over.

Vic continued to run, ducking and yelling, "Incoming!"

Adam clambered out of the pool, squishing down the sides, and squealed as Vic chased him across the yard. Vic scooped him up and deposited him in Jordan's lap. The sun, splashing in the pool, and all the running around must have tired Adam out because, for once, he didn't put up a fuss. His gray eyes—the same shade as his father's—squeezed shut, and he lifted his chin so Jordan could rub on the pink lotion. She bent over, carefully, and kissed the top of his sweaty little head.

"His hair is so long!" Jordan called. "He looks like Mowgli from the Jungle Book."

I arranged the sandwiches on plastic plates and sprinkled potato chips next to the cucumber and carrots sticks. "I know. My sister keeps bugging me to cut it."

"No!" Jordan and Vic shouted in unison.

"Don't worry, I'm not."

I wasn't even tempted. Adam's hair was as straight and black as his father's, and now, it was nearly shoulder length. When he sat in the bathtub, I had to resist the urge to check for silver threads, which was ridiculous because he'd just turned three. I wished I'd thought to ask Adam when he'd spotted his first white hair. One day, his son would ask when his father had started going silver, and I wouldn't have an answer.

I didn't have answers for a lot of the questions he'd have one day. Like why his father left. To that, I could only offer the simple and agonizing truth.

"Your daddy didn't know about you. That you were coming." And he hadn't. I'd found out two months after Adam left I was pregnant. An accident. A beautiful, heartbreaking accident. I'd never felt more alone. If it weren't for Jordan and Vic, I'm not sure how I would have made it through that time.

Sometimes, my sister jokes all I did was carry the baby because little Adam looks nothing like me. He is a mini version of Adam, from the color of his skin to his mannerisms.

I'd long given up hope he'd come back. Too much time had passed. He was lost to us, somewhere in that strange, wooded area at the far eastern edge of the slough.

My only comfort was Adam and Darlene must have succeeded, somehow. Roy's Cottages are filled with people now, all three phases complete, and there's not been one sighting of anything other than otters and seals. Not one unusual incident, not one video of anything that doesn't belong in those waters.

I watched, heart squeezing into my throat, as my son escorted Jordan to the picnic table. When our eyes met, his little chest puffed up, and he gave me a proud smile.

"Look, I'm helping, mama," he called.

THE END

Author's Note

Thank you for reading *The Devil's Shallows*. If you enjoyed it, I hope you consider leaving a review on Amazon or Goodreads. A short review is fine. With algorithms in play, reader reviews are especially important to independent authors like me. Don't have time for a review? Totally understand. Please hit those stars and rate it before you go.

I'm currently writing my next horror novel in the Dark Earth Rising collection, *The Copper Man*, set in a Wyoming mining town.

If you are familiar with the Central Coast of California, you know there's no Devil's Landing, Roy's Harbor, or Roy's Slough. I invented them for the story. To be honest, I just couldn't stand the idea of subjecting an area I call home to such awful creatures. In real life, I'm a big chicken. The inspiration for Devil's Landing is Moss Landing, north of Monterey, and Roy's Slough is a rough stand-in for The Elkhorn Slough.

Now a few words about the character of Thomas Garcia, who suffered from Lewy Body dementia. How accurate were his symptoms and behaviors? I can only say they are based on those I observed in my father, diagnosed with the disease in his mid-seventies. My dad was never one to use foul language, but the dementia lifted his inhibitions, and he would curse up a storm when frustrated. He also suffered from hallucinations and insomnia. I'm sure the effects of Lewy Body vary, and if you know anyone dealing with it, my heart goes out to you.

Once again, thank you for choosing to read this story. If you'd like to receive the occasional update on future books, please sign up for my newsletter at www.debracastaneda.com.

More Books By Debra Castaneda

The Monsters of Chavez Ravine
A 2021 International Latino Book Awards Gold Medal Winner! Before Dodger Stadium, dark forces terrorized Chavez Ravine.

The Night Lady
A rebel curandera, a plucky seamstress, and a young reporter are pulled into the investigation of a killer terrorizing Chavez Ravine.

The Root Witch: An Urban Legend Caught on Tape
A horror novelette.

Surviving Hillside Series
Young Adult Supernatural Suspense Novels

The Box in The Cuts
Following the clues is as deadly as ignoring them.

The Fault in The Cuts
Seven teenagers. An 8.1 earthquake. One angry ghost.

The Cave in The Cuts
Surviving 'til graduation just got scary.

Printed in Great Britain
by Amazon